DEMON HEART

THE DARKWORLD SERIES: BOOK THREE

EMMA L. ADAMS

'A fiend like thee might bear my soul to hell.'
Shakespeare, *Twelfth Night*

.

1

PLAYING WITH FIRE

"ASHLYN TEMPLE! You spent the night in a haunted house and never told me?" I winced as Cara's voice turned static, and she leant so far towards the webcam that I half-expected her head to come out of my laptop screen. "AND you have a boyfriend? You have some explaining to do."

I should have seen this coming a mile off, but the truth was, things had been so mad lately that I'd forgotten to keep my best friend up to date on developments. Trying to stop a crazed underground organisation of sorcerers from arresting me had been higher on my priority list for the last couple of weeks than informing everyone about the change in my romantic status.

Now I was paying the price.

Cara leaned back from the screen, brushing back her short cropped hair with one hand. She'd dyed it jet black since I'd last seen her, and it suited her. She pulled off the Goth look far better than I did, her eyes shadowed and outlined in liquid black.

"I'm coming to visit," Cara informed me, folding her

legs underneath her. Like me, she sat on her bed, except hers looked like a make-up explosion had taken place on top of it. "Next weekend. No excuses. And I'm meeting Leroy."

"*Leo,*" I corrected her. "And one of us will have to sleep on my crappy camp bed."

"I'll sleep on the floor if I have to. But I'm meeting Mr Prince Charming. Did you say he took you to a ball on Valentine's Day?"

"Nope, we spent that night scaring the crap out of the Literature Society at that haunted house. But he did take me to see a film last night."

"Fair enough." Cara rearranged her legs, knocking what looked like half the contents of a Boots make-up display over in the process. "Did he pay?"

"Uh, yeah." I felt kind of guilty about that, but it wasn't as though Leo didn't have money. His dad worked for the Venantium and they hardly paid their employees a pittance, unsurprising as they supposedly risked their lives on a daily basis. Leo had hardly seen his father in years; like many people who joined the organisation in charge of maintaining the magical Barrier that kept demons from invading our world, Mr Blake had sacrificed responsibility for his children in favour of trying to get into the highest ranks of the organisation. But he still gave Leo, and his brother Cyrus, a pretty decent allowance.

"Was it really romantic?"

"We watched a zombie sci-fi film with lots of explosions."

"Awesome."

Admittedly, I couldn't remember most of the film. I'd never felt self-conscious around Leo before, but knowing we were on a *date* suddenly made me hyperaware of every-thing from what I wore to whether I breathed too loudly. It was ridiculous, but I supposed this was what it felt like to be a *normal* teenage girl. Speaking of which, watching that film had been the first time we'd spent any time alone together in an ordinary situation—in other words, not sneaking around underground tunnels or haunted houses. Not ideal first date spots, however much fun it had been to hide in the cellar of the supposedly-haunted old house on Tombstone Hill and scare the living daylights out of the Literature Society members who'd decided to stage their postponed Halloween Sleepover there. I wasn't entirely sure Alex and Sarah, who'd also been there, had entirely forgiven me for that.

Of course, Cara really wanted to know if we'd kissed. I said, yes, we had—omitting to mention, of course, that our first kiss had been in a crypt, near an open grave I'd almost died in. Yeah, normal dating didn't exactly seem to be my thing. The truth was rather more complicated, of course. The crazed sorcerer, Jude, had been convinced I'd witnessed him murdering vampires, not realising that instead of me, he'd actually seen the doppelganger, the lost spirit of a dead half-demon who'd sneaked under the Venantium's radar. The leaders of an organisation well-known for its paranoia about magic-users certainly seemed to have missed a few issues with its members.

If it hadn't been for Leo and the others, I'd have died that night. I'd originally gone along with Leo to help find out why his guardian, Mr Melmoth—also a vampire— had been murdered, and what connection that had to the murderous ghoul who'd been walking around pretending to be me. Instead we found ourselves in the middle of Jude's plot to fight demons by seeking the advice of a lunatic sorcerer hiding in the Darkworld. Instead, a higher demon had intervened and killed the doppelganger.

"You set so much by the so-called virtue of your humanity? You don't even have a heart. You can't love. You can't be loved."

So the doppelganger had claimed… but the fortune-teller had told me otherwise. *I'm human. In all the ways that matter.* What I felt for my family and friends was no illusion. And Leo… he was fun to be around, a great friend, but it had been a revelation to know that he thought of me like that at all. And when I'd really thought about it, I wondered how I'd missed the signs when they were right in front of me. I'd thought I'd liked someone before and turned out to be mistaken, so I'd asked him to take it slow, and he'd respected that. So far, though, it was going well.

Except for the part where he didn't know I was a human-demon. The truth would come out eventually, I knew, but I'd barely wrapped my head around that revelation myself, let alone considered how to share it with someone who'd seen more of me than I'd ever thought I'd share.

I'd never been the type of teenage girl who had a different crush every month. I'd wondered if romance was something I wanted at all, though the fact that I was an unrepentant workaholic had made my social life entirely disappear during the time that everyone else in my peer group had started serious dating. But with Leo came warm fuzzy feelings and when he'd kissed me, it was like I'd been waiting for him to do it all along. I might not be certain of a lot of things, and I couldn't imagine doing the same with anyone else, but Leo and I had had a real connection before shit had hit the fan last term. Which was more than I could say for a certain former flatmate of mine.

"Next weekend," Cara reminded me, and switched off the webcam.

I stared at my screensaver. *Okay,* I thought, *I can deal with this.* I hadn't seen Cara since Christmas, anyway, since she lived in Edinburgh now. She was the only person from my secondary school I still kept in touch with, partly due to my life turning into a horror film in the middle of my final year. Seeing sinister eyes everywhere had driven me into my own private world, and in the end, most of my former friends had gone their separate ways. But Cara was different. She wouldn't even let even possible insanity ruin a twelve-year friendship, let alone a hundred-mile distance between our universities. I was lucky to have her.

Sometimes I wished I could tell her the truth, but I knew it would do more harm than good. Cara didn't need to know that her fear of the sinister unknown might be any more than superstition. I wouldn't wish that knowledge on anyone else. Leo and I were a part of it because we had to be. We could see the Darkworld, and it could see us. I envied normal people sometimes, but I couldn't change something I had no say in. Besides, it had brought me to Leo.

I'd told Cara we'd met at Gamesoc, the same story I'd told my flatmates, Alex and Sarah. I'd never had a boyfriend before so her opportunities to tease me about guys had been limited—not that she hadn't tried. Last term she'd encouraged me to make a move on my former flatmate David, who'd seemed to have a thing for me, but it he'd turned out to be a spy for the Venantium. I'd liked him, but whether the feeling had been mutual or not, I hadn't been able to forgive what he'd done. I'd acted pretty irrationally, but thankfully, no one other than me and Claudia know about the accidentally-turning-him-into-an-ice-statue fiasco. After that, forgetting about him seemed the simplest solution. At least we no longer lived in the same flat.

Leo was different. Being with him made me feel more alive than I'd felt in months.

My phone buzzed. I smiled when I saw Leo's name.
Pizza 2nite?

Sure, I replied.

The on-campus pizza restaurant was hardly a five-star date, but I couldn't have cared less. Leo and I never ran out of things to talk about, and his easy-going smile made me feel I could talk about anything on my mind—well, almost anything. It was the perfect bridge between being with my flatmates and Cara, who I couldn't talk to about anything concerning magic and demons, and being with Claudia and the rest of our group, who would talk of nothing else. I didn't even have to concoct an alibi to tell Sarah and Alex, like I did when going to the group meetings where a few of us—magic-users, that is—gathered to discuss the kind of thing we couldn't say in the outside world without being carted off to the madhouse.

As I left my room, I found my flatmates, Alex, Sarah and Mandeep, gathered in the corridor.

"What's this?" I asked.

Alex stepped forward, arms folded. "We need to have words, missy."

"About what? I'm going out."

"To see this mysterious boyfriend of yours?"

"Yes, I'm meeting Leo outside." I turned to lock my door, hitching my bag on my shoulder.

"As in, outside the flat?"

"Yes…"

"Great! We can all meet him, then."

"Oh, no," I muttered. I'd managed to stop her from interrogating Leo so far by meeting him on the woodland trail, but I supposed it was only a matter of time.

"Oh yes. I'm not convinced he's real."

"Not this again," I said, exasperated. "Look." I held up my phone. "Text, from Leo. Totally real."

"Uh-huh."

The buzzer rang, and I jumped. Alex laughed, grinning at Sarah and Mandeep.

"Here we go," she said. "Let interrogation round one commence."

"You're joking," I said. "Please. No interrogations. Not all guys are psychopaths."

"Hey, if you brought a girl back, I'd do the same."

"Remind me never to bring a girl back to this flat," said Mandeep, shaking his head. "Is it always like this?"

"Unfortunately," I said, resigning myself to the inevitable and going to answer the door. I supposed we did have a history of weirdos in our flat, namely Terrence the demon-summoning lunatic. Well, my flatmates knew no more than Cara did about the demon part.

Leo stood outside, curly dark hair fluffed up by the wind. His eyes widened when he saw that I'd brought an entourage.

"Um… hi?" he said, uncertainly.

"So you are a real person," said Alex, looking him up and down.

"Last time I checked," said Leo, flashing me a grin. "So these are the flatmates."

"And this is the boyfriend," said Alex. "Do you like *The Lord of the Rings?*"

"Uh… yeah? Any reason?"

"Good." Alex looked him up and down again. "You pass."

I bit back a laugh at Leo's incredulous expression. "Sorry," I said. "She won't let anyone in here who doesn't like LOTR. It's like her rule."

"Where are you going?" Alex asked Leo.

"We were going to get pizza. I'm assuming that isn't against the rules? Wait, do you have an actual rule book?"

"Don't get any ideas," I said firmly to Alex. "Right, we're off. I'll see you later."

"Have fun!" said Sarah.

"Round two starts as soon as you get back! *If* you get back," Alex added, loud enough for everyone nearby to hear.

"Honestly," I muttered, as we crossed the student village. "Please ignore everything Alex says. She's not pleased with us for the prank we pulled on LitSoc."

"Hmm." His hand slid into mine, and my heart stuttered. It never failed to take me by surprise how *alive* that simple gesture made me feel. So this was what I'd been missing out on. Even the miserable weather didn't bother me. I felt as light as air. Though it was still a relief to reach the warmth of the on-campus Pizzeria.

When I told Leo he'd be meeting Cara, he pulled a face. "She's the superstitious one?"

"Don't say that to her face," I said. "Probably best not to mention demons or vampires, even as a joke."

"I take it setting myself on fire's off the cards, too?"

"Unless you're planning a circus act, then sadly, yes."

"Shame. I had a whole performance lined up, along with a speech about how the demons are planning a mass invasion from the Darkworld."

It wasn't unusual for us to joke about these things, but all the same, his words triggered a memory of something the fortune-teller had said, before she'd disappeared like she usually did. *This isn't over… there's no doubt about it.* She couldn't really see the future, but she had an uncanny knack for foreknowledge due to her close connection to the spirits in the Darkworld.

I pushed all thoughts of the fortune-teller from my mind. She infuriated me enough in person without invading my thoughts as well. I returned my attention to Leo.

"So, do I have to prepare for any more interrogations?" he said.

"Sorry about Alex," I said. "She's very… um… distrusting."

"I like how at the end she said, 'You pass'," said Leo. "What does she do to people who don't pass?"

"Throws them out, I imagine," I said, never having actually witnessed this. "My flatmates are a little strange."

"Funnily enough, I'm used to that." He grinned at me. "I'm dating it."

My face turned the colour of the tomato on my pizza. "It?" I said, "or did you just call me 'little'?"

"Well, you are."

I nudged him with my elbow and we ended up in a kind of half-wrestling match under the table. People started giving us odd looks, but I didn't care. I deserved some fun. So did Leo. His guardian had died only a month ago, killed by Jude. Mr Melmoth had taken Leo and Cyrus in after their father had abandoned them, effectively making them orphans after their mother had been killed by a demon. I couldn't imagine how awful that felt, but Leo never complained about anything.

Recent events haunted me enough. Especially witnessing the doppelganger kill a member of the Venantium, and that horrible night in the crypt.

My heart fluttered as he slid his hand into mine on the walk back, even though he'd done it so many times before. I felt so alert around him, my skin tingling as though I'd been plugged into a live wire. When he kissed me on the doorstep of my flat, shivers raced up and down my spine as I wrapped my arms around him.

"Night," he whispered in my ear.

I leant on the door, telling myself to get a grip and stop acting like a cliché romance heroine.

"Are you planning on standing out here all night?"

I must have jumped a foot in the air. My happy visions of kissing Leo were replaced by the unwelcome scowling face of Berenice Payne.

"What're you doing here?" I said blankly.

"Duh, I live in this house, and you're blocking the door!"

I moved aside, muttering an apology. Berenice and I had never seen eye to eye, mainly because she'd been a bitch to me ever since we'd met. I'd never quite figured out her problem. The others in the group tolerated her, and I had to do the same, since she'd guessed my secret.

Berenice flounced past me, her curly hair brushing my face and making my eyes water at the overpowering smell of perfume. "Have you told him yet?"

"Told him what?" I said, feigning ignorance, even though I knew it wouldn't do any good.

She rolled her overly-outlined eyes.

"You're playing with fire, girl," she said. "He'll figure it out, trust me. He isn't stupid. And then what?"

"Nothing," I said. "I'm not planning a demonic invasion. I didn't even know what—what I am until a few months ago. It won't change a thing."

"So why haven't you told him yet?"

"None of your business," I retorted, mirroring her own response when I'd asked her a couple of weeks ago why she and Howard weren't dating.

"Well, don't say I didn't warn you." And she sauntered into the building.

Like I needed anyone else trying to bring down my confidence. The demons and the doppelganger had done enough of that already.

Berenice confounded me. I couldn't puzzle out why anyone would *want* to be that unpleasant to people. Various hints I'd picked up over the past few months suggested she'd had a bad experience with a demon, but that went the same for all of us. Her father lectured at the university, and from what I gathered, her mother worked in the higher levels of the Venantium and had completely ditched her family, which I guessed excused her general attitude towards other magic-users. Still, she didn't *have* to hang around with us. She only came to meetings to try to get in Howard's pants—and admittedly succeeded, not that Howard saw her as much more than a diversion.

Personally, I thought that both of them were blind to how the other felt—but suggesting anything to Berenice was like poking a sleeping cobra with a stick, and just as likely to result in a venomous bite.

Other than Howard and Berenice, the group included Claudia, the first magic-user I'd met, and Leo's older brother Cyrus. All six members of our group had our reasons for not joining up with the Venantium. Howard held a constant grudge against them for arresting his parents, whilst Claudia's had left to keep her safe. As for me, I was the only person without any magic-users in my family, and as far as we could figure out, no one related to me had ever been registered with the Venantium. We hadn't yet had the opportunity to check if this was true of the *Sorcerer's Almanac*, the book that held accounts of all registered sorcerers, because it had been missing from their library for months.

I wasn't sure of the procedure for human-demons, but there was no concrete way of telling whether someone was a human-demon or just possessed—and considering there hadn't been any records of a human-demon in years, no one had suspected a thing. The only clue, as far as I could tell, was that human-demons were better at demonic magic, and that sometimes our eyes changed to the violet colour of a demon's. I hoped that now the doppelganger had gone, I had that particular quirk firmly under my control.

"Ash!" Alex, predictably, accosted me as soon as I stepped into the flat. Thankfully, no one waited to ambush me in a Grim Reaper costume this time around. "Tell me everything," she demanded.

"You're as bad as Cara," I informed her, shutting the door behind me. "Oh yeah—she's coming to stay this weekend."

"Don't change the subject. Did you sleep with Leo?"

"In the middle of the Pizzeria? What do you take me for?" I strode over to my door, sidestepping the small mountain of lager cans Pete had left lying in the hallway.

"I meant in his flat, stupid." Alex banged on Sarah's door. "Sarah! Ash is back."

"I'm asleep," Sarah's voice drifted into the corridor.

"Don't wake her up, you cruel person," I said. "She's got an early shift tomorrow."

"Oh yeah… sorry. I'll pester Mandeep instead."

"I still have your scythe." Mandeep's voice came from behind the door that used to be David's. I was privately glad our new flatmate hadn't picked the other vacant room—Terrence's. "Don't make me come out there and use it!"

"Oh yeah, I forgot about that," said Alex. "We'll need it in our epic revenge plan." She narrowed her eyes at me.

"You started it," I told her.

"You were more evil." She referred to my hiding in the cellar of the abandoned house in Crowley's cemetery and scaring her and the rest of LitSoc to death. "How did you even know that cellar was there? None of us could see it."

"I told you, Leo and I found it by accident. I kind of fell into it."

Alex snorted. "Sounds like you."

"Cheers." In truth, we'd come into the cellar by accident via the underground tunnels that snaked underneath Blackstone and Crowley—probably the whole area. With the way Alex relentlessly asked questions, it had been tough to think of a valid cover story as to what the hell we were doing there in the first place—I'd just said we'd left early to give everyone a scare.

"But that would mean you were there for *hours*," Alex said. "Like… seven hours in a cellar. Tell me you weren't screwing him in there?"

I laughed. "Yeah, right. I just fell asleep. And… so did he."

I really need to practise my cover stories. Unlocking my bedroom door, I turned back to say goodnight to Alex.

"You can't fool me," she said, wagging her finger. "I know you're up to something."

"You can have the blueprints for my evil plan tomorrow," I said. "Night."

In my room, I sighed, shrugging out of my thick coat. Whenever I speculated on the possibility of any of my friends learning about my other life, Alex came top of the list. She didn't mean to be nosy, but her questions downright exasperated me sometimes.

I turned up the heating, since I still felt the chill from outside nipping at my skin. I genuinely didn't know why I could suddenly feel the temperature change—up until recently, I'd been constantly cold but unable to really *feel* it, something I'd attributed to being part demon, as demons thrived in the cold atmosphere of the Darkworld. But on the night I'd nearly died, I'd realised that I could feel warmth again like normal people could. It took some adjusting to, and now I could no longer get away with walking outside in winter without a coat. But it also meant that when Leo touched me I could feel his body heat burning like a flame.

Of course, he could *literally* set himself on fire, a skill most magic-users had no difficulties with. Fire was demonkind's one weakness as it had the power to destroy their demon heart, a crystal anchoring them to this world when they were summoned. Because of this, I was doubly susceptible to burning, as I'd found out when Jude had attempted to destroy my own demon heart, an amethyst crystal that held my family's magic, and very nearly killed me.

My own magic was mostly centred on lowering the temperature and even freezing things, as well as killing demons using ice that burned them like fire. I didn't *like* using it, but I'd been forced to, twice. The others saw it as an eccentricity and had no idea that it was a sign that I wasn't completely human. Except for Berenice, who'd seen my eyes flash purple when we were battling the Skele-Ghouls and hadn't bought my excuses. I just hoped she wouldn't use it to blackmail me.

My phone buzzed again. I picked it up, thinking it was Leo, but the number came up as unknown.

The devil knows your secret.

I stared. *Who has my number this time?* I'd had cryptic messages before, but as the number came up as 'unknown', I couldn't tell if it might be the same person. This time, however, a number appeared, an unfamiliar one.

It had been so long since the others that I'd all but forgotten about them. But just before I'd first encountered the doppelganger, someone had messaged me with the claim that **A shadow has your face**.

Was it the same person? Who else could possibly know? *Is it a warning? Or a threat?*

"It's not a very good one. Nice try," I told my phone.

It buzzed back at me and I nearly dropped it. Another message had crossed wires with the first. **Tell no one else what you are.**

I felt half-tempted to dial the number, but something stayed my hand. *Tell no one.* One person always said that.

The one person I wanted to avoid.

Great.

2

THE GIRL IN THE FLAMES

Fire sprang up all around me, orange flames licking at my skin. I flinched away from the writhing wall of fire, which cut off any chance of escape.

I stood in a large room, a bedroom. Through the haze of smoke I could see a four-poster bed, its feathery curtains ablaze. Flickering tendrils of fire ate away at the posh-looking furniture, smoke gushing out in clouds. On the wall opposite hung a magnificent, gilt-framed painting of a girl with long, curly black hair. As I watched, the paint peeled away from the background as the ever-spreading blaze devoured it. Underneath the roar of the fire I heard a whimper, and realised I wasn't alone.

A girl crouched in the corner of the room, arms wrapped around her knees, apparently oblivious to the fire raging around her. I tried to walk over to her but a wall of flames barred my way, flaring out of the lush carpet.

"Stay… out…"

The girl raised her head, but she didn't seem to see me standing there. She was older than I'd thought; her hunched position had made her look like a child, but she was probably around the same age as me. Her dark hair spilled from a bun, and her gown, similar to the one in the painting, was crumpled and stained, as though she'd fallen in the mud outside.

"Stay… out."

Her eyes looked right through me, and I gasped. They shone violet. A demon's eyes.

She doubled over, coughing. I tried to call to her to get out of the burning room, but it was like something had stapled my mouth shut. *Dreaming. I'm dreaming.*

"Stay… out!"

Her eyes flashed again, turning grey-black, ordinary, human. I recognised it. She was fighting possession with everything she had.

"Is this what you want?"

The demon used her mouth to speak, but didn't need to; its voice sounded in my mind, sliding through me like an ice-cold knife.

"I'll burn you," she said, in a tremulous voice. "I'll burn with you."

"Then burn."

A single tear fell from the girl's eye before the demon's replaced it again, and with a cry, she leapt across the room, towards the flames.

Her skin ignited like paper, and her scream ripped through me. Darkness crowded my vision and I awoke.

"Are your dreams always this violent?"

Crap. I wriggled around, disorientated. I still couldn't see. For a second I wondered why I lay on the floor, then I remembered that Cara had commandeered my bed for the night, leaving me to sleep on the camp bed. Somehow I'd ended up underneath it, tangled in my covers—which explained why I couldn't see anything but darkness. I hoped I hadn't been shouting in my sleep.

"Only when I'm sleeping on the floor."

I wiped away the tears as I clambered awkwardly back onto the camp bed. It attempted to tip me off again.

"You sleep okay?" I asked her, groaning as my back protested against lying back on the collapsible bed.

"Not great. You need to turn down your heater, it's boiling in here."

So it was. No wonder I'd been dreaming about fire.

I still felt thoroughly unsettled. Generally, when my dreams were that vivid, it was because of a demon. The fortune-teller had explained that demons had license to enter the dreams of anyone with a close connection to the Darkworld. Lucky me. They'd enjoyed giving me sleep paralysis, dreaming of being frozen then awakening to find I'd unconsciously used magic in my sleep and couldn't move a muscle. But fire? Not exactly a demon's friend. I'd figure this one out later.

Cara stretched, groaning like she'd been the one sleeping on a camp bed. "What's the plan for today?"

"Want to walk to Blackstone?"

"Sure. I wanna take a look at the market."

Cara had arrived the night before, straight from Edinburgh. We'd got take-out from Bargain Burgers and watched movies until the early hours.

"Sarah's working this morning," I said. "And Alex is out at one of her clubs. Archery, I think."

"You aren't a member?"

"God, no. I'd take my own eye out."

Cara laughed. "Fair point."

Mandeep had gone out, too, so Cara and I left the flat alone. We ran into Pete on the way out, on his way back from last night's fifteen-hour bar crawl and looking decidedly worse for wear.

"Are you new?" he asked Cara blearily. "You have the most beautiful walk."

"You look like shit," Cara said, raising her eyebrows as he hugged the kitchen door.

"Yeah," I said. "We'd better get out before he vomits on one of us."

We hurried outside. Pete had most likely spent the night in pursuit of Danielle, the girl from the flat upstairs, on whom he'd nurtured a hopeless crush for the past six months.

Flakes of snow drifted around us as we began the walk through the woods towards Blackstone village. The strong gale bent the spindly trees backwards, and the rain from the day before turned the leafy path to mush.

"I should have brought hiking boots," Cara muttered.

I grinned at her. "Y'know, we could have signed up to this weekend's hike to Ben Nevis. It's supposed to be buried under six feet of snow."

"No thanks." Cara huddled inside her thick coat. "I'd prefer to keep all my fingers and toes."

We more or less slid down the last part of the path, and Cara swore as our feet sank into marshy grass.

"Holy hell! Where's the path?"

"Um… here," I said, apologetically, trying to lead her onto the least swampy part of the track that led towards town. I tried to distract her by pointing out the ruin of the Blackstone family house, and succeeded because she forgot all about the mud and stopped to stare at it.

The old manor house lay like a sad, sagging skeleton, its walls ripped away to bare the foundations. The surrounding area was scorched, and nothing grew there even though it had been undisturbed for a century and a half.

"Jesus," she said. "A whole family died in there?"

"Yeah," I said. "The town's named after them; the survivor built it as a monument to their memory."

That was the official story anyway, the one all the locals believed. But every magic-user in the area knew that the Blackstone family had been sorcerers, and their daughter Melivia had fallen for the promises of a rogue sorcerer who had tricked her into summoning a demon. That event had triggered the Demon Wars, as a group of demons led by a power-crazed sorcerer had invaded our world. The Venantium had defeated them, but it was far too late for the Blackstones. They'd all died, and Melivia had burned herself alive to kill the demon possessing her—

A sudden image of a girl running into an inferno ripped through my mind. It couldn't be— could it?

Was that what I dreamed?

I'd never dreamed of an actual place or event before. Usually my dreams of suffocating or freezing were the demons playing tricks on me. But this... could it be simple coincidence?

"Ash? Where are you going?"

I left the track and walked towards the house. I stood on tiptoe to get a closer look at the first floor, trying to see if any of them bore any resemblance to the room in the dream... but it was hopeless, I realised almost instantly. The rooms had burned away to ashes, and the entire right wing of the house had been completely obliterated. Rotting floorboards hung over empty air, with gaping holes where the windows had been. I almost fancied I could still smell the burning, feel the smoke in the back of my throat, choking me.

Shaking my head, I turned back to Cara, and my heart jolted. The fortune-teller stood beside me, her long black coat billowing in the wind.

"Ashlyn," she said, in her soft voice. She, like me, stared

at the house, with an expression I couldn't quite read. I'd known she could change her appearance using magic for ages, but tended to forget about it. Now, however, her carefully blank features really did look artificial.

"What are you doing here?" I said.

"I could ask the same of you." Her gaze remained on the house, like she could see something I couldn't.

"I'm giving Cara a tour of Blackstone," I said, gesturing behind me. "Showing her all the, uh… sights."

Cara stared openly at the fortune-teller as though she was a ghost. I supposed her ghostly-pale face and silvery hair didn't help that impression.

"I don't believe we've met. Delighted to make your acquaintance, Miss Cara."

Cara finally remembered how to close her mouth. "Um… hi." She gave a nervous laugh.

"Well, don't let me interrupt your tour."

The fortune-teller strode off in her usual brisk manner, before I had the chance to blink. *She didn't say what she was doing here.* And I'd totally forgotten to ask her about the weird messages. *Dammit.*

By now, her retreating figure headed towards Blackstone. I could never figure out that woman. She defined mystery, a powerful sorceress who masqueraded as a fortune-teller by the name of Madame Persephone. She'd helped us—hell, saved our lives—on more than one occasion, most recently when we were trapped in the crypt with Jude, and it was her who'd got us off any charges of misusing magic from the Venantium—even me, after the doppelganger had made them believe me to be a dangerous rogue.

That still didn't mean I trusted her. She'd spent most of my life also pretending to be my Aunt Eve, supposedly for the purpose of watching over me. It had been her who had sent me the amethyst pendant, my demon heart, on my eighteenth birthday. Lucifer, my higher demon ancestor, had given it to her to watch over—after she'd had an affair with him, something that completely stumped me.

Not that I was likely to get any more answers from her about *that*. I wasn't sure I wanted to, really.

Cara still gaped after her. "Who the hell was she? She talks like she's out of a book!"

"Local fortune-teller," I said. "She'll be on her way to the market now. You should get her to do you a Tarot reading."

"No freaking way!" Cara shuddered, wiping mud off her boots. "She'd put a curse on me."

"Nah, she wouldn't."

And Cara gave me a lecture on associating with fortune-tellers all the way into town. We made our way through streets that twisted like ribbons around Victorian houses and cosy cafes. Like all market days, stalls had sprung up all over the square selling all kinds of paraphernalia, from second-hand DVDs and books to charms and jewellery. Cara typically made straight for the stall proclaiming to sell amulets to ward off evil, although even she declined the 'lucky charm' woman's offer of a regular amethyst crystal shard which cost as much as a holiday to the Bahamas. She did, however, buy a pendant made of small crystals threaded onto a piece of string—in my opinion, still hugely overpriced, but nothing would deter Cara from her mission to repel supernatural forces. If only that kind of thing actually worked for me.

Ironically, Blackstone was probably safer than back home despite its appearance—not just because, as a village in the middle of nowhere, the level of crime was practically zero, but also due to our proximity to the Venantium, who controlled the Barriers between our world and the Darkworld. The strengthened Barriers repelled demons so effectively that they couldn't come close enough to manifest in the waking world—a great relief since they followed me everywhere else I went. Not that they could harm anyone from the other side, but seeing sinister eyes everywhere? I wouldn't wish it on anyone else.

Cara, of course, knew nothing about this, although like my parents, she hadn't missed how jumpy I'd become over the past year and a half, ever since the demons had first invaded my life. Speaking of, I needed to call my parents. I still hadn't told them about Leo. Our weekly phone calls had turned into fortnightly ones, when one of us remembered. It made me feel a tad guilty for forgetting so often, but Dad often joked that he had a memory like a leaky sieve and Mum wasn't much better. Half the time they even forgot my name, for crying out loud.

The fortune-teller's tent wasn't out at the market, but I saw it tucked away in a corner of the town square, where it usually stood when the market wasn't on—invisible to most eyes. She'd put a level of subliminal magic (or Influence) on it, which meant only people she *wanted* to see it could find it; in other words, me and the other members of our little group.

I wondered, again, what she'd been doing at the Blackstone house. Not that it would do any good to ask. That woman traded in questions, not answers.

When we'd finished checking out the market stalls, I took Cara to the Art Gallery, since we could get in for free. The grand brick building crouched at the top of a set of concrete steps. The town's cathedral towered over it, looking like something out of a Victorian Gothic novel, all black spires and towering roofs.

"What the hell?" said Cara. "That's some freaky giant bird."

A large black shape sat perched on one of the cathedral's spires. It looked bird-like from a distance, but I knew it to be a harpy, one of the Venantium's spies. They didn't usually fly this close—not in front of non-magic-users, anyway. Most ordinary people couldn't see them except those extra-sensitive to the paranormal, but I guess it shouldn't have surprised me that Cara could.

She reacted exactly as I'd predicted to the gallery's collection of Hell-themed paintings—by retreating as far away as possible. I had to admit, some of them were pretty gruesome, depicting people being torn to pieces by monstrous creatures from the abyss. They reminded me of the illustrations in the *Seven Princes* book Howard had 'borrowed' from the Venantium's library of ghouls and shadow-beasts. Hell, maybe the artists had drawn inspiration from real life.

Thinking about it, David had said that the painter was Melivia Blackstone. She seemed to be haunting me today.

We walked down to the coast afterwards, since Cara hadn't believed we were that close to the sea. I chose a longer route rather than short-cutting through the cemetery as David and I had the first time I'd been here; I doubted Cara would appreciate that. She wasn't overly pleased about having to walk through the mud again, either. I tried to lead her away from places where there was a risk of slipping over and into a thorny bush. Brambles and nettles grew everywhere, and the few grassy parts had absorbed the rainwater and turned into a spongy sort of swamp. *Maybe this isn't my best idea.*

But the path through the copse was the quickest way to the coastline other than going via the graveyard, and soon we heard the rushing of waves. Calmness settled around us, disturbed only by faint birdsong and the rustle of tiny life in the undergrowth.

The tide was in today, and the waves crashing on the rocks sent a fine, salty spray over our heads. At this point the bay curved around, and I could just make out the cliffs on the other side. I squinted, frowning. I could swear I saw a figure standing on the distant precipice.

The waves crashed down again, and goose bumps rose on my arms as I squinted as the shape. Not a person. A dark space. I felt it, prickling at my skin, creeping down my spine. The Darkworld had been opened. And something hovered in front of the space.

"Ash?"

I stared at the cloud of pitch-dark birds flying over the sea from the dark space.

Harpies.

I'd never seen so many at once—I'd never even seen them come from the Darkworld. The ones the Venantium used lived more or less permanently in our world, or so I'd thought.

The screeching, wheeling flock headed right towards us.

"Let's go," I said, barely managing to keep my voice even, and backed up into the woods again.

"What's up?" said Cara.

"We can't get down to the beach, the waves are too close. We'd better head back."

"Why'd you even bring me here, then?" Cara grumbled at me, but at least she turned away and began to walk back, swearing as her feet stuck in the mud. With one last uneasy glance at the flock of harpies, I led the way back through the copse.

Instinctively, I pulled out my phone to text Leo, and when it buzzed in my hands, I almost dropped it. The message was from Leo.

Shit's going down at the V HQ, I'm going there

with Cy. Sorry I can't meet ur friend—next time? xx

Great. Now Cara had another reason to be annoyed with me.

But she took it pretty well, being more concerned with getting the mud off her shoes once we got back to the flat. She didn't ask any awkward questions, thank goodness, making me wonder if she'd seen the harpies at all.

I just wished I could be open with her.

But it looked like there were bigger problems than that. Trouble at the Venantium's Headquarters… it couldn't be coincidence that I'd just seen so many harpies on the move.

Something's wrong.

3

THE MISSING BOOK

I didn't get to find out what had gone down in the Venantium's Headquarters until Monday. I texted Leo on Sunday to make sure he was okay, but he replied saying he couldn't tell me anything over the phone in case someone was listening in. Considering weirdos kept sending me cryptic messages, it was probably a good call—but it bothered me all the same.

I probably looked a mess on Monday morning, after another sleepless night, but this completely went out of my head as Leo pulled me into a hug and kissed me so hard I practically lifted off my feet.

"Okay," I said, when I'd got my breath back. "What's going on with the Venantium?"

"You want to know now? Or we could do more of this." He kissed me again.

"Come on, we're going to be late," I said, but the smile on my face didn't make me sound particularly convincing. Alex and Sarah pushed past on the way out the flat, making mock-gagging sounds.

"Very mature," I said, shaking my head, and started to walk through the student village.

"First Monday lecture I've made all term! You should be proud."

"Glad I'm a good influence." I slowed my pace, making sure Alex and Sarah were well out of earshot. "Come on, tell me what's happening. I've been going crazy."

"It isn't anything major," said Leo. "They're just being paranoid idiots. Basically, one of their demon hearts has gone missing. They think it's been stolen."

"Demon hearts?" I frowned. "They have demon hearts?"

"Only from dead demons. They keep them in a safe underground in case a sorcerer tries to use them again. Some of them still have magical energy trapped within them. But it's just paranoia, really, they're pretty harmless."

Harmless and *demons*—not two words I'd usually put together. A demon's heart, also known as an anchor, bound a summoned demon to its host, and through that, to this world. Most rogue sorcerers used a precious stone as the anchor because they could store magical energy, becoming power sources which drew demons like high-powered magnets. When the demon attached itself to the magical source and possessed someone, the stone became fixed in position in the centre of the host's forehead, like a third eye. The only way to send a demon back to the Darkworld was to destroy their heart—generally by burning it with magical fire. But demons couldn't die, so I guessed it made sense that their hearts would remain in this world even after they'd left their host behind.

"Do they have any idea who took it? I mean, it couldn't be…"

Who? Jude might have been a murdering maniac, but he was gone. Was there another traitor? I wondered about the group to which Jude had belonged, the so-called Righteous, who believed that those with a strong connection to the Darkworld, such as people who suffered from the Vampire's Curse, deserved to be punished by death. Jude had taken it upon himself to root out these 'vampires' himself by pretending there was a cure. It was twisted beyond belief—and I couldn't believe no one in the Venantium had had any clue what was going on.

Leo looked thoughtful, but shook his head. "Well, they've got a lot of interrogations on the go. Pretty much everyone who knew Jude has been questioned. They're tearing themselves apart to find any hint of a traitor, it's no wonder they're misplacing things."

"So why did you and Cyrus have to go there?"

"Well, the heart was one of the demons Melmoth killed, so they wanted to check we didn't know anything about it. But it was before I was born. I've never met Mephistopheles."

"Isn't that the name of Satan's second-in-command in *Doctor Faustus*?"

"No one ever said demons don't have a sense of humour. But this one was around twenty years ago, so neither Cy nor me would know about it. It was during Lucifer's attack on the Venantium."

Lucifer. The fortune-teller had said that the Venantium were secretly afraid that this sorcerer, Lucifer, would be making another attack. Supposedly, he'd been hiding in the Darkworld for years, an idea that still confounded me. Usually when a sorcerer used the rare magic that separated their spirit from their body and allowed them to enter the Darkworld, they were stuck there for eternity. But if the fortune-teller was worried Lucifer could return, then it must be a possibility…

"Weren't the harpies guarding it or anything?"

"They lost a lot of harpies in the Skele-Ghoul attack. I don't think they ever expected anyone to go down there, anyway. They're not great at guarding the library, either."

"But these are *demon* hearts we're talking about!"

"Dead demon hearts. They're supposedly harmless, anyway. Trust me, they're just trying to make up for that total failure with Jude and the Skele-Ghouls."

I looked at him suspiciously. "Sure you aren't just saying that?" Leo was rarely as offhand as he pretended to be.

Leo shrugged. "Best not to worry about it until it attacks us."

Nothing attacked us during the lecture, thankfully, although even a demon would probably have steered clear of the lecturer's rambling monologue on Victorian religious poetry.

We ran into Claudia on the way out, who looked rattled. "There's a problem," she said.

"What?" I said, my heart automatically starting to beat faster.

"Nothing serious… well, I hope not." We moved away from the growing crowd leaving the lecture theatre, into an alcove. "The *venators* are tightening security, and they're doing a full check of everything in their inventory. Including the library."

"Oh," said Leo. "Crap. We have to return the books?"

"We don't want them accusing us of anything again." She looked at me as she said this, and I knew that she meant she meant me in particular. The Venantium had been a breath away from blocking my magic permanently when they'd thought I was abusing it, and it was only the fortune-teller's intervention that had stopped them doing so. I didn't want to go back into that Angel Box ever again if I could help it.

"We'll have to," I said. "I only have the *Seven Princes* one in my room, but I guess there were a few more. Did you ever find the *Almanac*?"

"No. Hope they don't think we took it."

We walked across campus wrapped in an uneasy silence. Back at the student village, Claudia and Leo headed to their respective flats to retrieve the books they'd 'borrowed' whilst I tried to track down the *Seven Princes*.

Due to Cara's visit, my room had been rearranged to make room for the camp bed, and for a panicked ten minutes I thought I'd lost the book. I resigned myself to another interrogation, at least until I tipped the mattress off the bed and found the old, yellow-paged volume wedged down the side.

Hurrying outside with the book tucked under my arm, I swore when a gust of wind flung raindrops in my face and swiftly stowed the book in my jacket. Looking to left and right, I spotted Leo, who carried a large sports bag on one shoulder and wore his hood up against the rain.

"Did you take half the library?" I said, indicating the bag.

"Nah, half these are Howard's. He dumped them on me, since the *venators* are always knocking on his door."

"Fair enough," I said, re-zipping my jacket to make sure it covered the book. I had an inkling the punishment would go beyond mere library fines if I returned it in a damaged condition. Not that they'd know *I'd* taken it, but still.

I turned as a voice behind me said, "Hey. What're we standing in the rain for?"

Claudia held the remains of a bedraggled umbrella in one hand and a carrier bag in the other.

"Waiting for you," I said. "Is Berenice not coming?"

"Says she has flu." Claudia shrugged. "I'm voting we take the bus. No more wild excursions in the forest for me."

"Agreed."

"Ash… are you sure about this?" said Leo. "I can take your book back with me, it's not a problem."

"Yeah, come to think of it, you don't want to get dive-bombed by a harpy again," said Claudia. "And if we get caught, it's our asses on the line."

"I'll be fine," I said. "I thought most of the harpies were gone, anyway."

Apart from that massive swarm I'd seen. But I pushed that out of my mind. The thought of Leo in the Venantium's lair alone made me all the more determined to conquer my fear of those tunnels.

"Yeah, but the Venantium…"

"I'm wearing a shield," I said. "See?"

I'd learned that particular trick from the fortune-teller, the last time I'd paid her a visit. It had been a few days after that night in the crypt, and I'd gone to her in another futile attempt to get some answers from her. Instead, she'd given me a lesson in camouflage. Now, invisible to the naked eye, a thin layer of shadows cloaked me. It was the same principle as creating a shield to repel a demon, but on a lower scale. Even *venators* would think I was an ordinary person unless they got close, and if I used magic in the tunnels, no one would be able to detect it.

Leo sighed, taking my hand. "I just don't want you getting into trouble because of me. You'd never have known about the tunnels if I hadn't taken you there."

Warmth rushed through me as his finger stroked the palm of my hand.

"It's fine," I said. "I made my choice when I joined the group, right? Besides, I'm not turning down an opportunity to sneak into a *library*."

Leo flashed me a grin. "Sure thing, bookworm. Okay. We're good to go?"

"I am," said Claudia, rubbing her hands together and shivering. "Come on already."

We caught the bus from the top of the hill and rode the five minutes to Blackstone, where Cyrus met us at the stop. He carried an overflowing bag the same size as Leo's.

"Howard," Cyrus said, as we walked through the dark cobblestoned streets. "He left all these books at my place when the *venators* were searching his flat."

"Did the same to me," said Leo. "I take it he's not coming tonight?"

"Says he can't be bothered. Asshole."

Leo shrugged. "All the more fun for us. Do you have the key?"

"Yeah. I hope they're not onto us. I've only got a month of uni left, I don't want to spend it in prison."

Cyrus was in his final year of university and had purposefully picked out modules without exams, meaning that he was free to leave in April. I had the impression that he just wanted to get away from the Venantium.

I tried to ignore my own misgivings as we crossed the town square, under the looming spires of the cathedral. It helped that Leo walked at my side, but I'd never been one to flirt with danger, unlike Claudia. Part of me kept nagging that it was a stupid idea, that I didn't have to go with them—but another part won out. The part that had a taste for playing with fire.

We went into the tunnels via the usual path, unlocking

the hidden entrance behind a gargoyle statue in the cemetery. My chest tightened as we descended down the stone staircase, the walls gradually narrowing. All four of us had conjured lights, which mingled, surrounding us in a halo-like glow. To compensate, we all wore shields that would make us invisible to any harpies—not that it would do any good if we ran into *people.*

Eerie blue candle-flames sprang up ahead as we reached the main tunnel, from candles held by harpy-statues. Their cruel, sharp eyes seemed to pierce through me, even though I knew they couldn't see us.

I held the *Seven Princes* book close to me, breathing in its musty old-book smell. I didn't want to give it up, even though I'd read it cover to cover at least twice. It had taught me more than anyone else about human-demons, because few other books even mentioned the subject. I owed my sanity to it, at least. But avoiding the Venantium's bad side was paramount right now.

The usual awe descended on me as we entered the library, a gigantic underground chamber with soaring stone pillars and towering bookshelves that seemed to go on for miles. They'd been built into the walls themselves, lined with more leather-bound volumes than I could count.

"I've no idea where I picked this up," I said, staring at the rows and rows of books.

"Just shove them onto a shelf at random," said Claudia. "This place isn't particularly organised."

I looked around and saw a likely gap in a nearby shelf. Pushing the book into place, I turned back to Leo to see he'd walked down another row of shelves, towards the heart of the massive library.

"Leo? Where're you going?" I went after him, my footsteps clacking on the stone floor.

"Don't go running off!" Cyrus's exasperated voice sounded behind me.

I caught up with Leo at a pedestal that stood at a junction between rows of shelves. A large, heavy volume sat on top of it; close to, it looked like a stereotypical spell book, etched with runes and bound in red and gold.

"Someone else must've had an attack of conscience," Leo remarked.

"Is that—?" I said, stepping closer.

"Yeah, it's the *Sorcerer's Almanac,* alright." He rested one hand on the pedestal and turned the thick embossed cover to the first page. Curiosity seized me, and I moved closer. Leo ran his finger down the list of contents. No—a list of names, surname first. This book held the details of every sorcerer who had ever lived. For the first time, I wondered who updated it. *It can't do it by itself.* Magic only went so far.

"Temple, Temple… what was your mother's maiden name?"

"Francis," I said, reading over his shoulder.

But none of the listed names rang a bell. As far as I knew, I was the first in my family to move away from Manchester, so none of the people who'd lived around here could be my relations unless it went back more than a few generations. I tried to think to any conversations I might have had with my parents about my ancestry, but something strange happened every time I tried to focus. It was like a mental hand pushed me back whenever I zoned in on the conversation. I closed my eyes, picturing my parents and me in a café in Blackstone, discussing family trees… and Aunt Eve. But as soon as her name flashed through my mind, a bolt of pain lanced through my temples. I winced, rubbing my head.

What was that?

"Ash? You okay?"

"Yeah," I said, opening my eyes to meet Leo's concerned gaze. "I was just trying to remember if I ever talked about this with my parents."

But I couldn't tell him about Aunt Eve—about the fortune-teller's secret—not without revealing my own. Berenice's words came back to me, then: *"You're playing with fire, girl. He'll figure it out, trust me. He isn't stupid. And then what?"*

Shut up, I told the voice.

"Maybe have a think about it?" he said.

I nodded, frowning as something occurred to me. I'd assumed I'd avoided thinking of my erstwhile Aunt Eve out of habit, but maybe... maybe I *couldn't* think about her, because she didn't exist anymore. When we'd used that mind-magic trick on David to make him forget he'd seen me use a spell, it left gaps in his memory without him being able to tell the difference. Likewise, whatever the fortune-teller had done had altered my impression of her, making me and my parents think her to be our relation. But after the spell had been taken off, I had barely thought of her, even though memories of summers spent at her cottage had been some of the most vivid recollections I'd had from my childhood.

Something definitely felt wrong. I poked the memory again, and winced as pain lanced through my temples again.

Okay. I'm having a talk with her. Messing with people's minds was downright creepy in my book, whatever excuse she'd used.

I jumped as Cyrus's voice echoed from nearby. "Guys, it's getting late. We should make a move."

"Could do with making a copy of this, really," said Leo, who still skimmed through the *Almanac*. "I wish we could stay longer, but the *venators* will be on the prowl soon."

"True." I gave the page one last look, then closed the book with a sigh. If I got tempted, I'd never leave.

As I returned the book to its former position, something slipped out from between the pages to land at my feet. A smaller book, a journal really, leather-bound with wafer-thin, yellowed pages.

"What's this?" I picked it up, flipping it open. Several of the pages shifted in my grasp and I had to hold them together to stop them from falling out.

"Blackstone?" Leo opened the *Almanac* to the page where the journal had slipped from. A double-page spread almost entirely given over to the Blackstone family.

I held up the journal, to where my conjured light still hung overhead. A name stood out on the cover. Melivia Blackstone.

"No way," I said.

"Magical concealment," said Leo. "That book wasn't there before you touched it. Something triggered it."

"What, you think someone left it there for *me*?" I turned to the first page. The handwriting was so intricate I had difficulty making out the words, but the name stood out clearly. Melivia Blackstone.

Was this her journal?

I gave Leo a quizzical glance, and he shrugged. "Let's clear out, anyway."

Cyrus bounced on the balls of his feet at the entrance, impatient to leave. In the end, he'd had to drag Claudia away from the volume of advanced alchemy she'd been immersed in.

"It was talking about spirit travel," she protested. "It's interesting, is all. Yeah, I know I can't take it. I'm not stupid."

Cyrus gave an exasperated sigh, turning to lead the way out. We'd barely entered the tunnel when he halted. "There's someone else coming."

I backed up, but it happened too fast. Before any of us could conjure an excuse, we found ourselves stared down by two Venantium members, a guy and a girl. Both wore the usual navy-blue uniform and matching scowls.

"Excuse me? What're you doing down here? This area is off-limits."

Shit. It was none other than my old flatmate, David. *Well, this is awkward.*

The same thought had clearly hit David, and he flushed, shifting from one foot to the other. Now he looked like a schoolboy playing dress-up in his fancy uniform. Not remotely intimidating.

"What are you doing here?" asked the girl beside him. She looked about our age, too, with thick dark hair and a scowl worthy of Berenice's.

"Just browsing," said Claudia, with a shrug. "I didn't know it wasn't allowed."

"This area belongs to the Venantium. It isn't for unregistered sorcerers to wander into as they please." David spoke to the air in front of him, avoiding my eyes.

"Sorry," said Claudia, unconvincingly. "Won't happen again."

"It better not."

"Since when was it a crime to go into your library?" Leo broke in. "You don't own the place. It belongs to the sorcerers who built it, and it was originally a sanctuary for *any* magic-users. Technically we have just as much right to be here as you do."

David flushed an even deeper red. "It specifically states in the rule book that all these tunnels are the property of—"

"Bullshit. You just claim what you need at any given moment. You *venators* are all the same." Leo moved towards David, and my heart sank. *Don't start a fight!*

"You don't know what you're talking about," said David.

"I'll bet I know a damn sight more than you do. Don't you ever question your employers' motives? Do you think they have the world's best interests in mind when they ban anyone but their own flunkies from accessing any information on magic?"

He'd stepped right up to David, staring him down. David looked back defiantly, but I knew him to be a coward already. He'd never win the argument.

"It's not for you to question our leaders."

"Precisely the same mentality that got you totally fooled by a traitor right under your nose. If you'd actually had minds of your own enough to question, a bunch of people might still be alive."

"We aren't responsible for the actions of traitors!" David shouted, his voice hoarse and almost desperate.

"Excuse me," said Claudia, "the testosterone is kind of choking me. Can't we just call it quits and get the hell out of here?"

"Yes, you should leave." David nodded, pulling himself upright in an attempt at dignity.

"Don't you dare think about reporting me to your boss," said Leo, aggressively, as he stalked past. The girl met my eyes in a stony glare. I looked back equally stonily. *Jesus. What's with these people?*

We walked out in silence. Leo didn't take my hand, or even turn back to make sure the rest of us were keeping up. My chest ached to see him like this. It was usually Howard who went out of his way to start fights; Leo had never snapped at anyone like that. Did he blame the entire

Venantium for their failure to realise Jude was a traitor? As much as I disliked David, I'd hardly put the blame on him. He hadn't been involved this time.

"For God's sake," came Leo's voice from up ahead. I caught up to see that the drizzle from earlier had turned into a raging storm. Within seconds of leaving the tunnels, the rain drenched us to the skin. We ducked into the Coach and Horses, where Leo proceeded to order what seemed an excessive amount of Jagerbombs.

"Might as well make a night of it," he said, to my questioning glance. "Let the bastards rot in their tunnels. We're *living*."

"You'll be dying in the morning," Cyrus said, but his brother ignored him.

I ached to ask Leo what was on his mind, but Claudia got there first.

"The hell's up with you?" she said.

"Too many dickheads in the world," he said, slamming a beer down on the table so foam overflowed everywhere.

I didn't think that was it, but I felt awkward asking with the others there. Besides, a part of me was afraid he wouldn't answer, or lie and say he was fine. If Leo didn't want to talk about it, then I wasn't about to push him. I had enough secrets of my own to fill one of those underground chambers.

Even though I was soaked, freezing and tired, I stuck around until closing time to keep him company. I also wanted to get a closer look at that diary. Thankfully I'd had the presence of mind to slip it into the pocket of my handbag, which was waterproof—kind of a necessity in a place where the sun shone once a year.

By the time we left the pub, Leo could barely string a sentence together, so I knew it was no use questioning him now. The three of us had to guide him back to campus, and he leant on Cyrus all the way up the hill, who bore it with a mutter of "You owe me for this, bro." I thought Leo was going to stumble off to his room alone, but he turned and suddenly hugged me so tight it squeezed the breath out of my lungs, and kissed me hard.

The confusion went away, for a moment at least, and the voice in my head was, for now, silenced.

4

RACHEL

I dreamed of the fire again that night, the Blackstone house burning. Again, I watched the girl throw herself into the flames, and scream as her skin ignited. The demon screamed with her, a harsh, cold cry lost in the roaring of the fire.

Then the dream pulled me out of the house, and suddenly I stood outside on the scorched grass, next to the fortune-teller. Clouds of billowing smoke poured from the tall windows before us. Sorrow was etched on her face as she watched the house burn.

"I'm sorry," she whispered, so quietly I barely heard her over the crackling flames. "I'm sorry you had to die."

She turned to face me—and my heart plunged into my feet as she looked at me with violet demon eyes.

I couldn't move, couldn't speak. *Not her. No.*

"I'm sorry," she said again, but her voice was her own, not the demon's.

Then she screamed, a high-pitched, inhuman cry. Darkness spread around her, forming wing-like shapes extending from her shoulders. Her arms opened wide, and she cried out something unintelligible as the shadowy wings turned to flame, and engulfed her.

I could still feel the heat licking at my skin as I awoke to the siren-like bleep of my phone alarm. I rolled over, heart pounding, skin sticky with sweat. *Dreaming. Just a dream. Chill out.*

Even after showering, I still itched all over, and the crackle of flames sounded in my head as I dressed and picked up my bag.

"Morning," Alex yawned, as I came out of my room. "You look like hell."

"I'm entitled to, it's too early for human beings to function," I said, locking my door. Nine a.m. seminars were a bitch on a good day.

Sarah looked even worse than me. Her new job at the campus shop had once again put her on a late shift despite her protests.

"You," said Alex, "need to tell them where to shove it next time they give you a late-night shift."

"I'm fine," said Sarah, bumping her head on the door frame as she passed it. "Sleep is overrated anyway."

"You're as bad as Ash," Alex told Sarah, glaring at me as though it was *my* fault.

"What?" I said innocently.

"You were sneaking around last night again. I heard you."

"Sneaking around?" I said, with a feeble attempt at a laugh. "What is this, *Mission Impossible*? Leo and I went to the pub with GameSoc people last night, that's all."

Another rain-storm greeted us outside. I pulled up my hood and resigned myself to spending another lecture dripping water everywhere.

"Hmm. What do you even do on those socials, anyway?"

"Drink and talk about nerdy stuff," I said.

"Y'know," said Alex, "That does sound fun. Rex was telling me about it, he's just joined up. I did wonder why he was looking for Sonic the Hedgehog costumes on eBay. He said it was for a social."

Crap. If Rex was a member, he'd know I never showed up for meetings. It looked as though I needed a new alibi. I supposed I could just say I was with Leo.

Still, the way Alex looked at me, I had a feeling she saw through my excuses. We'd lived together five months now, after all. I pictured Alex's face if she saw me doing magic. She loved that kind of thing.

Demons, though? Not so much.

"Anyway, I'm thinking of joining the self-defence club," said Alex, totally changing the subject.

"Um… why?" I said. "Aren't you already in every society? I thought you loved archery."

"Shit, their meetings clash, don't they? Dammit. Maybe next year, then."

"What do you need to defend yourself from?" said Sarah.

Alex shrugged. "Aliens. Weirdos like that Terrence. Did you know he's been marked as missing?"

My heart skipped a beat. She didn't think *I'd* had anything to do with that, did she? Only six—eight counting the fortune-teller and David—of us knew he'd been a power-obsessed sorcerer who'd tried to take my demon heart and use it himself. If I hadn't been immune to possession, the demon he'd summoned would have killed me. As it was, it had turned on its summoner and, at one touch, Terrence had died.

I knew nothing about him, really, whether he'd had a family, nor how he'd become involved with illegal magic. He'd vanished from existence after that night, but I guessed that the Venantium would have had to come up with a cover story.

"That other guy disappeared a couple of weeks ago, too. It's weird."

"Who, that politics student?" said Sarah.

Jude, I thought. He'd been in his final year here as well as working as a receptionist for the Venantium... but he was actually a cold-blooded killer. He'd fled in the chaos after the doppelganger's death. It didn't sit well with me, knowing he was still out there. He wanted me dead, too, since I was a human-demon.

"Yeah, it's strange. Especially for a university this small. You never know, there might be a dark history buried beneath campus." Alex gave me a ghoulish grin.

"If there is," I said, not sure whether she was joking, "then tell me in advance so I can plan my ambush."

"Don't you try that again," said Alex. "You almost gave poor Sarah a heart attack."

"Hey, you were the one screaming," said Sarah. "You hid in Rex's sleeping bag, if I remember rightly."

"I did *not*!" Alex hit her with her bag, and the two ran shrieking across the quadrangle.

"Honestly," I said, when I caught them up at the building where we had our seminars, rolling my eyes."

"Hey, Miss Mature Student." Alex pouted. "I'll bet you haven't done the reading."

"Nah, she'll have done it a week ago," said Sarah.

"Two days," I admitted.

"You give students a bad name," said Alex. "When else are we going to get to be childish?" She hit Sarah with her bag again.

"Cut it out!"

"People are staring," I said. Or, one person in particular. Berenice had stopped in the corridor to give me a snide look.

"Ash, did I ever tell you how middle-aged you sound?"

"Frequently." I glared back at Berenice, who stalked off, to my relief. *Don't be stupid—she wouldn't say anything in front of my friends.* Would she? "Anyway. I'll meet you guys out here in an hour, right?"

"Sure thing."

I was far from in the mood for an intelligent discussion of Victorian poetry, with Leo's behaviour last night still weighing on my mind. I had the feeling he wouldn't be making it to any classes today.

After my seminar, Alex, Sarah and I headed to the library to do some research for our essays. I was surprised to see Cyrus there, up to his neck in books. I'd forgotten his final deadlines were approaching soon. Right now, he was surrounded by a mountain of complex-looking psychology volumes. Third year looked like a barrel of laughs.

Still, this was what I'd signed up for when I came to university. Not narrow brushes with death. Not demons.

Not freaky anonymous messages.

Speaking of texts, I decided to send Leo one around midday, figuring that was an acceptable time: **How r u?**

Fucked, came the reply. *Figures.*

And that was all I heard from him all day. After several hours in the library, Alex, Sarah and I returned to the flat. The other two swiftly disappeared again—the former to Rex's flat, the latter to her shift at work. I logged into my laptop and tried to find something to occupy me which wasn't work-related. I'd been experimenting with blogging lately, as it seemed a good way to get some writing experience outside of my course. I still didn't know what I wanted to do after I graduated, but I'd considered journalism, or maybe reviewing books.

That would do. I opened Word and started typing a review of a book I'd read recently.

Needing to check something, I reached up towards my bookshelf and another book fell onto the desk. It was the journal I'd found in the library. Melivia Blackstone's diary. I picked it up carefully; the binding was fragile and looked as though it could crumble at a touch. The edges of the pages were slightly darker, as though... they'd been singed.

A shiver ran through me. I opened the book, flipping through page after page of cramped, intricate handwriting, the review forgotten. *This might take a while,* I thought, turning back to the first page.

It proved to be as dry as the old pages themselves. As an English Literature student I was no stranger to dense prose, but this was singularly the dullest thing I'd ever tried to read. I concluded within the first few pages that the girl, Melivia, was incredibly shallow, self-absorbed and just plain *boring*. Her only interest seemed to be her horse, which she spent long interludes gushing over, and each entry inevitably began with a meandering description of her morning ride over the hills. About the only interesting part was that she wrote about the same area I lived in now. She really had lived in that old house in Blackstone.

I usually loved all things Victorian; Dickens, Hardy and the Brontë sisters were some of my favourite authors, and I'd happily read through a volume of Tennyson or Browning for fun. But I found myself falling asleep as I read this, and I was tempted to just skip ahead to see if there was anything worth reading.

I'm probably not cut out to be a historian.

Still, at least part of me was still curious, so I laid the book aside with the page marked before I went to sleep.

～

Leo didn't show up to lectures the next day, either. I texted him as I left the flat, but received no response. I hurried to catch up with my friends.

"Does he ever come to lectures?" Alex enquired.

"Sometimes," I said.

"Is he like Pete? Only here for the lifestyle?" Alex wore her not-impressed face. "It's not cool of him to stand you up like this."

"I don't think so." I'd never asked why Leo had picked this particular university. I'd been drawn here unknowingly because of the Venantium's presence, but Leo had already known about that. Maybe it was because his brother came here, and he lived in the area. Maybe he wanted meet people like him, magic-users. It was easier to meet sorcerers here than at a big university.

Alex gave me a hard look, as if scrutinising me for something. "Have you two done it yet?"

That came out of nowhere. "Um, no."

"Thought so. You don't have the look."

"There's a look?" I said, blankly.

Alex laughed at me, and exchanged a glance with Sarah. "I'm joking. You can be so dense sometimes. So, why haven't you?"

"Haven't I what?"

"You're not fooling anyone, Ash. Why haven't you and Leo had sex?"

"Because we've been dating a fortnight?"

"Pfft."

"What, you and Rex—"

"It's not about me and Rex, it's about you and Leo. Are you sure you're actually attracted to him?"

"Of course I am! Don't be ridiculous. Not everyone jumps into bed on the first date."

"Are you sure he isn't gay?"

"Positive."

"Are you sure *you* aren't?"

"Why is this 'Let's Interrogate Ash' day?"

"Just curious."

"No, I'm not! We haven't done it because… because I guess we aren't ready yet. That enough of an answer?"

"Chill out, Ash. I'm just… concerned about you."

"Why?"

"You aren't all lovey-dovey. You know? Where are the sparks? The chemistry? I don't think I've ever seen the two of you together. You didn't see him last night, did you?"

"What, you think we should be slobbering all over each other in the lecture theatre like you and Rex?" I said defensively. I could feel my face flushing like a beacon.

"We weren't *slobbering*."

"The poor people sitting behind you would probably disagree. There are other ways of showing affection."

"Such as?"

"Never mind. This conversation is over."

But I was restless and distracted throughout the lecture. Not so much because of what Alex had said, but because I still hadn't asked Leo if he was okay after the other night. Should I have gone to see him yesterday? I knew certain people who hated to be disturbed when recovering from a hangover, so that was why I'd decided to leave it alone— but maybe I should have at least checked…

I decided to go over to his flat after the lecture. I hadn't met his flatmates yet, but he'd said they all got on pretty well, with the exception of a girl called Rachel who was reportedly a bit odd.

Naturally, she opened the door.

I could see instantly why she'd been labelled their flat's resident nutcase. Her face looked as though it had been painted with finger paints, which would have been fine if she'd been in costume for a fancy-dress party, but she just wore an overall and jeans, also splattered with paint. Her pupils were oddly dilated.

"You're Leo's girlfriend? Come in."

Apparently she spent most of her time smoking weed and painting lurid pictures. There were rumours she was into harder drugs, too. She certainly seemed unsteady on her feet, and she kept staring at me with those warped eyes as I knocked on Leo's door and waited. It started to creep me out.

Coldness suddenly gripped me, and a voice spoke in my head, "*He's coming.*"

I jumped backwards in shock—just as Leo opened the door.

"Ash!" he said. "Hi. Sorry, it's a mess in here."

"It's fine," I said, hardly knowing what I said. That voice had sounded so close, and so... like a demon.

Impossible.

Leo closed the door. I had a fleeting glimpse of Rachel and I could have sworn she was grinning at me.

"Sorry you had to meet her," he said. "She didn't try and sell you any dodgy plants, did she? She grows them in her room."

"Nope. I don't go near drugs if I can help it."

"Same here, but the flat always smells of pot. You can't escape it. Anyway. You can sit here."

He shoved a pile of clothes off the bed. His room wasn't actually that messy, at least not compared to Alex's, whose 'floor-drobe' covered every inch of her carpet. He did have a lot of Playstation games and DVD cases scattered around, but it was pretty much in the same state as my own room.

I sat down. My heart still raced from that weird voice I'd heard.

"Did you hear that?" I said.

"What?"

"Just before you opened the door, I heard a voice. It said 'He's coming'. It sounded like…"

I trailed off, bemused. He was laughing.

"What?"

"Rachel got you, did she? I admit she freaked all of us out on the first day. Threw her voice so it sounded like someone was outside. It scared everyone half to death."

"Oh," I said. "But… it really sounded like—like a demon."

Leo still looked amused. "Don't underestimate her. It's kind of like living in a horror movie. Her zombie impression's spot-on, she actually scared people on the Halloween bar crawl. And as for her Jigsaw impersonations… well, you don't want to know. But we're used to it now."

"Sounds fun." I tried to will my heart to slow down, but it wasn't quite convinced. After the week I'd had—the strange messages, the library… I'd almost forgotten the demons. But the doppelganger had made it clear they could get into my head at any time. I shivered at the thought, hands curling into fists. Sometimes my own imagination made a worse enemy.

"Hey," said Leo. "Don't worry about it. She's harmless. No evil stuff. Honest."

Then his lips were on mine. Taken off guard, I fell back onto the bed, our legs tangled together.

He stroked my hair with one hand as the other held me, and my heart quivered. His hands moved down my spine, and then he was easing me out of my jacket. I shrugged it off and hugged him back, feeling his heart beat against me, almost as fast as mine.

Then his hands were stroking my face. It brought me out in goose bumps, in a good way. He kissed me again, slowly, and slipped his hands beneath my hoody, beneath my shirt—

A buzzing sounded. My heart jumped.

"Shit." Leo pulled back, grabbing his phone from the desk with one hand.

Great timing, I thought, but relief flooded me all the same. It wasn't *my* phone. Not the anonymous messenger.

"Shit," Leo said. "Shit. No—don't move. I'm coming."

He was already on his feet and pulling a jacket on.

"What's happening?" I sat up, pulling my shirt down, the relief evaporating.

"Howard got taken down by a shadow-beast."

"Taken down?" I echoed, grabbing my own jacket as he shoved his feet into shoes. My heart beat in my throat, this time not in a good way.

"He's hurt, and Berenice can't get out of there. I have to go to Redthorne."

"I'm coming," I said, and followed him out the door. Rachel stared at us as we ran past.

"Hurry, or you might be too late!" she called.

"She doesn't know what's going on," Leo told me as we left the flat. "That's just the drugs talking."

"Are you sure?"

"Positive. Now when's the next goddamned bus?"

5

INFLUENCE

The buses to Redthorne ran fairly frequently, as it was the nearest town with a decent nightlife, and one arrived at the campus bus stop not long after we did. As usual, the driver steered the bus like a maniac, sending us flying off our seats at every hill. But for once I was glad of the breakneck pace. It had started to rain outside, and the raindrops peppered the windows like pellets as we hurtled downhill.

"What happened?" I asked Leo, gripping the top of the seat in front for support.

"Berenice and Howard got attacked by a bunch of shadow-beasts. Well, at least that's what I think happened. Berenice was kind of hysterical."

"Is it… serious?" My breath caught. I didn't particularly *like* Howard, but he was one of us, after all.

"I don't know." Leo shook his head. "Sometimes Howard underestimates shadow-beasts, since they aren't on a level with demons. But they can tear you to shreds if you make a mistake, even that idiot knows that. *Dammit.*"

I swallowed, tightening my grip on the headrest. I

wouldn't wish that on anyone. Shadow-beasts were vicious, but the reason the Venantium ranked demons higher was because of their ability to manipulate human minds, even though they didn't represent a physical threat on their own. True demons specialised in possession and telepathy, and could read the thoughts of any human they chose. And, of course, they could kill in a painless, final heartbeat.

But unless it possessed someone, a demon's ability to affect the physical world was limited to minor telekinesis, lowering the temperature, and sometimes the manipulation of electricity. Put them in control of a human mind and they could cause chaos. I'd never seen this because the only time I'd encountered a demon possessing—Terrence—there had been only one. But on a mass scale they could be far more deadly. They could move from one host to another, killing at will; and if the person they possessed was a sorcerer, they had access to the human magic as well as their own. The Venantium feared a demon invasion above everything else.

Alone, a demon was powerless. But the cases the Venantium had to deal with usually involved a demon's power combined with a sorcerer's—twice as deadly, and much harder to send the demon back to the Darkworld.

But demons couldn't simply possess anyone in an instant. They had to have permission, a kind of contract. I didn't know how it worked, only that they usually ended up killing the host to save the bother of arguing. Either way, the human wouldn't get out alive once a demon had picked its target.

All in all, getting involved with demons was a bad idea.

We leapt off the bus as soon as it pulled to a stop, and raced up the main street, past the blazing lights from the bars. We dodged around inebriated clubbers, slipping on the wet pavements. Leo swore as we took a turning into a side street and almost ran smack into a wall of shadows.

Something like a huge clot of darkness leapt at us. It crashed into my shoulder, knocking me off my feet. I fell down, and the Darkworld answered almost before I touched it, ice flowing from my palms to break my fall. The rain turned to ice in the air, glittering crystals suspended around me, blocking the beast as it leaped at me again. Shadows folded around the edges of my vision, the demon inside me awakening. I had to finish this fast.

Luckily, the Darkworld was more than willing to answer. I summoned icy fire to my right palm, and threw it at the shadow-beast. The shadowy mass distorted as the monster screamed, its jaws gaping wide, a fist-sized hole smoking in its flank. It shrank from the size of a lion to more like a large dog, but its sharp teeth were still bared. It jumped at me, trailing streams of darkness, and I responded with another palm of ice-fire. A horrible scream tore from its throat as the fire ripped through its semi-substantial coat. The demon within me blazed with approval, and for a brief moment, violet flashed across my vision. *Go back to the Darkworld,* the demon in the back of my mind hissed.

That was enough for the creature, which backed off and ran, scattering shadows like torn pages.

I looked up to see Leo, outlined in flame, face down another shadow-beast. It stood like a living shadow, several times the height of a person and with the mad, roving eyes of a wild beast.

But it was afraid of the flames. Leo blazed all over, and the creature cringed away. A hiss crept between its jagged teeth as it turned its purple-red eyes on me.

I was ready. The ice on my hands coalesced into a glittering dagger, and I stabbed wildly at the creatures as it lunged at me. *Burn*, whispered the demon inside me, and the icy weapon met shadowy flesh.

As it touched the shadow-beast, the dagger melted, its form becoming flame-like, and the Darkworld bit deeper into my skin. The beast howled, the ice-fire searing its flank. It broke apart, pieces of its shadowy skin falling to the ground, and it leapt through a hole in the universe, leaving the alleyway deserted.

Deserted except for the body on the ground, and the figure crouching over it.

My feet skidded, and my stomach lurched as I realised I was treading in blood. Lots of it.

Howard lay on his back, his arms flung wide, unmoving. Berenice knelt at his side, shaking with sobs. I'd never seen her cry before. She had her arms over Howard's body, as though trying to protect him.

Don't let him be dead, I thought desperately. But he *looked* dead—his face and chest were crisscrossed with deep lacerations, and my insides twisted when I realised I could see *bone* poking through one of the face wounds. His eyes were closed.

"He's… alive," Berenice choked. "I didn't know what to do—we need a healer."

"The fortune-teller?" I said. "Or the hospital? But they'd ask too many questions…"

Berenice glared at me through red-rimmed eyes. "How're we going to move him to Blackstone, genius?"

"Magical concealment," said Leo. "Influence. The three of us could carry him."

"You're shitting me," said Berenice. "It'll never work. Someone would know something was up."

"Well, you're the one who called me. If you've got a better idea, why'd you bother?"

"Leo!" I said. Why were they wasting time bickering when Howard might be *dying*?

"Look, we could try the hospital, but Ash is right. These are Darkworld-inflicted wounds. They aren't like regular injuries. The fortune-teller's the best person to go to."

"Okay," said Berenice. "You'd better be ready with some serious Influence."

"Been saving it up."

Berenice was so shaky she could barely support her own weight, let alone Howard's, but she wrapped her arms around his waist. Leo joined her, and I felt an irrational spike of jealousy when he put his arms around her to support her.

"Little help, Ash?" Leo grunted. Even between them they couldn't carry Howard's bulk.

"Sure," I said, awkwardly positioning myself next to Leo with Howard's arm draped around my shoulder. A faint groan escaped him. He *was* alive.

I wondered how in hell we were going to get him onto a bus.

Then a hole in the Darkworld opened in front of us. A familiar chill rushed through me as I met the eyes of the creature on the other side.

A demon.

"Ashlyn." The familiar voice, devoid of any emotion. All demons sounded the same to me—sinister, otherworldly, and beyond life or death.

"What?" My voice came out toneless, but a new wave of panic rose inside me. We didn't have time for this.

"I can help you."

"The hell you can," I muttered. "You won't get me that easily."

"Not all of us are your enemies."

"Doesn't mean I trust you," I said, and alarm flickered as I felt the demon respond inside me—I pushed the presence aside, conscious that Berenice and Leo were staring. But more urgent was the blood rapidly pooling on the pavement and Howard's limp form.

"Come on," said Leo, taking a step toward the dark space and pulling Berenice and me along with him. "You leave her alone," he told the demon. It merely grinned at him, its teeth flickering in and out of existence behind the black smoke.

Together we managed to get Howard to the edge of the street. Leo told me that Influence worked by being unnoticeable, by constantly repeating the same mantra in your mind. *We're not here. We're not important. Don't notice us.* I'd done it before, albeit unconsciously. I used to put it down to coincidence that at school, people often simply failed to notice me if I didn't feel like talking, teachers would sometimes forget I was there if I was having a particularly bad day. And sometimes people would look right through me. It wasn't like I was particularly noticeable anyway—just one in a thousand students—so it never crossed my mind to wonder about it.

This was different. I could feel my connection to the Darkworld like something burning inside me, paradoxically ice-cold and yet hot as fire. The combined strength of the three of us meant that tendrils of the Darkworld surrounded us in a cloud, a usual side effect of using strong magic. But it surrounded me in particular like a thick dust cloud; if it hadn't been semi-transparent, I wouldn't have been able to see where I was going. We waded through black fog, and a chill rushed through me as I saw Leo and the others fade in and out of view, like ghosts.

But when we walked down the main street, I could tell it was working. No one gave us a second glance, even the obviously sober bouncers outside night clubs watching out for anything suspicious. The bus driver didn't even glance up as we heaved Howard onto the bus; luckily, the door didn't shut on us. We laid him down on the back seat and I slumped down in the seat opposite, exhausted. My arms ached like crazy. I tried not to look at the trail of blood leaking onto the floor.

"How are people not noticing that?" I whispered to Leo, not sure if I was supposed to keep my voice down or not.

"Because we're keeping their attention away," said Leo in a strained voice. "I've never done it on this level before. You holding up okay, Berenice?"

Berenice was still chalk-white and shaking. "Yeah," she croaked.

Why wasn't it having as much of an effect on me? I wondered. Maybe I was doing it wrong.

But I knew I was doing *something*, because otherwise the Darkworld wouldn't be responding to me so strongly. Shadows danced around us, and I saw the flicker of violet demon eyes. *Shit.* There was a demon on the *bus.*

I looked away from the shadows, fixing my gaze on my feet instead. *This is absurd. There's blood all over the floor, and no one's looking. We're invisible in full view. We didn't even have to pay bus fare.* A strange, wild giggle bubbled up in my throat.

"What're you grinning at?" Berenice snarled at me. "You glad it got us and not you? Or is it because you think *you're* invincible? You make me sick."

"Don't be ridiculous." The overwhelming feeling faded, and now I just felt confused, shaken by the strange thrill part of me got from being this close to the Darkworld. And I didn't miss the demon grinning at me out the corner of my eye before it vanished as the bus lurched down a hill.

After the doppelganger had gone, I'd thought the demon inside me would stay back. The doppelganger had taunted me, brought the dark presence within me to the surface, but the fortune-teller had insisted that I wasn't dangerous. The demon was part of me. And yet… for a couple of seconds there, during the fight, she'd felt like an entirely different person.

"Berenice, stop snapping at Ash," said Leo. "We'll find the fortune-teller soon, and she'll sort everything out."

"She'd better."

We hauled Howard off the bus at the stop at the far end of Blackstone and made our way through the dark streets towards the town centre. None of us had ever been in this area before, but we used the towering cathedral spires as a guiding point. It was hard going. My arms burned, and Berenice stumbled so many times that if Leo hadn't been supporting her on the other side, we'd have crashed to the floor in a heap.

There was clearly a pub crawl going on, judging by the number of people in rainbow-striped outfits and superhero capes in the square. But none of them gave us a second glance as we walked right through the centre, to the corner where the fortune-teller's tent sat hidden in plain sight. Like us.

We dragged Howard over the tent's threshold, Leo shouting for the fortune-teller. It was dark in there, and even the incense candles no longer burned. I stumbled into the desk as we laid Howard on the wooden bench. In the gloom, I could make out the shapes of glittering charms hanging from the ceiling, and the faint glow of the crystal ball on the desk, which presumably was a fake.

No reply came. I conjured up a light, and directed it upward to illuminate the entire tent. The fortune-teller's usual seat was empty.

"Shit," said Leo. "You're kidding."

"She's not in?" whispered Berenice. "But we need… we need to help… him." She sank down onto the floor and made choked sobbing noises.

"Oh, pull yourself together!" I snapped. I shook all over from the exertion but something in me felt alert, and for some reason, angry. "Where does she keep her healing stuff?"

"Here," said Leo, who was already pulling out bottles and containers from behind the desk. "This is the one she used when the harpies got you, Ash—I think it works on all wounds from Darkworld creatures."

Berenice took the bottle from him with shaking hands. She still looked like living death, but my yelling at her had snapped her to her senses, at least.

"This one's for stopping heavy bleeding." Leo examined another bottle. "These instructions are handwritten. I think she makes all these herself."

"I don't care, just hand it over!" said Berenice.

"Okay, okay."

Berenice unscrewed the lid. The strong smell of herbs mingled with the lingering aroma of incense. For a minute, the only sounds were Berenice's sharp breaths as she tenderly rubbed the lotion into the worst of the wounds.

"The bleeding's stopping," said Berenice. "But he's not waking up. Why isn't he waking up?"

"We need to find Madame Unreliable," said Leo. "Seriously… she can't be far. It's not like her to leave her tent unguarded."

"Maybe she wanted to make sure we could get inside, just in case," I said.

"Sounds like her. But she couldn't have known this would happen."

"You never know," I said darkly.

Howard groaned from the bench.

Berenice let out a startled shriek. "Howard!" She threw herself onto him.

"Ow."

"Sorry—sorry!"

"Son of a bitch," Howard groaned. "Did it get away?"

"You crazy mother-fucker," said Leo, with a relieved laugh.

Howard squinted at him, tilting his head up. "The hell are you doing here, Blake?"

"No, 'thanks for saving my ass?'"

"You didn't save my—"

Howard sat up and promptly fell backwards again with a groan of pain. "Where the hell am I?"

"In the fortune-teller's tent," said Berenice. "You weren't moving, I freaked out and called Leo. He came here with… Ash." She gave me a distasteful glance. Typical. "Cyrus is blocked to the outside world and Claudia didn't pick up her phone. We had to move you here, I didn't know what else to do."

"So where's Madame Whoosit?"

"We don't know," said Berenice. "She wasn't here when we arrived, but this place was open."

"Bitch," he said. "Fuck, my head kills."

"You probably need painkillers." Berenice snapped into caring nurse mode again in a rather disconcerting way. "Are there any in here?"

"No, just natural medicines," said Leo. "It's like I said —I think the fortune-teller made them herself."

"I have ibuprofen in my bag," I said.

Howard practically snatched them from my hand.

"Hey, a thank you would be nice."

"Thanks," he muttered, dry-swallowing two painkillers.

Well, that's friendly. Not like we'd dragged him all the way from Redthorne or anything.

Leo looked like he was going to say something, but without warning, the entrance to the tent blew inwards and the fortune-teller entered. Her fair hair streamed behind her, and she wore her usual long, black coat.

"About bloody time!" said Berenice. "Howard's injured."

"I'm fine," said Howard, unconvincingly. Although the wounds had sealed somewhat, bloody lacerations covered his face. But it could have been much worse. A shiver went through me at the thought.

The fortune-teller moved to examine him, kneeling down beside the bench.

"You're lucky they used the right solution," she muttered. "Did you have any idea what you were doing?"

"What choice did we have? You weren't here." Berenice glared at the fortune-teller. "Is he okay?"

"He should be, but he was lucky. You shouldn't use these medicines lightly."

"There was a *hole in his face*." Berenice looked positively vicious. "Where the hell were you when we needed you?"

The fortune-teller gave her a cold look. "I was protecting this town from a shadow-beast attack."

My heart missed a beat.

"You what?" said Howard. He, Leo and Berenice all stared at the fortune-teller.

"It's worse than that," said the fortune-teller, and looked at me grimly. "Jude was there, and he was possessed."

6

FORSAKEN

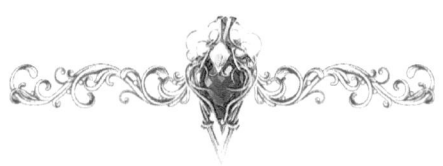

"*hat?*" Leo stared at her. "Jude? He let one possess him?"

"I do not know how this happened," she said. "But the Venantium have finally sorted out the evidence from the robbery the other day. They tracked the magic down to one person. It was Jude who broke in and stole the demon heart."

"But… why?" I said. The thought of Jude wandering around free after he'd nearly killed me had never filled me with confidence, but possessed by a demon? That was… I hesitated to say *worse*, because as a human, Jude had tried to kill me, tried to burn the demon out of me. He was as pitiless as a demon himself. And yet… demons had powers even Jude, as a sorcerer, didn't.

Either way, cold fear struck my heart and the demon inside me seemed to shrink away at the memory of the pain when Jude had set my demon heart ablaze.

"I have reason to believe that he isn't acting alone," said the fortune-teller. "Someone is playing him, and I fear they intend to attack the Venantium."

"How?" I said. "I thought their security was up again."

"It is. That's how they were unable to get through tonight. Jude must still have been human when he broke in last week. But when I saw him tonight in the tunnels—"

"You were in the tunnels?" I said.

"Patrolling. The Venantium don't like it, but ever since the crypts…" She shook her head. "Something's been wrong. The spirits are enraged, and now the heart of one of the most vicious demons I've ever met is out in the world again. Mephistopheles—"

With a sharp intake of breath, Berenice stumbled, clutching at the bench.

"Did you say—Mephistopheles?" Her face was ashen, genuine terror etched on her features.

The fortune-teller looked at her, gravely. "Yes. He is a known manipulator of humans and has managed to get out of the Darkworld numerous times, but his true heart contained the majority of his powers. Now he has it back, he is the most powerful demon in existence."

"You call a demon 'he'?" said Leo.

At the same time, Berenice gave another sharp gasp. She trembled all over. I stared at her. She'd faced demons before, right?

"Shit," she said, and then let out an unconvincing laugh. "Well, we're all fucked now, aren't we?"

"Care to elaborate?" said Leo, looking at her curiously.

"What part of 'most powerful demon in existence' do you not get?" Berenice made an attempt at her usual indifference. But I had a feeling there was more to it than that.

"Is he the one possessing Jude?" I asked the fortune-teller.

"Yes." She sighed. "If ever a demon could be called unhinged, it's him. Most are indifferent to humans the majority of the time. But he's ancient, and powerful, and I'd almost say he gets pleasure out of torturing people."

Berenice gripped the bench convulsively, her hands stark white.

Leo said, "It makes no sense. Jude, a demon's slave? He wanted to kill them, not join them."

True—however twisted his methods had been.

"Never underestimate the persuasive power of a demon," said the fortune-teller. "But tell me what happened to you. Was this a shadow-beast, too?"

Leo told her—including how we'd carried Howard here from Redthorne. I watched Berenice, who seemed to be composing herself, while Howard half-sat up, groaning to himself and running a hand over the wounds. I tried not to look too closely at them. *We were lucky,* I thought. All the times we'd been attacked by shadow-beasts before, we'd been lucky. Really lucky. It could have been any of us, any of the times we'd been attacked.

And Jude—no, a demon wearing his face—was the one summoning them. I half expected the fortune-teller to announce that she'd been playing us all, even if it'd be out of character for her.

When Leo finished speaking, the fortune-teller sucked in a breath.

"That was incredibly risky."

"What else were we supposed to do?" said Berenice. "He was bleeding to death!"

"Was the attack provoked?"

"Of course not!" said Berenice. "There were six shadow-beasts and they just pounced on us. There wasn't anywhere to run. I've never seen so many at once."

"Well, you were both lucky to survive. And lucky that your friends were able to help. But using that level of Influence, I'm surprised you made it back. Even the four of you combined..." She trailed off, and I didn't miss her significant glance at me. "You should go back to campus. I'll take care of him. He needs to go to the hospital."

"Why?" said Berenice. "He's okay, isn't he?"

"I'm not a doctor, Miss Payne," said the fortune-teller. "Alchemical medicine will only get you so far. There's not much I can do for the scarring, but an ordinary doctor may be able to help more than I can."

"Fine." Berenice pouted. "But I'm coming with you."

She shot Leo and me a dagger-like glare, like we'd been the ones who'd attacked Howard. Back to her usual self. But I couldn't forget her face when the fortune-teller had mentioned Mephistopheles. *She knows him. Somehow.*

"I'll take him myself," said the fortune-teller, firmly. "Go back to campus."

Berenice started to argue with her, but Leo and I didn't need any encouragement.

"The ungrateful shit," Leo said, as we walked back through Blackstone, accompanied by a sullen Berenice. "Almost makes me wish we'd left him."

I couldn't manage a smile.

"Hey," he said. "Don't worry about it. We beat the Skele-Ghouls before, we can beat them again. And Jude possessed is probably less dangerous than Jude non-possessed."

"We don't know that. Something really weird's going on."

"Yeah," said Berenice, suddenly. "I can't *imagine* why."

She threw me a significant look, and I glared back. *Don't you dare say a word*, I thought. But as long as she held the knowledge of my status as not-quite-human over me, I was at her mercy. Like we needed to be fighting amongst ourselves now.

"Well, that's nothing new," said Leo, seeming oblivious to the silent conversation between Berenice and me.

He had a point. Normal didn't exist here, not for us.

"Come on," he said. "Let's head back."

JUDE'S GRINNING face greeted me every time I closed my eyes. Last time I'd seen him, he'd tried to kill me by destroying my demon heart, and I'd never felt pain like it. Fire was as deadly to me as to any demon, and I'd felt part of me screaming, dying. When I did fall asleep, I relived the last part of the dream about the girl running into the flames, and jolted awake, breathing fast, the memory of facing my own death in the catacombs vivid in my mind. Rolling over, I drifted off into an even more disturbing nightmare.

I walked through a hall of mirrors, and each time I glimpsed my reflection, my own face grinned at me, violet demon eyes gleaming. I kept my eyes on the path ahead, but when I turned the corner, the mirrors turned at right angles, and four demon-eyed faces stared at me, split down the middle so my face looked distorted. Not real. Dreaming.

Then in another mirror, I saw another me. Younger. On either side of her stood two taller figures, but when I turned that way, they faded to the background.

"Ash," whispered my younger self. "Why do you run from the truth? Why do you hide what you are?"

Her eyes gleamed, violet and cold. "You've been her all along, Ashlyn. You're as much a demon as I am. More."

"Who are you?" I said, my voice echoing. "The doppel-ganger? Get out of my dreams."

She stepped forwards, hands splayed across the mirror like she stood inside a glass case.

"You trapped me here," she hissed, her voice no longer recognisable as mine. "You're going to pay. He'll make you pay." Her face twisted into a smile. "Oh, he'll make you suffer. Count on it."

"Who?" I said. "Are you talking about Mephistopheles?"

"Don't speak his name, you idiot. He'll hear you. He'll hunt you down." She reached out of the mirror, hand stroking my hair. I recoiled in horror.

One foot stepped from the mirror to the floor, and she came forwards. I moved aside, elbows striking the mirror beside me, and a hand gripped my arm.

Mine.

I pushed the hand aside and stepped back, into another Ash. All my reflections had stepped out of the mirrors, silently, like ghosts. Ash after Ash turned to face me, moving in a zombie-like fashion. Dread flooded me. I'd backed myself into a corner. Nowhere to run.

As another hand grabbed my arm, I panicked and lashed out. The girl fell clumsily, and her pain hit me as she struck the stone floor. As she sat up, her face twisted, and before my eyes, the skin peeled back from the bones. I watched my own face disintegrate in almost-fascinated horror, unable to look away from the ghastly unreality of seeing my face turn into something resembling a corpse. Blood leaked from the corners of her eyes. I stumbled into another Ash—and screamed as a decaying hand gripped my shoulder.

Zombies.

The rational part of my subconscious yelled at me to wake up.

Pushing zombies aside, I flat-out ran, kicking bits of flesh out of the way. Hands grabbed me, decomposing feet appeared to trip me up, and I almost ran headlong into a mirror at the next corner. Another Ash faced me—normal, not a zombie.

"You have to wake, Ash," she whispered. "They can't harm you—wake up…"

And I did.

Well, that was weird, I thought, breathing heavily as though I really had run headlong down a hall of mirrors with zombies on my tail. Zombie Ash, that is. I sat up in bed, groaning. At least this dream had left no marks.

A stream of greyish light seeped through a gap in the curtains. I pushed them back. The sun had barely risen, and a thick mist cocooned the forest. My room was on the ground floor, but I still liked the view from the window of the fields running down to the woodland. The early-morning sky was pale grey-white, and the grass sparkled with dew. Sheep lay sleeping in white huddles, and birds circled overhead. Restlessness seized me. Time to brave the woodland trail, I thought. Campus was safe again now that the Skele-Ghouls had gone, and Jude wouldn't be able to get back past the Barriers now he was possessed. I supposed one good thing came out of the situation.

As I left the flat, someone ran into me so hard I dropped my keys in the mud. I took in Claudia's dishevelled appearance and concluded that she'd just come back from a night out.

"Ash! Shit, what happened! My phone died when I was in Satan's Pit, I only just got those missed calls."

"Oh God." She didn't know. "Come on, we'd better go somewhere else."

We walked downhill towards the woodland path, where I'd been going anyway. The weak daylight filtered through the thick canopy, painting zigzag lines on the ground. Birds sang in the trees around us, oblivious to their human company.

I had a feeling of deja-vu as we walked until we reached a clearing—the same one where she'd first told me about the Darkworld.

"Okay. Spill it." She swayed slightly, like she was tipsy, but her gaze held mine steadily.

I drew in a breath. "Howard got attacked by shadow-beasts," I said.

"Shit! Is it serious? How bad?"

"It was pretty bad, but the fortune-teller patched him up." I shuddered at the memory. So much blood, and we'd barely made it in time.

"Crap. Was it in Redthorne?"

"Yeah, he was out with Berenice and they got jumped. They managed to fight them off, but I think Howard underestimated them. One of them clawed him up, and Berenice couldn't get him out of there alone."

"How'd you manage it, then?"

"We used Influence, then carried him back on the bus."

"Seriously?" she said, her eyes wide.

"Yeah. I don't know how we did it. But we got back to Blackstone and took him to the fortune-teller. Then Berenice basically told us to bugger off."

"Nice. I'm guessing she's with Howard now?"

"Probably," I said. "He's in hospital, though."

"I can't believe it happened to him of all people," she said. "I mean, he's killed dozens of shadow-beasts, not to mention those Skele-Ghouls. Of course he's never gone up against a true demon, but I suppose none of us have, except you."

My breath caught in my throat. This was the first time

in a while that she'd alluded to the incident with Terrence, when I'd nearly died because he'd got hold of my demon heart, like Jude had. No one except the fortune-teller and me knew the truth about that night in the Lake District, but they did know I'd killed the demon possessing Terrence. Maybe now was the right time to admit the truth. If Berenice knew and had accepted it, and she wasn't even my friend, then Claudia would surely accept it. She'd know I wasn't evil—right?

Coward, I told myself, as I let her carry on talking and missed my chance.

"I'm knackered," she said, kicking off her heels, apparently oblivious to the muddy ground. "I should probably get to bed before I curl up and fall asleep here and die of pneumonia."

I rolled my eyes at her melodramatic statement. "Sure," I said. "I was just going for a walk because I couldn't sleep."

"Enjoy it!" she said, and walked off, bare feet slipping in the mud.

Why did it have to be so difficult to tell the truth? I was usually a pretty honest person, except when it came to keeping my other life a secret from my flatmates and friends, of course. But that was more for their sakes than mine. They didn't need to know that I was connected to a sinister world of nightmares none of them could see. They didn't need to know I wasn't fully human, or that there were dark creatures seeking to possess the human race. Hell, I'd probably be arrested by the Venantium, too, if I told them, though I didn't think they had an official law against talking about the Darkworld to non-magic-users. Most people would never believe something like that. Actually using magic was different, because the Venantium saw it as dangerous activity which attracted the attention of demons. But, at least according to Cyrus and Claudia, both of whom had family members who'd worked for the Venantium, there was no rule saying you couldn't talk about it.

It came to my attention that my feet had wandered off on a tangent along with my thoughts, and instead of walking the woodland trail around campus, I'd instead come out on the other side on the country road that led to town. The ruin of the Blackstone house stared at me from a distance, and the memory of the dream broke through my thoughts again. I had to be imagining it was the same place. History didn't literally repeat itself, as far as I knew. Even in a world where demons hid amongst us, unseen.

Just another weird-ass dream.

I turned my back on the house and walked away, towards campus.

AFTER LECTURES, Leo texted me inviting me over to his flat. I felt a quiver of nervous anticipation as I rang the buzzer, remembering how we'd been interrupted last time I'd been there. But he greeted me wearing his coat and shoes.

"I thought we could visit Howard," he said.

"Are you sure he'd appreciate it?" I said, trying to keep the disappointment out of my voice.

"Probably not, but I feel like being nice to someone today. Good karma and all that bullshit."

More like he wanted to avoid starting our next essay— the deadline was creeping up on us. But I went along to the hospital anyway—and so did Claudia, who joined us as we left the village.

"I'm really sorry I couldn't help you guys," she said. "I'd have got there in a second if I'd known."

"Don't worry about it," said Leo. "One more person wouldn't have made a huge difference. I still can't believe we got away with it. I've never used Influence on that scale before."

"Yeah, sounds like you really went for it. I can't believe you managed it, either. Are you sure the fortune-teller wasn't helping?"

"No, she didn't show till later."

The fortune-teller was an expert at influential magic, if the way she'd pretended to be my aunt was anything to go by. That kind of Influence was way beyond any of us. She'd essentially manipulated me into living a total lie for eighteen years. I remembered the heady reckless feeling that came with using Influence, the feeling of absolute control and freedom, and felt nausea rise in my throat. If it hadn't been for the urgency of the situation, I couldn't have—ordinarily I'd never do that to someone. Never.

Are you being honest? a voice asked, and the memory of manipulating David's memories came to the surface.

"Berenice will be there," said Leo.

"Oh yeah," I said, remembering something else. "What do you think her deal was yesterday? I mean, when the fortune-teller mentioned Mephistopheles, I thought she was going to pass out."

"No clue," said Leo.

"Did she?" said Claudia. "I wonder if that was the demon that attacked her. I know she had a bad experience once—not that she ever told me about it, I sort of inferred it."

"Sounds about right," said Leo. "But I think she was just freaked at the idea of the most powerful demon walking around in the human world."

"What?"

At that moment, the bus pulled up the hill and we stopped talking as we climbed aboard. The driver was one of those pedants who counted every penny twice and scrutinised us as though we were going to cause trouble. It was weird thinking of how we'd walked onto a bus last night completely unnoticed. The whole experience almost seemed like another bizarre dream.

As we climbed to the top deck, Claudia said, "Most powerful demon?"

"I forgot to tell you," I admitted. "The fortune-teller had to deal with a shadow-beast attack outside Blackstone last night. And Jude was with them."

"He's possessed," said Leo. "Like, honestly possessed. I'd never have thought it of him, but that demon—Mephistopheles—must have got to him. Apparently he stole that demon heart from the Venantium, too. Something about a demon's true heart containing most of their power."

"What?" said Claudia, aghast. "Are you serious?"

"Yeah, course I am," said Leo. "Well, it's what the fortune-teller said, and she's usually brutally honest about this stuff. God knows how it happened, but Jude's a demon's puppet now."

"That's crazy." Claudia shook her head. "So he's summoning shadow-beasts?"

"Supposedly. I don't know, it doesn't add up at all, but you know the Venantium won't tell us what's going on. Maybe we'll get lucky and run into Madame Enigma at the hospital. I'm wondering what story she told them about Howard's injuries."

As it turned out, she'd told them that he'd cut himself on broken glass in the street in Redthorne. The cuts were nowhere near as serious as they'd been the night before, but the hospital had insisted on keeping Howard in overnight regardless. He wasn't particularly pleased about this.

"I'm fine, dammit!" he said, even though the entire right side of his face was bandaged. Berenice sat at his side, her eyes red-rimmed and her usually immaculate make-up peeling off.

"You don't look it," said Claudia. "When will you learn not to be reckless?"

"When monsters stop attacking me!"

"Keep your voice down!" said Claudia, with an anxious look around the room. The few other patients looked either asleep or too far off to hear what we said.

"Don't yell at him, he's injured," said Berenice. "Why the hell are you lot here, anyway?"

"Being nice?" said Leo.

Berenice snorted.

I'd had enough of her crap. "Not like we were any help. You'd both be dead if we didn't come, so quit whining and actually talk to one another for once, seeing as you're in the same room."

Berenice flushed brick-red. "Get out," she snapped.

"Could you keep the noise down over there?" a nurse called from the other side of the room. "Mr Lloyd isn't allowed more than two visitors at a time."

Oh, she means Howard. I wasn't in any hurry to stay.

"Come on, let's leave them to it," I said. Claudia shrugged helplessly, and Leo took my hand. Berenice narrowed her eyes at me. I ignored her.

I could almost see the awkwardness hovering between her and Howard as she avoided his eyes, whilst he looked at her with a faintly puzzled expression. Unless that was the pain drugs.

As Leo, Claudia and I walked back through

Redthorne, it seemed quieter than usual in the town centre. A strange feeling descended on me, like the beginnings of a migraine, a fist pounding at my temple. It felt vaguely familiar. My connection to the Darkworld tingled, and I looked around, realising that dark spaces were even more numerous than usual. Voids in the universe unfolded everywhere, revealing blackness beneath the world where dark things crept to stare at us. At me.

I thought of the demon that had spoken to me last night. Demons never offered help for nothing. Did it really think I'd accept its help?

My fingernails bit into my palm. Darkness followed me, even in daylight. Why couldn't they just leave me be?

"'Your leaders have forsaken you," said a harsh, cold voice.

I ignored it, although I felt the eyes on me from across the pavement. Leo squeezed my hand.

"Ignore it," he whispered.

"Why will no one tell you what chases you? Do you truly trust them? Why do you lie to yourselves?"

"Leave me the hell alone," I said, turning around in time to see the violet eyes fade back into the shadows.

Leo squeezed my hand again. "Ash. It's okay."

It didn't feel okay. My head pounded, like a pressure built up behind my skull, and I felt lightheaded and feverish.

Something's wrong.

"Ash, your skin's ice-cold. Are you feeling alright?" Leo squeezed my hand.

I shook my head. "I have a headache," I said. But it wasn't just that. I shivered in the same way that over-exposure to the Darkworld usually caused. Like something was freezing me from the inside out. The demon in the back of my mind pushed at the edges of my awareness, like she felt, it too. But I thought we were the same person.

I gripped Leo's hand, trying to focus on his reassuring warmth. It helped, slightly.

"We'll talk to the fortune-teller later," said Claudia. "She'll explain all this, count on it."

7

SUMMONED

Since I'd already had several sleepless nights, I all but passed out when I got back, waking with a headache even worse than the day before. I didn't usually get migraines, but the strange, horrible pressure on my forehead couldn't have any other explanation. At least my dreams played nice this time. No more Zombie Ash apocalypses.

I spent the day in bed, alternately reading and napping, with the result that when it came to midnight, I felt wide awake and restless. I paced the room, checking my phone for messages every so often. Those anonymous texts still stood out in my inbox. I'd forgotten to tell Leo. *Does it matter? You don't mention every time you get spam messages or emails.* But this was different, I knew. Either someone had something against me, or the demons had something to do with it. Could they tap mobile phones? I didn't think so, somehow, but it still felt like the kind of head-game someone like the doppelganger might come up with.

Paranoia. Stop being stupid and go to bed.

I picked up Melivia Blackstone's journal again, hoping

it would bore me enough to send me properly to sleep. Seven pages of Melivia's monologuing about her new dress —seriously?—and it started to work. Reaching a new entry, my eyes skidded over the first paragraph. I had to reread it.

"I am concerned that I may be suffering hysteria or delusions. Nothing like this has ever happened to me before. Yesterday, Mother and I took the carriage to the town of Redthorne, and I saw a strange apparition. Mother is very concerned about me."

Apparition. Could she be talking about… a demon?

It must be. The Blackstone family were magic-users, I knew that much—but they'd clearly kept their daughter in the dark, no pun intended. She had two older brothers who travelled a lot; one was a sailor, the other worked in London with their uncle. They must have known about demons and magic. Maybe it was because Melivia was their youngest daughter. Her mother certainly sounded overprotective.

Of course, it was 1868. Not exactly a time when women had a lot of freedom. What were the options for a female magic-user? As a member of the gentry, presumably Melivia was going to be married off to another high-class family. Yeuch. Another reason I was glad to live in the twenty-first century. For the first time I began to pity the girl.

Sleep forgotten, I read on. A chill ran up my spine when I came to her description of the demon. *"It was like the landscape was a leaf of paper, and someone had lifted it to reveal only a blank slate beneath. There was something stirring in the darkness. I saw a pair of violet eyes, not human eyes, but like a feral, ghastly wild animal. They looked at me, and I saw white teeth bared in a grin. I believe I must have fainted, because the next sight I saw was Mother bending over me. She told me that I should remain at home for a while."*

And so it went. I wanted to scream at Melivia's mother to tell her the truth. Anything was better than thinking you were mad.

But this was a real-life authentic document from the time. It was probably worth a fortune to any historian, but I guessed the Venantium wouldn't want it getting out there. At least, I assumed they'd been the ones to put it in the library. Who else could it have been?

My patience wore thin at Melivia's ten-page description of her eighteenth birthday celebrations, but one interesting detail was that she had stolen a priceless necklace from her mother's jewellery collection, an act that seemed out of character with her usual meekness. Not that you could tell everything about a person from their writing, but there was a simplicity to Melivia's style that suggested the naivety of someone who'd been sheltered for most of their life. Which, I supposed, was why the mention of the crystal stuck out to me. 'A glittering amethyst', she called it. *"When I touch it, it gives me the most peculiar feeling. I do not know why, but I feel like it belongs to me."*

That sounded awfully familiar to me.

I was right in assuming that she was being groomed for a husband. This 'Edgar Wilbury' who unexpectedly proposed to her sounded unbearable pompous, like a character from an Austen novel. I rolled my eyes at Melivia's naivety; *"I do hope he will be kind to me, and may learn to love me."*

This girl defines 'walkover'.

Although they became engaged, the wedding never happened. Edgar went away travelling for some reason— and that's when things got interesting.

One day, every member of the Blackstone family arrived at the house without warning. They were clearly in some kind of panic, but of course Melivia had no idea what was going on. I would have guessed that it had something to do with demons or at least the Venantium. But Melivia's diary stayed mundane as ever, describing such inane things as what shoes each of her relatives was wearing. That, as opposed to what they were actually talking about. The only clue was in the nightmares.

Every night, Melivia was plagued by strange dreams, of ice and fire, of voices whispering in her ears. It chilled me, because so many of them echoed my own.

"I feel so languid and depressed. Mother says I must be coming down with a fever. I do often wake with my skin burning…"

"I must have forgotten to blow out the candle on my bedside table last night, because I awoke to find a flame burning my skin. I blew it out, but the incident shook me enormously. I felt compelled to check on the crystal on my bedside table…"

"I am concerned that I may be going mad. What if I am? Will Edgar no longer want me?"

"You're better off without him," I muttered. "He sounds like an obnoxious prick."

She had been engaged to Edgar Wilbury for about eight months now, but there was no mention of a wedding. Then…

"Something has happened., something so peculiar I would dismiss it as a dream if I doubted the evidence of my senses.

For some time I have been dreaming of a voice. Now I have met its owner. He is an extraordinary man, and words alone cannot do him justice, but I will try.

I awoke early yesterday morning. I do not know why, but I felt compelled to rise and open the curtains. He stood outside our front door, and when I looked out, he glanced up at me and smiled. I felt his face was familiar although I am sure we have never met.

I rushed to dress myself without calling for Emily. Something told me that he wanted me to answer the door, and I did so. I must have looked a frightful sight, but his smile was kind.

"Who do I have the pleasure of addressing?" he asked.

"I… I am Melivia. Melivia Blackstone."

"Charmed," he said, and stooped to kiss my hand. I was astounded. He sounded vaguely foreign, German or Austrian, I would guess, but his English was flawless. He was certainly very handsome, and his attire spoke of wealth and comfort.

"Are you the lady of the house?"

"My mother…" I looked back down the hallway. Mother was nowhere in sight. "I believe she must be out. Are you here to speak with her?"

"I am here to speak with Lady Blackstone. May I come inside?"

He was so handsome, and so charming, how could I refuse him? He came into the sitting room and I sent Emily to prepare tea immediately.

"What are you here to talk to Mother about?" I said, embarrassed by the silence.

"I am not here to talk to your mother. But I would love to learn more about you. Tell me, Lady Blackstone."

No one has ever called me 'lady' before. I assume that was what led me to tell him, in five minutes, every detail of my life. It was most unexpected. I could not seem to stop myself from speaking. He listened politely and took an interest in my every word, far more than Mother or any of the others ever have. He stayed for an hour, then excused himself.

"Do you not want to speak to Mother?" I asked, when he stood to leave.

"I find you more fascinating. May I visit again?"

"I… of course."

What possessed me? This was most irregular. But it honestly happened, and as I sit writing this I can still see his carriage retreating into the distance along the road to Blackstone.

It only now occurs to me that he did not tell me his name."

I seemed to hear Mr Priestley's voice again, deep in the headquarters of the Venantium:

"Tell me, Miss Temple, are you acquainted with the story of the Blackstone family? The untold part is that around a century and a half ago, a stranger knocked on the door of the Blackstone family's manor. He was a sorcerer, a traveller, and they were happy to let him into their home. He seduced their daughter, Melivia. When her father found out, he unleashed his wrath upon the man. But he was too late. He had already tricked Melivia into summoning a demon."

This sorcerer was the man who had started the demon wars.

My phone buzzed on the other side of the room where I'd plugged it in. A rush of foreboding shot through me. I entered my passcode on the touch screen with shaking fingers. Two new messages.

Miss Temple. We request that you present yourself to us at 7 a.m. tomorrow for an emergency meeting along with your fellow unregistered magic-users.

The second message was from Leo: **The V have called a meeting 4 magic users tomorrow. Madame P is in trouble. We all have to be there at 7 xx**

What the hell? Who called emergency meetings at 7.00 a.m. on a Saturday?

What kind of trouble was the fortune-teller in?

LEO AND CLAUDIA looked about as much like death as I felt when they met me outside the flat at quarter past six. The early-morning mist enshrouded the buildings in the village, making it look quite eerie.

"You feeling better, Ash?" said Leo, hugging me. His hair was tousled as though he'd just got out of bed. I had to resist the urge to run my fingers through it.

"Yeah, I'm fine. What's this about?"

"I don't know, but I have a bad feeling. Maybe it's about those shadow-beasts."

"Do they know about it?"

"Wouldn't surprise me if they did. Shit, I hope they don't do a magic scan on us this time. Using Influence is illegal."

"Oh, crap," said Claudia. "If they do… well, you were attacked, weren't you? There was no other way to get Howard out of there. He'd have died."

"Of course," said Leo. "But you know what they're like."

"Yeah, you guys weren't here when they went psycho on that subliminalist cult last year," said Claudia. "They were using subliminal magic to burgle people's houses and make them forget they saw anyone. I think they're still chained down in the dungeons."

I winced. The memory of being locked in a cell and having my magic sealed was still fresh in my mind. The Venantium had gone as far as to block my connection to the Darkworld. I remembered the suffocating feeling, like something was squeezing the life out of me.

"I'm not going back in that Angel Box," I said.

They both looked at me. "I can't believe they put you through that," said Leo, taking my hand. "If I'd known, I'd have moved hell to get you out."

My heart beat faster. I wanted to hold onto him and forget all of this. But the clock was ticking and we needed to be at the Venantium's Headquarters before seven.

Berenice and Cyrus waited for us in the cemetery, the former looking incredibly pissed off.

"*There* you are," she said.

"Where's Howard?" said Leo.

"Sleeping. He's recovering at the flat. They came round this morning to *collect* us."

As much as I disliked Berenice, I felt a rush of anger. Who did these people think they were?

"So they didn't force him to come?"

"He can't walk, so no," she said. "They did a magic scan on him, and managed to get the answers they wanted. They know we're telling the truth about the shadow-beasts attacking us, at least."

"Does that mean we aren't going to get bollocked for using Influence?"

"I wasn't," she said. "They didn't even seem bothered, to be honest."

"That isn't the problem," said Cyrus. "They found out about the fortune-teller fighting Jude and the shadow-beasts, and now they think she's on their side."

My heart dropped to my toes. *No. She's not. Not her.*

"They haven't—" The words stuck in my throat. "They haven't arrested her?"

Cyrus's face said it all. Cold flooded me. *No.*

"What the hell kind of logic is that?" I said. "I mean, she was obviously fighting against them, right?"

"Their eyewitnesses saw Jude escape. They think she let him go."

"They're idiots," said Claudia, aghast. "She warned us… shit. She's a hell of a better fighter than they are."

"Um, I think you're missing the point," said Berenice. "Why would they summon the unregistered magic-users? They can't think *we* have anything to do with it?"

"God knows," said Cyrus. "I'm guessing they want to keep track of everyone, seeing as there's something crazy-wrong out there. I think they just want to know who summoned the shadow-beasts. Even now, I don't think they believe Jude did it himself."

"I can't believe this," said Leo. "Like we needed any more shit to deal with. Shadow-beasts and Jude of the Dead are running around, and they're blaming the one person who can actually help."

"Tell me about it," said Cyrus. "Right. Let's go face the music."

8

LUCIFER

Unsurprisingly, the Venantium Headquarters was wrapped in its typical eerie silence, like the subterranean tunnels that connected its different areas. We entered, as usual, through a doorway within the Blackstone family tomb, which involved falling into an open grave, the only remote hint I'd had that the Venantium possessed anything resembling a sense of humour. I couldn't for the life of me figure out why they just didn't use stairs.

I'd only been acquainted with the interrogation room and the prison cells, but today, everyone waited in the entrance hall to be summoned to the room Leo told me was the meeting place of the Inner Circle.

Maybe I'd finally get to meet their mysterious leaders. The thought gave me a thrill of horror. I couldn't forget how close they'd come to imprisoning me for life, even if Dr Philips had formally apologised to me.

I looked around for any familiar faces. A hundred or so *venators* milled around the entrance hall. Most wore sharp suits, embossed with a silver badge in the shape of a 'V'. I recognised David and the girl he'd been with in the library, who were in deep conversation. We were, I realised, the only people there who weren't wearing uniform.

The entrance hall looked exactly as it had the last time I'd been there, minus the scowling face of Jude lurking in the shadows. Lit with the eerie blue lights burning in brackets along the walls, it looked like a cross between the entrance to Dracula's castle and a sepulchre. Harpies nested in the rafters of the domed ceiling, and gruesome demonic paintings and tapestries adorned the walls.

The heavy iron doors at the end of the hallway swung open, and a figure glided into the room. Everyone stopped talking, almost stopped breathing.

The man was tall, his narrow face all sharp angles. He stood like a king amongst his subjects, and I knew before he spoke that he was someone very, very important.

And he looked right at our group.

Leo's grip on my hand tightened and he hissed, "That's my father. Looks like the rumours were true. He made it into the Inner Circle after all."

I stared at the man. *Leo's father?* I couldn't see the resemblance at all—his sharp gaze held no warmth; if anything, there was something unnaturally still and cold about him. His eyes roved over the crowd, calculating.

Then he spoke one word, "Come."

Everyone followed him through the iron doors in silence, into another hallway lined with doors. Through another door into a large room. It looked like the Great Hall at the university.

Several Venantium members stood on the stairs, directing people into seats. One pointed us to a row near the back. Leo's father didn't even acknowledge his children. Leo himself fidgeted at my side. Cyrus's mouth was set in a grim line.

Mr Blake stood at the front and waited for everyone to be seated, which took no time at all. There was no chatter, no noise like when people were coming into lectures. Leo's father didn't need to call for silence; there was already the kind of absolute quietness of a funeral.

"Magic-users and sorcerers," he said. "You may wonder why I have called you all here today. You may wonder why it was so imperative that you all attend—even those who have chosen not to register with the Venantium.

"As representative of the Inner Circle, I feel it is my duty to give you this warning in person," he said, blank gaze sweeping the room. I found myself automatically holding my breath, dread building in my chest.

"I am sure you are all aware that an alarming series of incidents has occurred of late, including the tragic deaths of several magic-users and the illegal magical activities of Jude Anders."

I saw Cyrus and Leo exchange glances.

"For many of you, your faith in us has undoubtedly been shaken by these events. But we remain steadfast in our stand against the darkness, and our full-scale investigation points to one person as the catalyst for these events: Lucifer."

This time, it felt like the entire room held its breath. That one word rang out into the silent room, and though no one moved, I could almost feel the tension pouring off the crowd in waves.

"Many of you would not have been here the last time Lucifer made an attack on our world. It was twenty years ago that he invaded last, but he has left his marks on our history, and we will do our utmost to ensure that he does not return from the Darkworld."

Several people were nodding. But the silence remained, unnatural, still.

"But in order to do that, we need information, and to that end, we have taken the sorceress Madame Persephone in for questioning."

I stifled a gasp. It was true. They suspected her.

"Here she will remain until we can ensure that she presents us no threat. Many of you have questioned this decision; after all, she has acted in the defence of magic-users for many years now. But what few people know is that she was unheard of before she moved here twenty years ago, and there are no records of her life anywhere else. What is this woman hiding? Is it coincidence that she appeared *at the very same time* that Lucifer made his last attack?"

No. They couldn't really think…? Yet more than a few of my own questions had gone in this direction. Not that I thought she was guilty. I'd never believe that. But she *had* hidden things, enough to make her a suspect in the eyes of the Venantium. I glanced sideways at Leo, but his expression hadn't changed. Claudia, however, fidgeted on my other side, looking as agitated as I felt.

"That is what we intend to find out, and I hope that I have answered any urgent queries about our decision to question her. If she is found guiltless we will of course allow her to join our defence.

"You may leave now. If you have further questions, you are welcome to direct them to any of our representatives."

And he strode from the room without a backwards glance.

Gradually, whispers broke out like fireworks. Leo hissed, "Let's go," and the five of us stood and followed the gathering crowd out of the room.

"Wait," I whispered. "Shouldn't we check on Madame Persephone?"

"Why?" said Berenice. "She isn't our problem."

"She saved Howard's life," I said, and a *venator* shot me a glare. *Oops.*

"I doubt they'll let us see her," said Cyrus. "But you're right, we should ask."

He made his way over to a *venator* standing near the door to the entrance hall, and spoke to him in an undertone. I saw the man shake his head. It was probably for the best that Cyrus was doing the talking; the rest of us looked like scruffy students standing awkwardly in a high-class building.

He came back over to us. "We can't see her until they've made sure she's not a threat."

Leo swore under his breath. "Let me talk to them."

"They aren't going to listen," said his brother. "Don't bother. We'll come back later. They *can't* find her guilty."

"If our delightful old dad has anything to do with it, they will," said Leo.

But we left the headquarters. There didn't seem to be anything more we could do.

The fog had lifted slightly, and the cemetery was bathed in bright sunlight that yielded no warmth.

"They didn't say anything about Jude or Mephistopheles," I said. "Do they not know about it?"

"I'll bet Madame Persephone's keeping quiet," said Leo. "Smart move, not that it helps us. So this Lucifer is running around as well?"

"Another enemy. Brilliant." Berenice gave a mock cheer.

"Lucifer," said Claudia. "They think Lucifer's returned. What evidence do *they* have?"

"The fortune-teller thought so, too," I said. "She told me just after we came back from the Venantium last time. She said it wasn't over, that the Venantium was really preparing for Lucifer to make a comeback. She said he lives in the Darkworld…"

"That makes no sense," said Claudia. "*Lives* in the Darkworld? The Darkworld isn't a physical place. You can't just hop over there whenever you feel like it. Even if a sorcerer managed to separate from their body—like astral travel—they'd never come back. It's a one-way trip."

"It doesn't sound like this Lucifer's a regular sorcerer," said Leo. "Man, what is with these sorcerers and that name? You'd think the Higher Demon Lucifer would be pissed off that so many magic-users are walking around using his title. Plus, you know, they don't exactly look like angels, fallen or otherwise."

"The fortune-teller said Lucifer thinks he's the greatest human sorcerer," I said, remembering. "She said he… he haunts the Darkworld like a ghost. And I'm sure she mentioned that it wasn't impossible to return to this world."

"A lot of people are turning out to be alive who shouldn't be," said Leo. "Melmoth *killed* Lucifer twenty years ago. He burnt him alive. I don't see how even the 'Greatest Human Sorcerer' could escape that one. Demons might be immortal, but this Lucifer's supposed to be human, right?"

"Unless someone else is using the same name," said Cyrus.

"But the fortune-teller seemed sure it was him," I said. "This is too confusing. Who's the enemy?"

"You automatically believe everything she says?" said Berenice. "She keeps more secrets than anyone else. How do you know *she's* not playing us for fools?"

I hated to admit it, but I didn't know that woman at all, not even her true face. All the same, she'd seemed genuinely scared of *something*, and the fortune-teller was usually indomitable.

"Well, the Venantium are convinced, and whether it's true or not, everyone will believe what they say. Their word is law," said Leo, bitterly. "And dear old Dad is their spokesperson."

"Yeah," said Cyrus. "Face it, little brother, we have one fucked-up family."

"I know that," said Leo, tightly. "Small pity that Jude didn't take out him instead of Melmoth."

"*Leo*," I said, shocked.

"What? I have no affection for the guy. Let him rot in hell." In that moment, for the first time, Leo wore the same cold expression as the man who was, by blood, his father.

And it terrified me.

"Leo doesn't mean it," said Cyrus.

"Yes, I do," said Leo.

"Well, you know it's only because of Mum that he—"

"Stop talking," snapped Leo. "I don't want to discuss that bastard any more, okay?"

"Alright," said Cyrus, raising his hands in a 'chill out' gesture. "So what now?"

I didn't want to go back to campus. It didn't feel right, chasing normality when everything was falling to pieces. The fortune-teller a prisoner. Jude—or Mephistopheles—on the loose. Shadow-beasts in Redthorne. Leo and Cyrus's father refusing to acknowledge them…

"Let's see if Madame Persephone left her tent unguarded again," said Claudia. "I want to see if she left us any kind of clues to get her out of there."

We walked down the narrow alleyway to the town square. Without the market, it always looked bare, with the single angel statue in the centre like a lone worshipper.

"It's not here," said Cyrus.

I walked around the outskirts of the square, checking every corner, but the black tent was nowhere in sight.

"I'm going back to Howard's," said Berenice.

"Well, *I* intend to find a pub and get raging drunk," said Leo.

"There must be something we can do," I said. "She wouldn't just have let herself get taken in like that."

"Unless she's planning an epic jailbreak," said Leo. "Come on, you remember the mind-tricks she used to get us out of the shit a couple of weeks ago? She completely got us off the hook. She can run circles around them and they know it."

"She went under testing then," I said, frowning as I recalled the interrogations. "What more do they want from her?"

"Maybe they know she tricked them to get us out of trouble," said Cyrus. "They can detect subliminal magic, can't they?"

"Yeah, but it's always been pretty obvious she's using it," said Claudia. "I know for a fact she's using magic to enhance her appearance."

"That's not illegal," said Cyrus. "Just hard to do. Like a mass-influence. No, it must be what they said. What happened twenty years ago."

"Well, it was before most of us were born," said Claudia. "My parents have never mentioned it before, but they don't really like talking about what happened when they were in the Venantium."

"Well," said Leo, "we all know the best place to look. I think now's the perfect time for a ninja operative."

"You're mental," said Claudia, shaking her head.

"You can't seriously be thinking of going back down there," said Cyrus.

"Well, why not? I already read Melmoth's accounts,

but there has to be more about this Lucifer guy." Leo had already turned around and headed back in the direction of the cemetery.

"Fine, I'm off," said Berenice, and stalked away, presumably back to Howard's.

Cyrus hurried after his brother, with Claudia and me close behind.

"Leo, wait!" I grabbed his arm before he could climb over the wall. "Look."

Several *venators* stood in small groups around the grave-yard. They were plainly still discussing the announcement.

"Fine. We can go underground, then," said Leo.

"Can't it wait for another time?" I said. "They'll be running around like crazy under there."

"Okay, good point," said Leo. "Come to think of it…" He frowned. "Some of those documents I found in Melmoth's study. There wasn't much on Lucifer, but he didn't mention Madame Persephone at all, as far as I can remember. I'll have another look."

"As long as you don't do anything reckless," said Cyrus.

"Who, me?"

"Seriously," I said. "Be careful."

He sighed. "Yeah. Sure. Careful."

He didn't say much on the walk back to campus, which was unusual, but none of us really felt like talking. Claudia said goodbye tactfully, leaving the two of us alone.

"You doing anything tonight?" he said. "I'm guessing you've already started your essay. I should probably do the same."

"Yeah," I said, hesitant. Why could I never think of the right words? "Are you okay?"

"As I'll ever be." He shook his head. "It's nothing. It just pisses me off that my own dad… he didn't even ask after Melmoth. He doesn't care that his kids are pretty much homeless."

"It's awful," I said, and I took his hand in a gesture that said more than words could.

He smiled at me, and it all but broke my heart. "I'll see you tonight, okay?"

"Sure," I said.

9

THE PARTY

Tiredness dragged at my limbs, and when I got to my room, I more or less passed out fully clothed. I slept most of the day, only waking when my phone buzzed again. 5.00 p.m.

Yawning, I checked my messages. I had a text from Leo inviting me to a party at Howard's that night. Apparently, Howard had recovered enough to want to 'celebrate being alive'.

My neck ached from the angle I'd been sleeping at, and I had a pounding headache. I was also pretty sure I hadn't eaten since yesterday afternoon. Groaning, I got dressed and showered before heading to the kitchen.

Sarah, Alex, and Mandeep had been in the middle of a conversation, which abruptly cut off as I entered.

"You feeling alright, Ash?" said Alex. "You didn't answer your door this morning. We thought—" She exchanged a glance with Sarah. "We thought you were at Leo's."

"I didn't get any sleep last night," I said, examining the contents of my cupboard with distaste. I really needed to go shopping; all I really had were a few ready-meals and some pasta. I tipped pasta into a pan, which was at least clean. "Guess I was more tired than I thought."

This was pretty normal for me, but Alex frowned. "Were you out?"

"No," I said, trying to sound casual.

"Are you coming to the English Lit social tonight?" said Sarah.

"I've been invited to a party," I admitted. "Not sure if I'm really in the mood, though. I should probably catch up on those lectures."

"Well, we're heading out in an hour," said Alex. "Is it Leo's party?"

"Nah, it's at his friend's house," I said.

"Ooh. Get you. Your first *real* party."

"What does that mean?" I said.

"Hello? Getting shitfaced and making out in the spare room?"

"How is that different from any other student party?"

"It's in a *house*," said Alex, and laughed at the expression on my face. I couldn't even begin to guess what was so funny.

"Well, I don't know. I don't want to walk into town…" I almost said *again*, but caught myself just in time. Living a double life got confusing sometimes.

"Never turn down a party invitation."

My phone buzzed again. **R u coming tonite? xx**

Sure, I texted back.

Alex watched me carefully. "It appears we've been replaced," she said.

"What? You told me to go."

"I'm only joking, you ass," she said. "Jesus, go and take out your sexual frustration on someone else."

Like *that* was what bothered me. Still, if Leo and I hadn't been interrupted the other day…

But was that the way I wanted it to happen? I'd always thought of sex as the ultimate expression of trust in another person. It wasn't that I didn't trust Leo—far from it. But I hadn't been completely honest with him about who I was, and as long as I kept secrets, could I guarantee that he'd forgive me if he found out the truth?

My nerves prickled as I waited outside the flat for Leo, ready to leave for the party. I was glad both that I'd brought a coat and that I hadn't bothered doing anything fancy with my hair, since the wind assaulted me as soon as I stepped out the door, whipping my hair around my ears and biting at my bare legs. I'd picked a short denim skirt and my nicest black top and wore the only pair of heels I could walk in. They had nothing on Claudia's six-inch platform shoes, but I had no intention of face-planting the floor in Howard's house. I didn't particularly want to see Howard or Berenice, but it'd be nice to have one night where we could hang out as a group without anyone nearly dying.

"Hey," said Leo, greeting me with a kiss. "You ready to go?"

We caught the bus to the far edge of Blackstone, since Howard lived some way from the town centre. His was one of many brick houses identifiable as student accommodation by the signs in the windows—in this case, a cardboard cut-out of Arnold Schwarzenegger. I rolled my eyes when I noticed a sign advertising the 'Sex Dungeon' in the basement.

Leo rang the doorbell, which was unnecessary as Claudia had already spotted us from the window. "Hey!" she called. "Glad you guys could make it!"

She stood on a table, half-gone already. God alone

knew how she kept her balance on those heels. Howard let us into the house, leading us into the living room. A game of Ring of Fire was underway, and the furniture had been moved against the walls to accommodate the crowd. I couldn't take a step without falling into someone or knocking drinks over, and the smell of sweat and cheap beer was almost overpowering.

"We're hitting Redthorne later!" Howard yelled at the crowd. "Gonna thrash the shit out of Satan's Pit!"

Several people cheered.

I stuck close to Leo as we moved through the crowd and found two free chairs next to the table where the game of Ring of Fire was still underway. In the centre of a mass of playing cards, a pitcher was full of what looked like absinthe mixed with seven kinds of beer. *Yeuch.*

"I'll sit this one out," I said to Leo. "I have no intention of projectile-vomiting."

"Good call," he said, handing me a glass and rummaging in the bag he'd brought with him. He tipped some cola into the glass and started measuring vodka shots.

"Cheers," I said.

Observing Howard's friends was kind of like watching animals in a zoo. Claudia challenged a guy to a game of battle shots and proceeded to drink him under the table— then *danced* on the table herself, to catcalls from Howard's friends. I stuck with Leo; Howard's crew were the sort who tried to grope girls from behind in night clubs and pass it off as an accident. Thankfully Leo kept his arm around me in a 'back off' gesture.

Three hours later and I wondered if anyone actually planned on going into town. Someone had brought a stereo in and turned the sitting room into a rave; someone else vomited into a plant pot; and Howard and Berenice made out in the middle of the 'dance floor' with no inhibition whatsoever.

I hadn't anticipated how fast the vodka would affect me. It was cheap store-brand crap and it went right to my head and made my legs forget how to stand. I ended up half-lying in Leo's lap, which he didn't seem to mind.

"Wanna go get some air?" said Leo.

"Sure," I said.

We stumbled over people on the way to the door. Leo grabbed my hand, swung me around and kissed me so fast it left me breathless. Unsteady on my feet, I leant on him for support.

"Are you having a good time?" he slurred.

"Uh," I said, my voice sounding odd. "Sure."

Really, I'd rather be alone with him, not stuck at Howard's, but my head buzzed too much for me to care.

He took my hand, pulled me down the hallway. "C'mon."

I stumbled after him. *Hell, I'm drunk,* I thought, as the world span.

He kissed me again, trailing kisses down my neck. My skin flared in response, and my fingers shook as I ran them through his hair.

An image flashed before my eyes. Leo no longer stood before me but slumped on the floor, blood pooling around him. My entire body went cold. I trembled, dropping to my knees.

Leo lay still, but as I inched closer, fighting all instinct, he moved, lifting his head. Violet demon eyes met my stare, and a cruel smile twisted his lips.

"Don't get too close or you'll get burned, Ashlyn."

"Hey, you okay?" Leo's voice broke through the vision.

The world righted itself, and a terrible pain shot through my head. I tried to say something, but my mouth had forgotten how to speak. Leo drifted in and out of focus. But he was alive. Not possessed. Not dead.

"You're very drunk. Want me to take you home?"

"No," I groaned.

Someone fell over us. It was Claudia, wild-eyed and dishevelled, but that barely registered. I just wanted Leo. I just wanted to hold him, to know he was alive.

"There you are," said Claudia. "Someone got killed by a shadow-beast in Redthorne tonight."

"Uh-huh," said Leo, pulling me close to him again.

"Wait," I said, the dull pain in my head receding. "Wait a sec. Um… shadow-beast?"

"Jesus. Yeah, a shadow-beast," said Claudia. "It attacked her. Remember Dianne Lester?"

"Who?"

"She worked for the *venators*. She was a student. She's dead."

Dead. That word had the equivalent effect of someone dousing me in water. The memory of the vision was replaced by stark reality.

"Seriously?"

"Why would I lie about something like that?" She shook her head. "I think you should get home."

Gradually her words worked their way through my mind. "Someone's dead," I repeated.

"Yes. I'm going home. I suggest you do the same. Redthorne's not safe tonight."

I staggered upright.

"Um, you should probably learn to handle your drink better. I know Leo's a terrible influence, but still." Claudia shook her head.

I looked at Leo as she walked away. "Someone's dead," I said. He didn't seem to be listening.

"Ash." He stroked my face. "You're beautiful. Ash."

"Leo," I said. "For God's sake. Didn't you hear a word she said? Someone got killed by a shadow-beast!"

"Not here?"

"No, in Redthorne!"

"Well, we're safe, aren't we?"

"Are you mad?" I pushed him away from me. "Don't you care that someone's dead, and the fortune-teller's locked up underground, and we're here getting pissed…"

That seemed to have more impact. "Of course I care." He stood up from where he'd slouched against the wall. "Come on. We have to get you home."

"I can walk by myself, thanks," I said coldly, as he tried to half-lift me down the hallway. My mind reeled. What had that vision meant? The demon had tried to warn me off Leo—why? Was it a threat? The very idea of something happening to him turned my blood to ice.

Yet I shook with rage, not fear. It was the culmination of everything that had happened recently, from the near-fight in the library to the fortune-teller's arrest, Howard nearly dying, the Venantium's warning about Lucifer, and now the shadow-beasts moving in for the kill. The feeling constricted like a vice around my chest. If we hadn't been pissing about, we might have been able to do something about it—we might have been able to save her.

Even though we knew no more than the Venantium about what was going on.

I felt tears spill over before I could stop it. I didn't even know who I cried for. Was it for the girl who'd just been killed, or for the rest of us? The fortune-teller, imprisoned. Howard, lucky to be alive. Melivia Blackstone, who'd died to rid herself of a demon.

It all came down to the demons. And the sorcerers who summoned them.

"Ash?" Leo turned to face me. "Ash, what's wrong?"

"Everything's wrong," I said. "Why is this happening?"

"Because there's a load of dickheads in the world," said Leo, pulling me into a tight hug. He seemed to have sobered up quickly. "There was nothing we could have done."

There's nothing the Venantium can do either, I thought. They'd predicted Lucifer's return, but plainly they weren't prepared at all. *And what about Jude?*

I CERTAINLY WASN'T PREPARED for my first hangover. It hit me like a jackhammer the instant I awoke from yet another dream of burning in the fire that destroyed the Blackstone family house. My head pounded and I groaned and pulled my covers back over my head.

When I dozed off, I fell into another nightmare. This time I lay in the grave where Jude had tried to kill me, watching him summon fire to engulf my demon heart. But the pain somehow brought everything into focus.

It wasn't Jude who burned me. It was Leo.

Horror ripped through me. Leo smiled sadly, conjuring another flame. I screamed as my demon heart flared up.

"Sorry, Ash. It's your fault. You have to burn."

I woke up drenched in sweat, the pendant searing my chest. I'd forgotten to take it off. Gasping, I tore it from my neck. It left a faint red mark on my skin.

Shuddering, I fell back onto the bed, too tired and sore even to think about the dream.

Too bad my subconscious wasn't done with me yet.

I lay in the grave again, but this time the fortune-teller extended a hand to pull me out. I clambered up the earthy wall, hands shaking with some horrible foreboding.

Coffins lay all around me, open. I ran to the nearest.

Claudia, eyes closed, unmoving. Next to her lay Cyrus. Howard. Berenice. Alex. Sarah. Cara.

And Leo stood in the centre, demon eyes shining.

"Sorry, Ash," he said. "Looks like it's just you and me. See, it isn't fair that you get to survive when I'm just another pathetic human. It's only fair that I get a dark side. Right?"

His face twisted into a smile. A flame danced in his hand, and he aimed it at the fortune-teller.

She didn't even dodge. The flame consumed her, and she cried out as she burned. Horror choked me, and I dropped to my knees. *No. Stop—Leo—*

"Stop!"

Knocking brought me back to the waking world. Someone banged on my bedroom door.

"Wait a minute," I muttered, sitting up. I pulled on my dressing gown and opened the door.

"You were yelling," said Alex, blinking at me. "Jesus. Good party? You look like crap."

"Thanks," I said, rubbing my eyes.

"What's up? Leo didn't take advantage of you when you were drunk, did he?"

"No," I shook my head hastily. "He'd never do that."

"That's good to know. Want to come watch a film later?"

I shrugged. "Might as well."

"Okay, seriously, Ash. What's with you?"

Alex's stare wore me down. "Bad dream," I relented.

"How bad? Like, apocalyptic?"

"Good word," I said, forcing a smile. "All death and destruction. The works."

"Neat. Write it down," said Alex. "Best way to exorcise your demons." She burst out laughing at the look on my face. "Now you look like you've seen a ghost."

"Nah, it's just your face."

"Very funny. I'm going to go write my essay and maybe die a little. See you in a couple of hours?"

"Sure," I said.

Exorcise your demons. The irony. I rested my head on the door frame with a groan. Maybe I should text Leo, see if he was in any state to talk.

I fished my phone out of my bag and skimmed through my messages. None from Leo. There was a text from Cara asking when I was next available to Skype, but I didn't think talking to her would help take my mind off things any more than a movie night with Alex and Sarah. I sent Claudia a quick text asking her if she knew any more about what had happened last night.

No idea, came the rather terse reply.

Was Jude involved? I asked.

I don't know. Meet me outside in 5?

Sure, I texted back.

Claudia already waited in the hallway when I opened the flat door.

"It was just a bunch of shadow-beasts, same as the other night," she said. "Whoever it is, they must be local. They're attacking people just outside the barrier limits."

"You know what we have to do," I said. "We've got to set the fortune-teller free. She was the one who really kept everyone safe, even the Venantium. And she's the only person who has any clue what's going on."

"I know," Claudia said. "We're going to have to do something about it. Maybe we should ask if they allow visitors. I can't think of anything else."

"Let's go tomorrow," I said.

"Sure thing. Just don't get your hopes up. Have you heard from Leo?"

"No," I said. "I don't think he's in any state to talk to

today."

"That figures." She gave me an appraising look. "Was that the first time you've ever got really drunk?"

"Yep." I grimaced. "Won't be happening again."

"That's what they all say," she said, with a half-smile.

I rolled my eyes. "It was an accident, okay? Trust me. I shouldn't have done it—not with the fortune-teller stuck down in the cells and us the only people who can help her."

"You can't take responsibility for everyone else's lives," said Claudia. "I know, I felt like that when I first discovered what I can do. It's why I considered working for the Venantium at first. The idea of saving people… but you can't save them from themselves. You can't stop them from deciding to meddle with demons. Leo knows that, too. Hell, his own mum did it, and it sent his dad crazy. You've seen him now. He's barely human."

I remembered Mr Blake's blank stare, his complete lack of any emotion.

"He's become like them. Like the demons. He thinks it's the only way to face them. He doesn't get it at all. Cyrus and Leo know that, even if they can't deal with it that well. They aren't like him."

"I know." I felt tears inexplicably pricking at my eyes. "I just wish I knew what he was thinking. He doesn't seem to care about *anything*…"

"Leo? I'm damned if he doesn't care about *you*. You're lucky."

There was something wistful in her voice. I looked at her. "You've never met anyone? You know, another magic-user?"

"I wouldn't date just anyone because they were a magic-user," said Claudia. "There's not much of a selection around here, is there, anyway? Just people like David."

"Weren't you manipulating him into giving you information?"

"Unfortunately, he saw through me and backed off when he realised he couldn't get any info on you guys from *me*." She pulled a face. "And Cyrus is leaving soon. Says he's going travelling."

"Oh yeah," I said.

"He never had any intention of joining the Venantium. I think he wants to get away from here. I'm kinda jealous. Wish I could afford to see the world."

"Same here," I said. "But… well, I mean, there are demons everywhere, right?"

"Yeah, but you can't let that keep you down. There's crap enough in the world with nothing to do with the Darkworld."

"True," I said.

"I'd love to see somewhere new. Guess I should have picked a university with a study-abroad programme."

"You picked Blackstone because of the Venantium, right?"

Her forehead creased in a frown. "I guess. My parents both came here, but they never forced me to do the same." She rubbed her head, like it hurt. "I don't know. It was the only place I got in, anyway, all my other university choices turned me down because of my shitty grades."

I felt an odd shiver of foreboding, like there was something I was supposed to have done, something I'd forgotten. I unconsciously reached for the pendant and remembered I'd left it in my room. For some reason, that made me feel even more uneasy.

"Anyway, travelling is definitely on the cards."

"Same," I said. Much as I liked university—minus all the people who'd tried to kill me—I couldn't imagine staying here in the middle of nowhere forever. Maybe that was my problem. I felt trapped, hemmed in by the Darkworld.

"What about you and Leo?" said Claudia.

"What about us?"

"Huh? Never mind. You've only been together a few weeks, right? I think you'll be alright. You just don't want any regrets."

Too right I didn't. Neither did I want to join the ranks of the all-night partygoers. I'd had a glimpse of that last night, and I wasn't keen for it to happen again.

Claudia seemed to guess what was on my mind. "Hey, getting shitfaced is hardly the worst thing you could have done. Think of it as a life lesson. Of sorts. Well, that's what I tell myself whenever I wake up on someone's floor after a night at Satan's Pit." And just like that, carefree Claudia was back.

"I'll keep that in mind," I said. "It's more, you know, that people died when we were at that party. Kind of makes the whole thing seem like a frivolous waste of time."

"You know what I said about no regrets? That. Wouldn't you rather have *enjoyed* your life, even if a demon got you in the end?"

"Well," I said. "There's that."

"Then go and do what you like doing. We'll bust the fortune-teller out of jail tomorrow."

I snorted with genuine laughter. "Now you sound like you're out of one of those prison-break movies."

"I did once say I wanted to star in a James Bond film."

Still laughing, she waved goodbye, saying she needed to go to the shop. I went back into the flat. At least our conversation had cheered me up.

If only the big problems could be resolved as easily. Despite everything, something told me that we were the fortune-teller's only hope.

10

DR PHILIPS

"**O**h," said Claudia, as we stood before the Blackstone family tomb. "I'm not sure how you get into Headquarters if you don't have an appointment."

The tomb's doors were resolutely sealed, and it wasn't like there was a doorbell or anything. *We should probably have thought this through.*

I examined the Blackstone memorial stone, which stood beside the tomb, wondering if it contained some kind of clue. The smooth black stone had been engraved with a list of names. Melivia's name stood out at the bottom; she'd been the youngest.

No one else ever seemed to come near here, though I could still see the town square through the alleyway alongside the cathedral. We did spend more time hanging about in this abandoned old cemetery than was probably healthy. No one ever went in the cathedral either; it had apparently been closed due to the unstable floorboards making it unsafe to walk inside. Instead of renovating it, the local council, who were based in Crowley, had merely left it to drift into disrepair.

Leo raised a hand and knocked on the doors to the tomb. A hollow, ringing sound echoed.

"Hey! Can we come see the Venantium?"

"It's urgent!" I added, feeling foolish to be speaking to the front doors of a tomb. Not even a harpy was around to hear us. The gateway remained sealed.

"Should we use the tunnels?" said Leo, stepping back.

"Doesn't look like we have much choice," said Claudia.

So, once again, Cyrus—who'd come along at Leo's insistence that he was our only way into the tunnels—unlocked the door behind the statue and we descended into darkness.

This time, we followed a different path to the one that led to the library, a winding track that looped on itself several times. The floor became damp as moisture seeped through the walls and ceiling; I heard the distant sound of rushing water.

"Are we going the right way?" I said, sidestepping a muddy puddle.

"Possibly," said Leo. "Ah, hell."

My arms prickled and my heart started beating fast. The walls had become metal rather than earth and a familiar burning smell crept up on us. I *knew* I'd been here before. The cells.

The pendant was cold on my neck, and I was glad I'd fetched it from my room before we'd set out.

"C'mon,'" Leo whispered, quickening his pace. "At least we know this way leads up to the surface."

"Are you mad?" I said. "They'll think we're here to help her escape!"

"I'm with Ash," said Claudia, whose pale face gleamed in the blue candle-light.

"These cells go on for miles," Leo whispered. "This is the quickest way."

"Unfortunately, he's right," said Cyrus. "Seriously, though—I'll kill you all if you get us arrested."

Sure enough, we soon reached the cells, a row of barred doors set into the cave walls. I couldn't help looking inside, but most were empty. None of the few inhabitants looked up, although Leo pressed his face right up to the bars.

"What're you doing?" I hissed.

"Looking out for Howard's parents."

"Do you think they might be here?" I'd totally forgotten that Howard's parents had been arrested by the Venantium when he was a child. This wasn't a fate I'd wish on anyone.

"No, I've been down here before and I've not seen them. But it's a force of habit. The least I can do."

"You think you owe it to Howard?"

"Well, I realise he's an ungrateful bastard fifty per cent of the time…"

"Ninety-nine per cent," I corrected. "I've never heard him say anything nice. Ever."

"Probably only Berenice has," said Leo. "Anyway, here we are."

We now stood in the corridor that led to the room with the Angel Box—and the way out. The silence unnerved me; last time I'd been here the tunnels had been swarming with activity thanks to the Skele-Ghouls. Now, however, not a soul was in sight.

Leo reached the door first, and pushed it open. We emerged through one of the archways in the entrance hall, and walked into a stern-faced *venator*.

"Shit," said Leo.

"What are you doing here?" she said.

Oh, hell. Dr Philips, the woman who had interrogated me before, glared at us.

"We were… we wanted to speak to the fortune-teller." Claudia was certainly brave to look her in the eyes.

"Madame Persephone," I said.

"That is not her name," said Dr Philips, frowning at me. "We might not be able to read her as we can any other magic-user, but she is not who she claims to be. And you shouldn't be here."

"She's not bad!" I said. "She isn't working with the demons. She's not a threat."

"That has yet to be determined. You heard Mr Blake. Her involvement with Lucifer, for instance—"

"What does it matter what happened twenty years ago?" I said. "People are *dying* now! Only she can stop Jude—I mean, Mephistopheles."

"Mephistopheles?" Dr Philips raised an eyebrow. "Clearly, she has confided in you, but refuses to divulge anything to us. *We* are trying our utmost to stop all threats. *She* works to her own agenda, and she has been known to have dealings with demons before. She is not trustworthy."

"Look," said Cyrus. "We understand your position, but there's no denying that she is an extremely talented magic-user. She could help you."

"Believe me, we are doing our best to get as much information from her as we can. She has alerted us to several attacks already."

"I thought you blocked her Darkworld connection," I said.

"Did you not hear the announcement? We are in a fragile situation. We need her help."

"Then why not let her help you of her own free will?" I asked. "She's working against Lucifer. You know that."

"That may be the case, but it is curious that a woman

who claims to be on *our* side has so many… unusual talents. She can modify her appearance at will, so how are we to know she is the age she claims to be? Her ability is disturbingly similar to Lucifer's. Are you aware of the Lucifer case?"

"Actually, we are—sort of," said Leo. "We were curious about that. Mr Blake… my father… he said that Lucifer lives in the Darkworld. That shouldn't be possible."

"I read something about it in a book," said Claudia. "It said astral travel's possible, but nothing about being able to come back. I'm not about to run off and do it," she added hastily, as Dr Philips's eyes narrowed. "I don't have a death wish. But you can't expect us not to be curious after what we just heard."

"Well, knowledge on the matter is restricted," said Ms Weston. "You know that twenty years ago, Lucifer invaded our world, bringing with him a host of demons. As a spirit, he possessed a body himself. That is the price of immortality. You must kill to return to life. But most who attempt it die before they have the chance. Lucifer was an uncommonly strong sorcerer. The Darkworld takes no prisoners, and spiritual travel is foolhardy at best. For most, it is a last resort to escape mortality. But you young magic-users are not my responsibility. By all means satisfy your curiosity, but the answers might not be to your liking."

"This… Lucifer," said Claudia. "He's human, right?"

"That would depend upon your definitions of humanity. He is more demon than human now."

"But he *was* human?"

"Once. Perhaps. No one knows. Not even the Inner Circle."

"Figures," said Leo. "So you've taken Madame Persephone prisoner just because you're hoping she knows something you don't. You couldn't have just asked for her help?"

"She is notoriously uncooperative. If you know her as well as you claim to, you will know that."

"Everyone has secrets," said Leo.

"Not everyone's secrets threaten everything we stand for," said Dr Philips. "Now, we are not currently permitting visitors to the cells. I might be persuaded to overlook your transgression, since it was apparently well-meaning… but if I catch you here again, I will have to take measures."

Her gaze lingered on me. I shivered. I hadn't forgotten the interrogation—even though at the time she'd thought I was my doppelganger, and had since apologised. Her face resembled a jagged cliff, her eyes like silver chips.

"I hope you learn a lesson from this about meddling with illegal magic," said Dr Philips.

"Not really," said Leo. "Since we've no proof that's what Madame Persephone was doing."

"You have faith in her even though she is known to have been complicit in the Lucifer case, supported his atrocities? The evidence suggests that she may have had a change of heart and turned on him, turned him into the Venantium. But that does not mean she is truly on our side. If he returns, she may turn again. That is my final word."

A clear dismissal. As we left through the tunnel she pointed us through, I whispered, "She's scary. I just want to know where they're keeping the fortune-teller."

"Bastards." Claudia's voice shook with anger. "They're just frightened because she's a better magic-user than any of them ever will be."

"But what if it's true? That she switched sides?" I swallowed. "What did Dr Philips mean about her being *complicit* in the Lucifer case?"

"I don't know," said Claudia. "I really don't know. The only person who can tell us is stuck in jail."

"I'd say we stay out of it," said Cyrus. "I think we're in way over our heads. The Venantium might not know what they're doing, but they're in a better position than us. If Madame Persephone's really helping them, I'm not sure what more we can do."

"Find Jude ourselves?" said Leo.

"What?" I said, staring at him. "Really?"

"He killed our guardian," said Leo. "I think that's a good enough reason."

"Leo," said Cyrus. "He's under the control of a demon, remember?"

"All the more reason," said Leo.

"You'd go after the most powerful demon in existence?" said Cyrus, raising an eyebrow. "Okay, bro, send me a postcard."

"Please tell me you're joking," I said to Leo. "We don't have a clue what Mephistopheles is planning, but getting Jude to walk openly into the Venantium and stealing a demon heart kinda suggests that he doesn't fear anything from magic-users. And let's face it, they know more about this stuff than we do."

"Too true," said Cyrus. "Don't do anything rash, little bro."

"Well, I'm not sitting back and doing nothing when people are getting hurt," said Claudia. "Ash? You in?"

"Huh?" The thought of hunting down a demon on purpose didn't exactly appeal, but there *was* something I could do. When I thought it, it seemed both simple and reckless beyond belief—*I could talk to the demons.*

As much as I hated it, they acknowledged me as their superior. They might be irritating and cryptic, but... maybe that was our best chance of getting information.

Are you mad? Demons don't give information for nothing. They want a deal. They'll try to get you to set them free.

But I'd resisted them before…

"Who is this Dr Philips, anyway?" said Claudia. "More to the point, who shoved the stick up her ass?"

"Her brother was killed by a sorcerer," said Cyrus. "Half the Venantium's made up of grieving families. That's why they're so persistent and unforgiving. Think what it looks like to them for Madame Persephone to potentially be mixed up with Lucifer. Even we don't really know what she's capable of."

How many dark secrets did the fortune-teller really have? She'd had an affair with a demon, and apparently helped Lucifer with his schemes. I remembered what she'd said to Jude, down in the sepulchre. *"The past has power. We may not forgive ourselves, but the memory gives us strength. And damn me a thousand times more if I allow you, yet another misguided child of the Seven, to try to take what you have no right to."*

At the time I'd been too scared to wonder what she meant. But now… had she worked with Lucifer? Summoned demons, even?

"Well, she's also on the board of governors," said Cyrus, who was still talking about Dr Philips. "She'll have influenced their decision."

"So what does the Inner Circle do?" I said.

"It's unusual for them to show themselves," said Cyrus. "There are seven of them, including the Chairman. I've heard it's a statement to the demons, since there are seven higher demons, too. The Inner Circle make all the decisions, and pass on the orders to the governors, who pass on their orders to everyone else. It's a strict hierarchy, and no one ever questions orders from above."

"Which is bullshit," said Leo. "Yeah, they maintain the Barrier, but that pretty much runs itself. They just make and impose their laws on all magic-users. And where did the last rogue magic-users come from? Within their very own ranks."

"Exactly," said Claudia. "I'm starting to think they're just as clueless as the rest of us."

"Damn right," said Leo.

I just hoped that they'd set the fortune-teller free before anyone else had to die.

~

THIS IS STUPID.

The voice in my head persisted, as much as I told it to shut up. I'd never deliberately tried to speak to a demon before. They'd always come to me—whether I liked it or not.

Now, naturally, as soon as I wanted to find one, they were silent.

I stood in an alleyway in Redthorne, feeling like an idiot for coming. On Sundays, the usual traffic didn't clog the roads and few people walked the streets. I felt reasonably confident that no one would walk past the alleyway I'd slipped into as soon as I'd stepped off the bus.

I reached out to the Darkworld, feeling my mind explore every corner I could find. I unconsciously tapped into a sense I barely knew about, a sense unlike sight and hearing but simultaneously a mixture of both. *Where are you?*

"We are always here. Need you ask?"

I jumped back as a dark space opened up inches from my face, and a familiar pair of violet eyes stared at me.

"Remember me?"

Um...

Truth to be told, I couldn't tell demons apart. They all

looked identical to me, and their 'voices' were all equally emotionless and cold.

"What do you want with us?"

I raised my eyebrows. If it wasn't for the fact that it was in my head, the demon's voice now sounded exactly like *mine* had the many, many times I'd asked the demons what they wanted with me. It would have creeped me out if the doppelganger hadn't rendered me immune to the fear of demons imitating me. As it was, I didn't appreciate being made fun of.

I want to know what you know of the fortune-teller. Madame Persephone. Do you know her? Can you take me to someone who can?

I realised my mistake as soon as I finished the thought. That was the problem with mind-communication.

Not take *me,* I corrected.

"You still don't want to take me up on my offer?"

No, I don't want to come into the Darkworld. I'd never do that. But she did it… didn't she?

"The information you ask for is worth more than your life."

Is it, now?

"Of course, I may be willing to cooperate… in exchange for assistance."

No thanks. I don't make deals with demons.

"Your Madame Persephone is in the worst position. She no longer has a choice. But you do."

I told you, I don't want anything to do with you! I just want to know if she's on our side or not.

"It depends what you mean by 'our'. I am on no one's 'side', for instance."

Is she on Lucifer's side? Or the Venantium's?

"Surely you already know the answer to that? The sorceress works alone."

My head felt like it was splitting, as though someone were reaching a hand between my brain and my skull. I switched to verbal communication and said, "I wish you wouldn't eavesdrop on me."

"You fascinate us, Ashlyn. A human-demon, poised on the brink of the Darkworld. You could have it all, but you choose to limit yourself."

"Yes, I do. And you know what? It's because both extremes would turn me into a monster. I won't become one of the Venantium, and I won't become like you."

"Because of your humanity?" An almost mocking note coloured the demon's tone.

"It's true. I told you. I'm human. And it's pretty obvious you aren't going to be any help."

I glared at the demon, which just grinned back at me.

"Is Jude planning to attack again? Is he the one summoning shadow-beasts?"

"Do you mean the Righteous?"

"Yes. I heard he's possessed. By... Mephistopheles."

The demon vanished.

"No! Hey—you can't run off now!"

No response.

"Dammit." I kicked the alley wall. The Darkworld responded almost instantly, ice coating my foot, and I fell backwards. Instead of a sharp pain hitting my foot, my hands scraped the ground as I tripped over.

Brilliant. So much for my bright idea. The demon had given me no clues whatsoever.

"You're already on the ground? I didn't expect it to be quite *this* easy."

Speak of the devil. Jude stood at the end of the alleyway, smiling an inhuman smile, violet eyes gleaming like knife blades.

11

JUDE OF THE DEAD

"Hello, Ashlyn," said the demon in Jude. I'd never seen him smile as himself; now, it looked unnatural, distorting his stern features into something grotesque. His eyes gleamed, alive and yet dead, animated by something that wasn't of this world. Something with intelligence far beyond humanity.

"You're… Mephistopheles." My voice sounded steady, which surprised me. Every nerve stood on end.

I pushed myself to my feet, using the wall as a support, wincing as my grazed hands scraped against the rough brick. The pendant burned cold against the bare skin of my neck, and I felt its vibration in tandem with my quickening heartbeat.

Jude smiled at me. His shirt and jeans were torn and filthy, as though he'd been dragged through mud. I wondered what has happened to him since he'd run away, how the demon had won him over.

"Which of my kin has been telling you tales, I wonder?" He tilted his head, and the way it hung, limp, dead, made bile rise in my throat. "Who were you speaking to?"

"Nobody," I said.

"Really, Ashlyn? This seems a rather unusual place to have a conversation with yourself." He smiled again, showing more teeth, and the fear in my veins crystallised. "You know my name, yet you lie to me. A bad idea."

"I wouldn't tell you if I knew." I shook all over, but I couldn't let the demon gain any advantage over me.

"Interesting. So you're as loyal to demons as you are devoted to your human friends? Lucifer will be interested to know that. You intrigue him almost as much as you intrigue me."

Anger rose within me, sudden and icy cold. "Fuck Lucifer," I said.

Jude raised an eyebrow. "Well, I happen to know a story or two…"

"Shut up." Out of the corner of my eye, I saw shadows edging in around me. My heart pounded. I knew goading a demon couldn't end well, but the presence of *my* demon in the back of my head, pushed the fear to manageable levels.

"You're rather… *bold*, for a human. This one was rather cowardly, in the end. It was most disappointing— one never feels truly triumphant if the victory is merely handed over. But I know I made the right choice, because this vessel knew some *interesting* things about you. There is only so much one can observe from the Darkworld, and it does feel oddly satisfying to walk amongst you mortal beings once more. With my own heart." He tapped the gem in the dead centre of his forehead.

"What do you want with me?"

"Patience, young Ashlyn. Your kind claim it to be a virtue, but I cannot see the appeal, personally… Very well.

I want you to tell me where I can find the woman who calls herself Madame Persephone."

"You think I'd tell you that?"

"I met her recently. I would quite like to continue our acquaintance, but I have reason to believe that she is currently in the custody of the Venantium. Is that true?"

"That's none of your business."

"You can't hide the truth from me, Ashlyn." Jude's eyes glowed purple, and the demon heart glowed crimson. *"I can see every thought in your mind. I know where your friends are. I know what you fear. I know where you keep your demon heart. And I know you have no inkling of its potential."*

The amethyst pendant burned against my chest again, as if in response to his words.

"I'm not giving it to you. Or Lucifer."

"We're not giving you a choice, Ashlyn."

The shadows rose around him, solidifying, and *things* emerged. Not shadow-beasts, but hunched shapes, emitting an awful keening sound like an injured animal, one after another. *Ghouls.* Horrible, deformed creatures, emaciated like wingless harpies. They stared at me with reddish-purple eyes sunk back in their skulls. Their mouths were like small pipe openings, and they exhaled darkness in streams that curled around me like ribbons. Dread sank its claws into me, dragging at my limbs.

Then came the shadow-beasts—two monstrous bear-sized creatures with tusks like mammoths. They flanked the ghouls on either side of the alleyway.

"Try not to kill her," said Mephistopheles. "Just… incapacitate her a little."

Come on, Ash, whispered the demon inside me.

I called the Darkworld and made a dagger of ice form in my hand, and a disconnected thrill rang through me as the first beast was impaled on it. The monster cried out, a horrible sound like a thousand glass bottles smashing at once. The second sprang forward to take its place. I dived for it, but suddenly there were ghouls grasping at my feet, pulling me down. Teeth closed above my head. *That was close,* I thought numbly, heart hammering.

Adrenaline buzzed through my veins along with a fresh wave of cold fury. I aimed another ice dagger at the first beast and caught it in the hind leg. It fell with a bellow of rage, but before I could throw another, a paralysing chill rushed up my right leg.

A ghoul clung to me like a grotesque parody of a monkey, claws digging into my leg. I kicked out, dodging more scrabbling claws, and reached for the Darkworld, trying to make a shield. I'd practised a lot since the fortune-teller had shown me, and now I barely needed to think before the darkness rushed to my hands and slid over my skin like a weightless cloak. The ghoul gave a keening cry and dropped to the ground, rolling over. Its skin blistered, and I shuddered with revulsion as layers peeled away to reveal greyish veins beneath.

Behind you!

I'd forgotten about the shadow-beast. It slammed into me, knocking the breath from my lungs, and I hit the concrete with an impact that jarred every bone in my body and ripped the skin from my elbows. I tasted blood on my tongue, bitter and metallic. The alleyway blurred before my eyes as I struggled to a sitting position.

There was nothing before me but a wall of shadow. I was backed into a corner. *Shit.*

The second beast bore down on me, a hideous specimen, a shambling mass of darkness with teeth like serrated knives and a tangle of clawed paws.

You can still move, Ash! whispered the demon in my mind.

I rolled away from the shadow-beast's claws and kicked

out, ice fire flaring from my feet. Its jaws snapped inches from my neck. Desperately, I reached out to the Darkworld and felt the shadows close in around me, forming a protective net. Just in time.

Blind it, Ash!

I conjured a light right in front of the beast's eyes, and it howled in shock, momentarily blinded. I used that split-second to pull myself out from underneath its jaws, wincing as my skinned elbows dragged on the pavement, and I stabbed it between the eyes with the ice-dagger.

The beast roared and leapt away, vanishing into a dark space.

"This is highly entertaining," said Jude, who was suddenly right in front of me, "but I have little patience, I confess, Ashlyn. My apologies."

And he seized my arm in a grip stronger than any human's had the right to be. I cried out as he squeezed my wrist, cutting the circulation off—but he let go without warning, swallowed by the shadows.

Someone else had just run into in the alleyway. Several someones.

"Ash!" shouted a voice, and everything erupted into chaos.

I saw Claudia and Leo running towards me, kicking at ghouls left and right. Claudia yelled something and hurled a handful of bright, fiery light into the sky, and the ghouls howled, scuttling away from the brightness.

More shadowy monsters leaped from the shadows, but Howard ran at them, blazing like a human fireball. Jaws snapped. Punches flew left right and centre, and fires sprang up so close that I backed away from their hot breath—right into a group of *venators*. As I got to my feet. I stared at the new arrivals, noticing in a detached way that they were dressed in a less formal-looking variation of their uniform, presumably some form of battle-gear.

Jude had disappeared, but another shadow-beast was fast approaching Leo and Claudia. I summoned another icy dagger and hurled it, striking the beast in the lower back. Leo and Claudia both threw handfuls of flame at the staggering beast, making it reel back in pain.

The *venators* took over, blue-clad figures weaving in and out of the darkness and driving the shadow-beast back into the Darkworld. A hand swiped at my leg, but I moved out the way, throwing icy fire at the ghoul.

Lights burst overhead as several *venators* summoned glowing orbs. That was enough for the remaining ghouls, who shrunk away. As the shadows cleared, only Jude remained.

He hissed as Leo sent a jet of flame that narrowly missed him.

"How nice, Ashlyn, that so many would risk their lives for you. I confess myself surprised. Nobody came to save this fool."

"You are a threat to everyone," said David. "Who are you, truly? Is Jude dead?"

"Naturally. What use would he be still living?"

"Demon," said another *venator*. "Are you working with Lucifer?"

"All demons are under Lucifer's rule," said Jude, the hint of amusement to his voice now gone. "The same will be true for humanity, too, soon enough. Now if you'll excuse me, I'll be leaving now."

He moved so fast he blurred. Several other people moved at the same time, lunging after him, and there was a headlong crash in the middle of the alleyway. A single figure rose into the air, hit the wall and ran upwards swiftly, vanishing over the rooftops.

"Shit," I said.

Groaning, Howard disentangled himself from the heap of bodies. He let out an impressive stream of curses when he saw Jude had gone. At least he had no new wounds to add to the scars which now criss-crossed his face. Glowering, he kicked the alley wall.

Berenice wasn't there, I noted. Had she and Howard had an argument? Or did she just not want to get involved in the fighting?

"Ash," said Leo, running over to me. "Thank God. I thought—"

He hugged me so hard that all my doubt and fear eased away, like a door had shut them out. I let out a shuddering breath, my limbs shaking with adrenaline. Mephistopheles gave off this aura of paralysing fear, so subtle I'd barely noticed it on top of the usual chill I felt when I saw a demon. And *my* demon must have muted my fear, somehow. In fact, her warnings had saved my life. Only now did it register that I'd been within a finger's breadth of death; my immunity to demonic possession aside, Mephistopheles could probably find another way to kill me. I shuddered and clung to Leo, oblivious to everyone around us.

"What on earth were you doing here?" he said.

I gave a shaky laugh. "Looks like I can't even come into town to go shopping without getting attacked these days."

"I'd like to know what his game is," said Cyrus, who'd come over to check that Leo was okay. Brushing tears from my eyes, I glanced over the group. It didn't look like anyone had sustained any serious injuries. *Thank God.*

"I think we'd all like to know that," said one of the *venators*.

"How'd *you* know he was here?" I said.

"Madame Persephone warned us that Lucifer would be making a move. We've been combing Redthorne all day."

So she is working with them, after all, I thought.

"How the hell did Jude defy gravity like that?" snarled Howard. "I'd have throttled the dickhead if he hadn't turned into freaking Spiderman."

"He's possessed, Howard," Claudia reminded him. "He could have done a lot worse. It was like he was holding back… but why?"

"That is what we need to find out," said one of the *venators,* a hard-faced youth with a crop of well-oiled black hair. "The Venantium need to know. What were you doing in this alleyway, Miss…?"

"Ashlyn Temple," I said. "Like I said. I was just taking a short-cut."

"Leave her alone," said Leo. "She hasn't done anything wrong."

"We need to move," said an older female *venator.* "We must discuss our next steps."

She led the small group out of the alleyway. It looked as though several were arguing amongst themselves, and more than one glanced back at us, distrustful.

"Running away?" said Howard. "I knew you *venators* were cowards at heart."

One of them turned back. David. "*What* did you call us?"

"Howard," said Claudia. "Come on. Let's go."

"Don't mess with me, *venator,*" said Howard, spitting the last word. "You didn't do any fighting yourself, I noticed. Scared of getting your face mauled by a shadow-beast?"

"I fail to see what business it is of yours."

"It's my business when we put our necks on the line for the likes of you and don't get so much as a thank you."

"The demon *got away*," said David. "You did nothing to prevent it."

Anger rushed through me. "Neither did you!" I said.

David looked at me. It was the first time we'd made eye contact since last term, and I honestly had no idea what I'd ever seen in him.

"Want a real fight?" said Howard. "I'll give you one."

"Howard!" said Cyrus. "Seriously. He's not worth it. Trust me."

David narrowed his eyes at Howard and stalked off. Howard flipped him off.

"What was that for?" Cyrus demanded. "You could have got us all into trouble."

"I don't give a flying—"

"Miss Temple, please come with us." The dark haired guy beckoned to me.

I felt an icy shudder run down my spine. Had they seen me speaking to the demon?

"What do you want with her?" Leo put his arm around me, protectively.

"That is none of your concern," said the hard-faced *venator*.

I took a deep breath. "Can't you just ask me here?"

"No. These questions are confidential. Speak to us when we're back at headquarters."

"Fine." Swallowing my apprehension, I followed the group out of the alleyway.

The bus journey back to Blackstone was incredibly awkward. I sat next to Leo, but I could feel the gaze of a dozen eyes on my back: the *venators* sat in a group a few rows behind us. Leo held my hand in defiance.

"They won't put you through crap again," he whispered. "I'll stop them."

Howard was far more vocal. "Interfering busybodies. We could have handled them ourselves."

"Howard," Cyrus hissed.

He kept up a continual mutter all the way back to campus. *Maybe he did have an argument with Berenice*, I thought. He certainly seemed on edge, not that that was anything new.

Cyrus and Claudia made a valiant effort to talk loudly about other subjects to cover Howard's grumblings. My mind kept straying to the Angel Box and the cells. When would these people leave me alone? Would they not be satisfied until they'd forced a guilty confession out of me?

But rather than taking me to their headquarters, the group paused beside the Blackstone family tomb without opening the entrance. Leo and the others had to leave, with the promise that they'd be right around the corner and be able to intervene if there was any trouble. I forced a smile and waited until they were out of sight. Then I faced the *venators*.

"There's no need to be nervous," said David.

"I'm not." I couldn't believe he spoke to me as though I was a stranger.

"We just wanted to ask you a question. What was the demon possessing Mr Anders talking to you about?"

Mr Anders? Oh. Jude.

"Who said he was talking to me? He appeared from nowhere and attacked me!"

"Did he say anything?"

"Only… that his name was Mephistopheles. The demon."

"That's…"

"The demon whose heart Jude stole." I said. "The fortune-teller told me," I added, in response to his raised eyebrows.

"I see." His mouth tightened into a line. "Have you anything else you can tell us?"

"No," I said. "He didn't say anything else."

"If we find out you're lying——" said the dark haired guy.

"Enough," said David, to my surprise. "She's honest. Let her go."

The *venator* looked displeased, but nodded. "Very well. You may leave."

So I went to re-join my friends. The *venators* watched me, as though they expected me to reveal something by my behaviour.

"Will the Venantium ever give up their quest to get me to admit to being in league with demons?" I said, once I was sure they were out of range. "I swear it's like talking to a wall."

"I could have a word with them," said Howard, cracking his knuckles. It kind of surprised me that he'd stuck around; normally he and Berenice would have disappeared by now. I wondered where she was, but no one had asked the obvious question.

"There's no need," I said. "I'm fine. See?"

"Yeah, whatever. They're asking for a fucking punch to the head."

"Seriously, Howard. Let it go."

"Anyone fancy a drink?" said Claudia, trying to placate him.

"Nah, I'm alright," said Howard, and he sloped off without so much as a goodbye.

"What's up with him?" I asked in a whisper, when he was out of sight.

"Guilt," said Claudia. "Him and Berenice… well, you know how they are. Only turns out he didn't think she ever really had feelings for him, so things have gone a bit awkward.'

"I heard you said something at the hospital," said Cyrus.

"Great, so it's my fault?" I said. "Berenice has been acting weird since the fortune-teller mentioned Mephistopheles, anyway. Well, she's always acted weird, really, so…"

"It wasn't Ash's fault, Cy," said Leo. "If anything, it's Howard's. Who cares, anyway? You up for a quick one?"

"Deadline's tomorrow," said Cyrus, with a martyred expression as though he faced the noose. "Three more to go, then I can drink myself into oblivion."

"What're you doing next?" said Claudia. "You going to stick around for next term?"

"Nah, I'm travelling at the end of March. Going to Vegas."

"You're not twenty-one yet, Cy," Leo reminded him.

"Shit, good point."

Claudia laughed. "Well, send me a postcard from wherever you end up."

"Will do."

We headed for the Coach and Horses, finding a table at the back where we could talk without people over-hearing us and thinking we were nut-jobs.

"There's one thing that just doesn't add up," I said. "Jude definitely wasn't possessed when he broke into the Headquarters. I think the demon must have been talking to him before that. Must have persuaded him, somehow."

"He wasn't acting on his own, either way," said Leo.

"Lucifer," I said. "He said he was under Lucifer's command. He said all the demons were."

I cut myself off, having forgotten for a moment that I hadn't intended to tell anyone else about the other demon

I'd been speaking to. That had been a stupid, reckless thing to do, and I should have known it wouldn't be worth it. *I could have asked the spirits instead.* I wished I'd asked the fortune-teller how to do that.

I wished I'd asked her a lot of things. But I'd never in a million years have thought she'd let herself be captured like that. If she did have an ulterior motive, it was beyond me to guess it.

We had to find a way to get her out of there. What use did the Venantium think keeping her out of the action would do?

What if Jude attacked again, and she couldn't help everyone?

It'll have to be us, I thought. *Me.*

"Ash."

The voice sounded chilling and familiar, both alien and disturbingly close to home. I opened my eyes, although I knew almost instantly that I was dreaming.

I lay in the centre of a field, although no grass grew around me, and the ground was scorched black. The ruin of the Blackstone manor sat nearby. A girl stood in front of it, smiling a sinister smile. The doppelganger. Her demon eyes found mine and her smile turned cruel, making me feel as though she stripped me down to the core.

"Long time, no see," said the doppelganger.

"Go away," I said.

"You wound me, Ashlyn."

"This is a dream. You can't hurt me, so don't even try."

"Have you learnt nothing from your dreams? I am more real than you are, Ash. And at least I'm not in denial about my true self."

"I don't know what you're talking about."

"You're a fool. You might wear your frail human heart on your sleeve, but your other heart needs nourishing, too. Otherwise it'll take what it wants for itself."

"What're you——?"

Before I could finish, cold pierced me all over and shadows sprung up, wrapping around my wrists. The pendant burned against my chest, and my vision darkened, turning into the purple-tinted monochrome vision of a demon.

I fought against the shadows, but they held me like the arms of a giant.

"Let me go!" I screamed.

Never.

The voice echoed, both in my head and aloud, both mine and not mine. But the doppelganger hadn't opened her mouth.

Was that me? The demon?

No. It couldn't be.

"Conflicted, Ash?"

"You. What have you done?"

"I've not done a thing. I'm trying to *help* you, even though you *destroyed* my second chance at life. You're like us, and the sooner you accept that, the better."

And suddenly the surroundings were clear again, including the building behind the doppelganger. But it was no longer a ruin. The mansion all but gleamed, its white walls and balconies as spotless and whole as if newly made.

No way.

"A word of advice, Ash. Choose your path wisely. There's no turning back from the Darkworld."

Now we stood inside, in Melivia's bedroom. The painting of the girl smiled at me from the wall. Another painting had been pinned to a canvas in the centre of the room, showing a whirlwind of flames engulfing a mass of shadowy black shapes.

And the room was burning, too. Flames leapt around us, devouring the gilt paintings, the rosewood desk, the plush carpets.

The doppelganger vanished, and in her place crouched the frail shape of Melivia, trembling as she faced the flames.

"Burn," she whispered, "burn with me." The fire answered, flickering toward her.

"That won't be necessary."

Another voice spoke out of the shadows. I tried to turn my head to see who it was, but paralysis gripped me. Out of the corner of my eye, I saw the figure offer Melivia a hand.

"I can help you," whispered the voice, and it sounded so… emotionless. Human, but chilling as any demon's. "Come with me."

Melivia shook her head, squeezing her eyes shut as though hoping to push the demon away. "I have to die. This is the only way. I… I killed them."

"Nothing dies forever," whispered the voice. "Not in the Darkworld. We can find them again. You *never* have to die, not if you don't want to. Let me show you immortality."

The hand appeared again, and this time she took it.

"Show me," she whispered.

The flames sprang up in front of me, cutting me off, singeing my skin, and I awoke with my skin afire.

12

THE PAST HAS POWER

Breathing heavily, I leant back on my pillow. Sweat soaked my covers, but no flames licked at my skin. Safe.

What the hell happened?

I got up and paced the room, trying to reassure myself that I was fine, that I was in the here and now, and that dreams were as insubstantial as ever.

Except I knew that to be a lie. My dreams were more real than most people's, because the demons liked to manipulate my deepest fears and use them against me. For some reason, they'd decided that I needed to see Melivia's past.

Let me show you immortality.

I'd thought she'd died in the fire. But now it occurred to me that anything could have happened. With no witnesses, there was no one to say whether she'd survived or not—save the demons. The demons alone knew what had really happened. If she had survived, what had happened to her?

What about the doppelganger? It shouldn't exist, not

even in my dreams. A higher demon had killed it. Unless…
Nothing dies forever. Not in the Darkworld.

Of course, there was no way of knowing whether single demon manipulated my dreams, or a collective effort. Given that every demon I'd met had been fascinated with me, I suspected that I might never be able to find out.

I still felt too hot, like I'd stood too close to a bonfire. I opened the window wide, inhaling the cool night air, feeling it soothe my skin. The sky outside was clear, like a jewelled gown of deep blue studded with stars. The forest, serene, barely disturbed by a faint breeze.

I needed to take a walk and clear my head of thoughts of demons. I dressed quickly and dragged a brush through my hair, banking on not running into anyone out there to notice or care that I looked like a scruff-bag.

Bar a single early-morning jogger, the path was completely deserted, and I walked swiftly through the woods, trying to escape my own thoughts. The cold air calmed my racing heart, but my thoughts continued to spin, turning back to demons.

The idea that they might be listening in on my thoughts crept up on me occasionally, and although I couldn't pretend it didn't disturb me, I couldn't do anything to prevent it. But when coupled with the knowledge that someone conspired against me in the real world, it made me feel like a wild animal caught off guard by a trap, a fish caught in a net.

Melivia's face flashed before my eyes, her facial expression turning from terrified, to fighting, to the blankness of possession. However uninteresting a person she'd seemed in her journal, in that moment she'd been braver and stronger than almost anyone I knew…

Crap. I really am an idiot, I thought. The diary. If

anywhere had any answers about what I'd seen in the dream, it was Melivia's diary.

I power-walked back to the student village. Back in my room, I opened Melivia Blackstone's journal to the last marked page. It was time to find out the truth.

I'd left off after Melivia's first meeting with the sorcerer who would go on to trick her into killing her family, and this knowledge made me determined to slog through the rest of the book until the end.

The diary became more fragmented at this point. From what I could gather, the mysterious sorcerer continued to visit, always when Melivia was alone in the house. She continued to naively believe that it was coincidence, that he really did meant to speak to her mother, but kept missing her. It made me uncomfortable, like reading one of Shakespeare's tragedies, knowing the characters hurtled towards disaster but knowing there was no way to avoid it; it had already been written. In hindsight, the tragedy of Melivia, too, was set in motion.

Now the sorcerer had started teaching her magic. She referred to him as a 'conjuror', making fire out of nothing, performing wondrous tricks, never thinking for a minute that he might be up to anything sinister. Reading between the lines, I could tell that Melivia had become forgetful, that she had gaps in her memory, that cold things wove their way into her dreams. *"I felt as though I lived a living death, like I was no longer in my own body but something separate, floating in a void... It entranced and terrified me."*

Sleep paralysis. I could see the spell the sorcerer had her under. *"He encourages me to express my inner thoughts through painting. With a brush in hand, I can make wondrous pictures."*

I thought of the paintings of demons rising from the depths of hell, now displayed in Blackstone Art Gallery. It didn't surprise me that they'd been painted under the influence of demons. She'd drawn sketches in the journal, too. Demon eyes.

"He showed me a dark place. It is his domain, he tells me. He has control over the darkness and can make the shadows dance.

He tells me his name is Lucifer, that it means light-bringer, and he will show me the light. He tells me he can guide me through the darkness…"

I stared at the word. *Lucifer.* This couldn't be the same man who threatened the Venantium. It *couldn't be. No way.*

If this Lucifer was human, then he'd be long dead by now. No one could live forever, not even with magic. I knew that much.

But the fortune-teller had said…

There might be some clues here. Maybe this diary *had* resurfaced for a reason.

The journal shook in my hands as I turned the page, feeling as though I hovered on the brink of a revelation. I skimmed over all the irrelevant passages, focusing on any mention of this Lucifer figure. She never really *described* him. Was he definitely human? Demons couldn't hide their appearance, as far as I knew—those violet eyes were a dead giveaway. But she definitely thought Lucifer was human.

Or was he a human-demon?

"He is teaching me to speak to the shadows. He says that I have a natural aptitude for it. No one has ever said that to me before. He is quite unlike any man I have ever met."

Poor Edgar Wilbury, I thought.

"He tells me he is going away travelling. It will be fine. If I am lonely, I can always speak to the shadows. They understand me, they comfort me. I have started to paint again. It is the only way to express my dreams; mere words cannot do them justice."

In the next entry, the handwriting was shaky, as though written in a hurry.

"Something terrible has happened. Mother saw me speaking to the shadows this morning and was very shocked. She cried out that I was partaking in dangerous sorcery, and locked me in my room. For some reason, I can no longer speak to the shadows. They do not listen to me, or they simply are not there. I try my best but I no longer feel the cold. It is as though a light has been extinguished inside me. I am dreadfully unhappy.

Mother wants to hasten my engagement. She says this place is no good for me. She got upset when I revealed my knowledge of the other place. She questioned me today about who taught me to speak to the shadows. I told her I taught myself. I must protect his secrets. She does not believe me. I think she is hiding something from me. Perhaps my entire family is hiding something from me. She said something strange. She said the shadows are both my family's gift and our curse. I do not know what it means. But I am afraid."

I shivered, a horrible, creeping feeling snaking up my spine as I turned the page.

"I tried to speak to the shadows again today, willed it so hard that I felt something shatter inside me, like I'd broken down a barrier in my mind. The shadows rushed into me and I felt alive again."

"I do not know what to do. I fear I have done something terrible. He came back today, and he seemed dreadfully unhappy. He told me that he had to take me with him. I was afraid, but I agreed. I trust him. He walked me to Blackstone and led me past the cemetery where my ancestors are buried, down the path I have walked many times. We walked through the forest. Spring is on the way; the trees are robed in white blossom, and buds are creeping through the soil. But I have only just noticed that coldness follows him wherever he goes, the chill of the grave, like he has risen from the very catacombs themselves. He took me underground, through a cave hidden deep in the forest. The tunnels were darker than the darkest night, and I could hear my own breath coming out in terrified gasps. He taught me to conjure a light as he did, but grew impatient when I was too nervous to maintain it. I feel as though I have failed him in some way.

He said something strange. He said that he had expected it to be more thoroughly guarded. I do not know what this means.

I could not believe what I was seeing. There is a whole other world beneath Blackstone, hidden underneath thousands of feet of soil, tunnels carved out of the very soil itself. It felt as though we travelled to the core of the Earth, like in Mr Verne's novel.

He led me in silence, only stopping after we had been walking for quite some times. We had reached an enormous chamber, and an astonishing sight met my eyes.

The chamber was lit by candles which burned with bluish light at five corners of a five-pointed star. In the centre was a circle drawn in chalk surrounding a mass of shadows, and he seized me roughly and threw me to the ground. I was unprepared and fell hard onto the soil. Then he told me to speak to them. I did not dare disobey. I spoke and the shadows answered, and eyes appeared within the circle. Then the shadows moved out of the circle and I was sure I heard a cold voice say, "Thank you", before they disappeared.

He took me home without offering me an explanation. But I feel dread creeping over me whenever I think of those mobile shadows."

"You idiot," I whispered.

"Something is wrong with Mother. She is behaving strangely. She has shut me away again. I could not meet him as planned today.

He is angry. He came to the house and demanded entry. Mother refused. He hit her. I was very shocked. Mother cried and told me I was speaking to the devil.

Maybe I am. But I do not know what to do."

The next entry was shakily written and horribly blotted, as though the ink ran whilst she was writing.

"I do not know what to think. I do not even know how to write this. How can Mother be dead? She was healthy as ever in her life this morning, and yet now she lies as cold and stiff as my ancestors beneath the ground.

The last time I saw her alive was when she came to lock me in my room. I saw no one all day. It was the maid who found her this evening, lying in the hallway, dead. There was not a mark on her. Uncle is here. He tells me it was sorcery."

A gap of several days occurred here.

"Uncle is dead, too, after being stricken by a sudden illness. My brother confides in me that he thinks there is a curse on our family. He wants to move far away. But Father disagrees. He says he will do everything in his power to stop what is happening."

"It is too late. They are all dead now. Mother, Father, even my brothers. I have nothing left. I sit in my room and cry, for what else can I do? I know that I am next. I know that the shadow has saved me for last, as punishment. All I can do is wait for it to arrive. But I know now. I should have listened beforehand, but the clues were right before my eyes. I know how to defeat the darkness. If I conjure fire, it will no longer be able to harm anyone. It is too late for my family. But not for everyone else. This may be the last time I write in this journal. I intend to burn it in the fire, so no one knows what I did, so no one knows the depth of my guilt. Perhaps it is the last act of a coward, but it is all I have left. It will be some small consolation to my cousin.

Farewell."

That can't be it. I turned the page over and found only blank space. It couldn't end there, surely? Where were the demons? And the fire? The Demon Wars had begun that night, but there was no mention of how she'd escaped the fire, presumably with the demon still inside her mind...

I turned the pages and found my answer. On the last page, there was a scribbled note. The handwriting looked different, but still recognisable as Melivia's.

"I had no idea this journal survived the fire. If I hadn't found the crystal, perhaps I would never have thought to search this house again. There are people who deserve to know the truth of my guilt, undiminished after all these years. Maybe this is my penance. These are but the naïve words of a child, confined within these pages. A hundred and fifty years in the past.

I do not think it should be made public. Perhaps there is a lesson to be learned, but I do not think this tale contains any clues as to how to defeat the monster. If I made any observations in my youth, they are lost to the depths of memory. It is painful for me to recall the days that led to my departure. I will never understand why he saved me, spared me, although I begin to suspect the truth. Perhaps he always intended the Demon Wars to be my burden, for me to bear on the part of my family, the last to resist the darkness. Today, no such family exists. The Venantium—yes, I have finally learned the name of the group my family was entwined in—are not as they were, and I am not welcome amongst them. I intend to travel and learn of the darkness of the world, in the search of eventual salvation, for what more can I do?

Now he is gone, but I know in my heart he will return. He is beyond life, beyond even death, and I could have been the same. But as I stared into the darkness of forever, I knew that I could not justify pursuing infinity, even in a good cause. I must make up for what I have done, and if embracing mortality is the consequence, then so be it. I will conceal this diary in a place where the right person may find it someday.

I hope you will forgive me.

Melivia Blackstone"

I stared at the last page, as though it might rearrange itself before my eyes into something that made sense. Melivia Blackstone hadn't died in the fire. Somehow, this Lucifer had taken her with him into the Darkworld, a place where it was possible to survive without a body.

And she'd come back.

Impossible. All the books I'd read had said separation was permanent. The body of Melivia Blackstone had long since rotted away beneath the ground. But…

Like Lucifer, she had been able to return to this world. Even though she was human.

It made no sense. Why her? I guessed Lucifer had targeted her because she was a Blackstone and naïve and vulnerable, but unless she'd been a *really* skilled magic-user—hard to tell from the journal entries—then I didn't see what Lucifer got from keeping her alive. A willing puppet? Or had he been depraved enough to want her to be the only surviving Blackstone, cursed to forever bear the burden of guilt?

So—assuming it was the same Lucifer—he and Melivia Blackstone had returned to this world twenty years ago. Presumably she'd had a change of heart, decided she didn't want immortality. Whatever had happened behind the scenes, Lucifer had been defeated, and sent back to the Darkworld with his demons.

Did that make him truly immortal? Had he spent so long in the Darkworld that he had no need for a physical body anymore?

And what did that make Melivia?

It hit me like a punch to the chest. *No. No, it couldn't be.*

Twenty years ago. He'd come back twenty years ago. And so had someone else.

Was the fortune-teller Melivia Blackstone?

13

DARK WITHIN

No *way*, I thought. No doubt that the fortune-teller had issues, dark secrets. But was she the woman who had—accidentally, admittedly, but still—started the demon wars?

I tried connecting the woman I thought I knew—as far as one could know someone who went out of their way to be unbearably cryptic—with the writer of the journal. It was impossible. Melivia Blackstone was… well, from what I could infer, pretty useless. I'd seen no hint that she possessed any unusual magic, unless she'd thought that less worth noting down than elaborate descriptions of her horse. The fortune-teller was… until I'd witnessed her struggle to face down Mr Priestley, I'd always seen her as seemingly invincible. Strong-willed. Melivia in the journal wept to see an injured squirrel. She'd never sacrifice another person's life, certainly not intentionally. But I couldn't say the same for the fortune-teller. She'd had no qualms about masquerading as my Aunt Eve for eighteen years with no thought as to the impact on the other people involved.

At that thought, something nagged at me, but I couldn't put my finger on it. Like a momentary lapse of memory, like something had slipped away from my grasp. It felt important, though. Something I'd overlooked.

Shaking my head, I returned to contemplating the fortune-teller. No single image fitted the woman I knew. The woman behind the counter offering advice. The expert in healing medicines. The fearless fighter. The bearer of some unbearable guilt. I had no idea what she really looked like, but in any case, if she *was* Melivia, her body wasn't her own. She possessed someone else's. Like a demon.

Oh, God.

If she could pretend to be someone's close relation with no moral repercussions, could she really take another's life in order to cheat death?

Or was it an accident? Had she not expected to return from the Darkworld? Had someone else—Lucifer—forced her to? It started to look like the only explanation, although the idea of her being dominated by *anyone* seemed totally at odds with her character. But not Melivia Blackstone's.

I needed to speak to the fortune-teller. Just to know the truth.

Guys. We need to talk. It's urgent. I sent the message to Leo and Claudia. I had to tell someone. I needed reassurance that I hadn't read the signs all wrong. The letter could be a forgery, after all. But the journal felt solid in my hands. Everything from the slightly singed yellowed pages to the elaborate binding looked genuine.

How could I know? I'd been fooled enough times recently to regard everything with scepticism. But this… this was something else entirely.

Did the Venantium suspect her true identity? Was that why they'd taken her prisoner?

The past has power. We may not forgive ourselves, but the memory gives us strength.

I paced outside the flat, waiting for Leo and Claudia. Claudia arrived first, yawning as she came downstairs.

"Ash? What's wrong?"

I held up the journal in a shaking hand. "I've been reading this," I said. "Does it look genuine?"

Claudia took it. "Sure, but why? What does it say?"

A knock on the door. Leo.

"What is it?" he said, as I let him into the building. "What's up, Ash?"

"She started the demon wars," I said shakily. "Melivia Blackstone. This is her diary."

"Where did you get this?" said Claudia, flicking through it.

"It was in the library. It fell out of the *Sorcerers' Almanac.*"

"You're kidding."

"Never mind that," said Leo, looking at me. He knew I'd have more reason than that to call him and Claudia out this early in the morning.

I took a deep breath. "I think it's the fortune-teller," I said.

Leo blinked at me. "You think what's the fortune-teller?"

"I think she's her. I think she's Melivia Blackstone." I breathed in again. My heart hammered. "I know it sounds crazy—"

"Um, yeah, Ash, she's been dead for over a hundred years," said Claudia. "Why—"

"I know, but listen. There was a note in the back of the

diary, and it was written in 1993. The handwriting's exactly the same. Look."

I took the diary and opened it onto the last page, and the final, scribbled message. *"I hope you will forgive me.*

Melivia Blackstone, 1993"

"It's a forgery," said Claudia instantly. "Come on. People don't live that long. Not even magic-users."

"I know that. I think she went into the Darkworld. I think Lucifer took her there."

"Lucifer? As in, the Lucifer who's supposed to be causing trouble now? Or the higher demon?"

"I… I don't know. But remember what Dr Philips said? It's possible for someone to come back from the Darkworld, even after years. It can be done."

"I don't know, Ash." Claudia shook her head. "She might be unpredictable, but I can't see Madame Persephone killing someone else to come back to life."

"Persephone," I said, something else occurring to me. "The Greek myth. She was the wife of Hades. He held her prisoner in the underworld, remember? For six months. Then she could return to the surface."

"So she's a fan of Greek mythology. That doesn't prove anything. Leo, what d'you think?"

Leo wore a frown, as though lost in thought.

"I don't know," he said, finally. "It looks like a set-up. But it would also explain a lot. The fortune-teller talks like she's out of her own time. You can't deny that. And it fits with everything we've heard about her and Lucifer. She'd have come back twenty years ago, right?"

"Yeah," I said. "That's what I thought. Well, if it *is* her, then it wasn't really her fault. She was young and naïve, and Lucifer took advantage. He tricked her into summoning a demon, and it possessed and killed her whole family.

Everyone thought she died in the fire, but if she went into the Darkworld and left her body behind, then no one would have known it. They thought Lucifer was dead, too…"

"How old is this guy?" said Leo. "Is he immortal? If he can keep going back to the Darkworld—like a demon—then it doesn't sound like he can be killed."

"I don't know. Maybe," said Claudia. "But that's beside the point. Why did he go after Melivia?"

"That's what I'm trying to figure out. There isn't much to go on in the diary," I said. "But I don't think she's on Lucifer's side. She knows what he did now. It'd explain what she said to Jude, about guilt."

"I just don't know about this," said Claudia. "It seems too convenient that the diary would appear right now."

"I don't think it's a coincidence," I said. "I think it might have been planted there. If it's genuine, then it might have been the fortune-teller herself who did it. Maybe… I don't know. Maybe she wanted me to know this. Perhaps it could help us set her free."

"Or maybe it was to tell us not to bother. Maybe she thinks she'll never atone for what she did. Assuming she did it at all."

"I don't think she's the type to give up," said Leo. "We might not know her, but you can't deny that much."

"Yeah. I just wish I knew what it all means. I need to talk to her."

"The Venantium won't let us into the cells," said Claudia.

"I know. But this is going to drive me mad," I said. "If I could just ask her one question—just find out whether it's true—"

"I don't think it's relevant, to be honest," said Leo. "Even if it is true, it won't change anything. Lucifer's still out there, and so's Mephistopheles."

"It *must* be relevant, somehow," I said. "Why else would I find that book right now?"

"Who knows what that crazy woman's thinking?" said Leo.

"He's right. Don't dwell on it, Ash. You'll get chance to ask her later. For now, taking down Jude's the priority, right?"

I sighed. "Sure. You're right, I guess."

"Next time you have a mad theory," said Claudia, waving her phone in my face. "Can you not wait till a normal hour?" *Oh. Right.* The clock on her smartphone read, 4:00 a.m. *Oops.*

"It's not crazy, but sure," I said. "Sorry. I just freaked out. It seemed so absurd, and yet…"

"No, I believe you," said Leo, taking my hand. "It's just like I said. I think we should focus on other things for the time being."

Claudia cleared her throat. "Well, I'm going back to sleep." She went upstairs.

"Same," said Leo. "You can come over tomorrow—well, today, I guess—if you want."

"Sure," I said. "Sorry about that."

"No need to apologise. It's not every day you find out a friend's a visitor from the past."

"It's not exactly time travel," I said. "You can only go forward in time, right?"

"Yeah. Kinda feel sorry for her, if she did. Imagine waking up in a hundred and fifty years and finding that hover boots are in fashion and the world's flooded and everyone you knew is dead. Well, the hover boots would be cool."

"Definitely," I said, managing a smile. "Later, then."

∾

I brought the diary over to Leo's flat, which we ended up skimming through. Leo found most of the first half as tedious as I had, although my running commentary on how little I gave a crap about Melivia's wardrobe made him laugh. "As for that loser Edgar Wilbury," I said.

"What ended up happening to him?" said Leo.

"God knows," I said. "Probably married some other girl. He's long-dead now, anyway."

"And I thought I had a messed-up family," said Leo. "Melivia's parents were *useless*. Her mum was obviously an alcoholic."

"How'd you figure that one out?"

"Subtext, Ash. I'm a literature student."

I raised my eyebrows.

"Just joking. I've no idea, it was a guess. Anyway. Her dad was never there, either. Now that I can relate to. I'll bet he was trying to save the world, same as mine. Moron."

"I'm trying to figure out her brothers," I said. "I'm guessing they worked for the Venantium, too."

"Reckon they all did. She was the only one who didn't know. Let that be a lesson, always tell your kids you're secretly a demon killer."

"How'd *you* find out about the Darkworld, anyway?" I asked.

"Cy told me. I was only about seven, he was nine. He'd overheard Mum and Dad talking about their work for the Venantium. Total accident, oddly enough, even though I was an expert eavesdropper. I always thought they were into something weird. I kept tailing them, but they always caught me. Even the time I lurked in the shrubbery and accidentally discovered a wasp's nest."

"Did you find anything out?"

"Only that my Dad hates wasps as much as I do. But they did tell me about magic, along with a hundred lectures about why not to use it. Which was probably better than leaving me in the dark."

"Could you actually do magic at that age? I thought you had to be older to get a Darkworld connection."

"Yeah, it wasn't until I was sixteen, but I'd been trying to use magic for years before then. Of course, Dad had left by that point—taken off to avenge Mum's death and become the Venantium's puppet. But Melmoth was an okay teacher. He didn't trust magic any more, but I don't really blame him. I read all his books, but I knew they had better ones here in their library. Cy told me, but the bugger refused to steal any for me."

"Is that why you came to uni here?" I said.

"Kind of," said Leo, with a grin. "Nah. I'm thinking I might have preferred somewhere further away, especially considering everything that's happened, but it's a good uni. The course is okay. Nice place. What more d'you want?"

I realised we'd gone way off topic. "Anyway," I said. "Back to the diary."

Leo pulled a face. "Can't we do something else?"

"Like what?"

He kissed me. "This?"

I put the diary down. We could figure that one out later.

For now, we watched Lord of the Rings, lying together on the bed, feet tangled, hands locked together, taking make-out breaks every few minutes—although I refused to take it further. As delighted as I was to have the whole day in Leo's company, the shock of what I'd discovered still hadn't worn off, and I just felt like this wasn't the right time. Not that there was necessarily a defined perfect moment to lose one's virginity—but now I just felt too shaken up to relax.

No one had ever been able to read me as clearly as he

did, and I didn't even have to say a word. With Leo, I could forget everything that was on my mind, even the fortune-teller. Even the doppelganger returning to my dreams again. I'd still not quite shaken off the chill of the Darkworld gripping me all over, and the voice that was both me and not me speaking, demanding to be set free. But now last night felt as harmless as the dream it was. I held onto him like he was an anchor against the insanity of the world.

Even if the insanity was in my own mind. This was the life I wanted. I'd never let the demon take over.

I settled back, resting my head against Leo, and actually fell asleep for real. And this time, there were no dreams.

14

A DEAL

"Ridiculous," said Howard, looking at me like I'd suggested we arrange a chess match with Lucifer. "You think Madame Persephone is a time-travelling ghost?"

"That's not what I said," I protested. I wished Claudia hadn't decided to announce my theory to Cyrus, Howard and Berenice at that week's meeting in a way that made me sound like a conspiracy theorist. "Look at this."

Howard snatched the diary from my hand.

"Hey, don't damage it!" I said.

"This is Melivia Blackstone's?" said Cyrus. "You're absolutely positive it isn't a set-up? Would anyone have a reason to trick you?"

"Not that I know of," I said. "I know it sounds mental. But it fits with the facts."

"It does," said Cyrus thoughtfully, "but so do a dozen other unlikely theories."

"I don't see what this has to do with us anyway," said Berenice, who as usual, looked as though she'd rather be anywhere than here.

"I didn't expect you to," I said.

"Well, I think you're trying to make unnecessary trouble for us. The Blackstones are dead and rotting in the earth, and it doesn't matter if one of them survived. It's hardly world-changing. The fortune-teller's messed-up world isn't any of our concern."

"What about Lucifer?" I said. "If it is the same person who's been living in the Darkworld all this time, he's a pretty big threat to everyone."

"Only if we provoke him," she said. "I'm not getting involved."

"I never said you had to," I said. "I'm not proposing we join the Venantium's fighting squad. I just want to talk to the fortune-teller."

"You know they won't let you," said Cyrus.

I sighed. "Yeah. I know. If there was just some way I could convince them... someone I could talk to..."

But there *was* someone, I thought. Someone at this university who worked for the Venantium. David.

The thought of speaking to him again didn't particularly appeal, but he *had* called the *venators* off harassing me the other day. Admittedly, I couldn't really count on him to question his superiors, but I could try.

I didn't stay in the meeting room for long. Howard and Berenice didn't say much other than to bicker, and Berenice's face flushed like a traffic light whenever she met Howard's eyes. Once we'd exhausted the conspiracy-theory stuff, no one had anything else to say. I left to get an early night, and to mentally prepare to make a total ass of myself tomorrow.

≈

AFTER THE LECTURE the next day, I followed David out of the lecture theatre, trying to psych myself up. I needed to do this. The fortune-teller might need me to.

"David," I said. "Can I talk to you for a second?"

He blinked at me, as if unsure if I was having him on. "Um, sure. What is it?"

"Um… can we talk outside?"

Alex and Sarah stared at me as I walked with him out of the lecture building—Alex's eyes practically bugging out. I had no idea what to tell my friends, but I'd handle that later. I'd already done the difficult bit.

"I was wondering…" I took a deep breath. Might as well cut to the chase. "Do you know whether there's any chance the Venantium might let me talk to the for—to Madame Persephone? It's just that I have something I really need to ask her."

"I don't know." David looked suspicious. "What's so urgent? I might be able to get a message to her, but I'm only admin. I don't really know the staff questioning her."

"It's kind of something I need to ask in person. I know they don't do visitors, but I think she wants me to speak to her."

"Look, what's this about? You look… I don't know, agitated."

"No shit," I said, feeling a flicker of anger at how unhelpful he was being. "I'm not letting you know my business. Forget I asked."

David hesitated. "I'm sorry. I didn't want them to take her in, you know. I don't think she's an enemy. But I don't have a say in the decisions."

"It's okay," I said, relenting. "Last time I went down there, Dr Philips told me I couldn't talk to her, but if I had permission, or there was something I could do…"

"I'll talk to my brother," said David. "He's higher up

than I am. As long as you aren't planning to help her escape, then I don't see why they shouldn't at least let you talk to her."

"If she planned to escape, she could do it without my help," I said.

"True," said David. So he knew that much, at least. 'Okay."

"Thanks," I said, and hurried to catch up with my friends and come up with a bogus story.

"I DON'T TRUST HIM," said Claudia. "He wants you to go there alone?"

"It's not like they can arrest me or anything," I said. "I haven't done anything wrong."

The text from David had come two days after our conversation—an invitation into the Venantium Head-quarters to speak to Dr Philips about a possible meeting with the fortune-teller. Whilst I didn't particularly trust either of them, this was the best chance I had.

Claudia and Leo had walked with me as far as the cemetery, and now we were waiting for David to show up. He'd said it was 'urgent', which sent alarm bells ringing in my head when we showed up and couldn't see him anywhere. David and I might have once been friends, but I knew he'd always put the Venantium before anyone else—the prime reason why I disliked him so much now.

"Come on, the tosser was probably having you on," said Claudia, the only other person who knew what had transpired between David and me last term. I wanted to keep it that way, if just because the past was the past.

But the way things looked at the moment, the past

didn't want to stay buried. Melivia Blackstone, for instance…

"Nah, there he is," said Leo.

I looked up and saw David, just across the other side of the cemetery.

"Hi, Ash," he said. "You ready?"

"Sure," I said, standing up from where I'd been leaning on the wall.

Leo gave me a quick kiss on the cheek. Claudia narrowed her eyes at David.

"Hurt her and we'll break you," she said, looking ready to kick someone into the next world. She'd never liked David, especially as she'd been the one to discover his secret.

David blanched. "No one's planning to hurt her."

"It's okay," I said, with more confidence than I really had. Anxiety prickled up my spine as the tomb of the Blackstone family swung open, but I refused to let my nerves show in front of David.

This time, the drop barely fazed me. One second of floating in nothingness later and we stood on the red carpet of the entrance hall. David made for a door which I recognised as the one that led to the interrogation rooms. I shot him a glare.

"We're just going somewhere quiet," he said, looking slightly cowed. It felt oddly satisfying to think that I'd intimidated him. "You never know who might be listening in."

Hoping I wouldn't regret this, I followed him through the door and down the darkened staircase. In the corridor, a door lay open on our left, and Dr Philips waited inside, her face in a familiar stern line. I wondered if she'd ever smiled in her life.

"Miss Temple. You are no doubt wondering why I

wished to speak to you, after I told you last time that I did not want you to come to our Headquarters again."

I said nothing. My insides felt twisted into knots.

"The truth is, we have need of your assistance."

I met her stare in surprise. "Me… why?"

"We have received a… message, which claims to be from Jude. It says that he plans to launch an attack on our headquarters tonight."

"*Tonight?*" My heart jumped into my throat.

"Yes."

"Why would he tell you that?"

"We do not know. But we cannot let it slide. Jude knows how to slip through our Barriers, as he did before. He may be possessed and unable to access this area, but we will nonetheless be alert in case he finds a way to send another emissary through. We are posting lookouts around the perimeter of our Headquarters, and we would greatly appreciate the assistance of yourself and your young friends."

I could never have expected this, but her stern expression and obvious agitation proved her to be serious. *They must be desperate.*

"But… what makes you think I can help?"

"We need all the combatants we can get."

"*Combatants?*" I said. "I'm not a fighter."

"You have encountered demons before, have you not? I understand that yourself and your friends played a pivotal role in defeating the Ghouls at their source."

"That was the fortune-teller, not us," I said. "I gave a statement."

"But you did take part in the fight. I hear you also have some… unusual magic, Miss Temple."

I shot David a look. Had he told her?

"I don't know what you mean," I said, standing my

ground.

"You have an aptitude for manipulating the Darkworld. I am told that you have a particularly strong ability to create demon-proof shields, and to freeze things… do you not?"

"Who told you this?" I said.

"Madame Persephone herself told me. I was curious as to your relationship."

Real fear coursed through me now. Had they put her under some kind of torture? Why would she willingly reveal things about me when she'd already told so many lies to keep me safe?

What had happened to the fortune-teller I'd thought I knew?

"We're… I don't know her," I said. "She helped us a few times. That's all."

"Be that as it may, will you not consider giving us your aid?"

"Consider what, getting myself killed?" I said, unexpected anger surging inside. I forgot I was talking to a senior member of the Venantium. The words flowed out without any control. "I can't believe you're asking for my help after what happened before."

"We have many deep regrets as to the way you were treated on your last visit—"

"Regrets? You locked me up and blocked my connection to the Darkworld, thinking I was a demon!"

"We were under attack. We had to take extreme precautions. We offered you a full apology, and now we are asking for your help."

"I…" Like it or not, I knew that if the Venantium was attacked, then we'd be the next targets. Maybe helping would be the best option. But would the others really go for it? I had my doubts.

"If you help us, I will of course grant you an audience with Madame Persephone."

No way. Was she blackmailing me?

I wished someone else was here to support me. Alone—David just stood there, looking uncomfortable—I had no clue how to negotiate with these people. I wasn't about to risk my life if there was no need.

But if the demon did come here, we could all be in danger.

"I will give you some time to consider, if that is what you wish."

I found myself nodding. "Okay."

"We will be meeting outside in the cemetery at sundown to prepare. If you join us, I and my colleagues will be most grateful."

"THEY MUST BE MAD," said Claudia. "We aren't their warriors. It's ridiculous."

"But what if Jude really does attack?" I said. "He won't stop here. The university'll be next."

"You're talking like he has an army. For all we know he's just planning to break in to steal something again."

"We can't be sure," I said. We'd called an emergency meeting in the Games Room, and so far, the group's reaction had been exactly as I'd predicted.

"That's exactly the problem," said Cyrus, who'd brought his laptop with him and was typing away on his essay. "We don't know what we're up against, and it's not much of a reassurance that the Venantium don't either."

"Well, *I'm* having nothing to do with it," said Berenice. "What're they planning to do if we get killed? What the hell do they plan to tell our families?"

"Good point," said Claudia. "My parents would never let me go into a fight on their behalf."

"No one to stop me," said Howard. "I've been itching for a fight."

"Howard, you nearly got *killed* last week," said Claudia, shaking her head.

"All the more reason to kick some ass."

"This is more than we normally deal with," said Cyrus. "Ash, what would your parents think if the Venantium had to tell them you'd gotten yourself killed? They don't even know about your connection to the Darkworld, do they?"

"I…" There it was again. That strange headachy feeling, like someone had slammed a blunt instrument into the back of my head. I tried to imagine my… parents'… reaction, and the image slipped away before I could grasp it.

Cyrus must have interpreted my expression as shock at his words. "I'm sorry," he said, "but you have to know what you're getting into. Howard, Leo and I haven't got any family ties, but you——"

"My parents are still alive, thank you very much," Howard snapped. "Why wouldn't the *venators* let me fight for them in exchange for getting to see *my parents* again?"

Sensing the danger, Claudia said, "I don't know—none of us know how their minds work. They just wanted to get Ash on their side."

"It's always her," said Berenice. "Again. Haven't you noticed?"

"Berenice, give it a rest," said Claudia. "Ash, you're going to say no, aren't you?"

"I… I guess so." But I couldn't shake off the feeling that I'd overlooked something crucial. It was a familiar feeling, but I couldn't put my finger on the source. She was right, though. *It's not our fight.*

15

MEPHISTOPHELES

I ended up agreeing to Claudia's suggestion that we go for a drink at the Coach and Horses in town that evening—that way we'd be in a position to help if anything *did* happen. But judging by the way the others kept glancing uneasily at the door every time someone came in, I could tell they wondered if Jude would come in and order a beer.

Leo stared absently into his pint glass. Howard perched restlessly on the edge of his seat, tapping his feet against the table and making it shudder. Even Cyrus looked nervous, and Claudia's feverish texting betrayed her anxiety. I had no idea who she texted, since we were all here. Except for Berenice, who'd stalked off back to campus, refusing to be involved.

"He can't break past the barrier," said Cyrus, reasonably. "He won't come here."

"I wouldn't put anything past him," said Leo. "He was a murderer and a monster even before he was possessed."

Suddenly, Claudia jumped to her feet and squeezed past Howard to the door.

"Claudia, where are you going?"

"To find Berenice. She isn't answering her phone."

"Oh, for heaven's sake, not now," said Cyrus, half-rising from his seat.

Howard said nothing but continued to tap his foot on the table, over and over again.

"I'll go with you," I said. Anything was better than sitting still and waiting. I joined her by the door. "What's up with Berenice, then? Apart from the obvious."

"Howard, of course," said Claudia, with a glance back through the pub door. "She was really ticked off that he ignored her at the last meeting. He's been dodging her all week. They're like a couple of kids who've fallen out."

"So where's she wandered off to?"

"She's just being melodramatic. We'll probably find her in the pub across the street."

"This is stupid. Is now really the time for her selfishness?"

"You know what she's like—shit."

We narrowly dodged aside as a motorbike roared past, leaving a trail of oil. Under his safety helmet, I recognised the rider as David.

"Forgot about that thing," said Claudia. "Is something kicking off?"

"No, he's just roaring around and being a nuisance," said a voice.

Claudia jumped. "Berenice! There you are."

Berenice glared at her with red-rimmed eyes. "Yeah, here I am. What?"

"We were worried about you."

"I'll bet she was." Berenice looked at me like I was some disgusting insect she'd caught in her room. "Looking for a chance to rub it in, more like."

"Rub what in?" I said blankly.

"You always have to have the last word, don't you? You aren't content with parading your love affair with Leo around, you have to have answers to everything. I know who the fortune-teller is! I know who Lucifer is! I can run circles around freaking *Mephistopheles.*"

"Honestly, Berenice, I've no idea what you're talking about," I said. "Leo's my boyfriend, and we've not been rubbing it in anyone's face. Just *talk* to Howard if that's what your problem is."

"He's not the talking type. And it's none of your business."

To my astonishment, I saw tears hovering on the edge of her mascara-lined eyes. She blinked furiously.

"Berenice, you should talk to him," said Claudia. "There's absolutely no reason to get mad at Ash. She has nothing to do with this."

"Yeah, she's the pure and innocent one, I get it."

"Pure and innocent?" I said. "What the hell does that have to do with anything?"

"Berenice, you're talking crap," said Claudia, shaking her head. "Talk to Howard. Tell him how you feel. Save me from having to make this lame speech."

"Same here," I said. "My life is *not* perfect. We're facing the same enemy here——"

"You think," said Berenice. "You don't have a fucking clue."

Ice shot up my arms, like the temperature had dropped ten degrees. The chill of the Darkworld crept along my skin.

"What's happening?" said Claudia, rubbing her arms.

"Trouble," said Cyrus, who'd just come up behind us with Leo and Howard.

Leo inched closer to me, looking about. The street looked normal. A student bar crawl——by the looks of things, a movie character-themed one—walked past, singing loudly. Groups of locals and students congregated around the pubs, whose doors lay open, welcoming. I couldn't see anything out of the ordinary, but with every second that passed, it became colder. The others wore expressions ranging from confused to—in Berenice's case—terrified.

Then the howling started. It made the hairs rise on my arms, sounding like a cross between the keening of an injured animal and the cry of a wild dog. I looked around, meeting the others' panicked eyes. But the other people on the streets carried on as normal. Only we could hear it.

What the hell is that?

"Town square," muttered Cyrus. "C'mon."

We walked swiftly, across square and down the alleyway beside the Art Gallery. If I hadn't known something was wrong the instant I felt the Darkworld close around us, I'd definitely know it now. The Venantium no longer guarded the cemetery. Which meant…

A motorbike roared past, kicking up dust.

"What the hell's going on?" Claudia shouted after it.

The bike halted, engine shuddering, and David lifted his helmet. "They're— there are shadow-beasts loose in Redthorne. It was a false alarm."

Dread sank its claws into me.

"Then what're you still doing here?" Claudia demanded.

"No one told me what was happening. I was guarding *her.* Madame Persephone. She told us about the attack."

"And you're leaving her there?" I said.

"I don't have a choice!" David cast one last desperate look around and drove away.

"Shit," said Claudia. "Must be bad if they left their Headquarters like that. Is it even still guarded?"

"Course it will be," said Leo. "Their defences still work. Jude can't get into the town again now he's possessed."

"They fell for his trick pretty easily," said Claudia. "Makes me suspicious."

"I agree," said Cyrus.

"What the hell's that *noise*?" I said, as the howling struck up again.

"Shadow-beasts," said Leo. "Must be an army. Most people can't see them, but… shit, he's really set shadow-beasts loose on Redthorne?"

"That noise isn't coming from Redthorne," I said. "It's too close."

Leo looked at me. "Huh? Sounds pretty distant to me. Maybe the Darkworld's amplified it."

"No…" I said, wincing as another howl assailed my ears. "Sounds more like it's coming from that direction…"

I pointed at the dark mass of trees that marked the forest behind the cemetery.

"Want to check it out?" said Claudia. "I don't think we'd get to Redthorne on time to be any use."

"You're fucking kidding, right?" said Berenice, whose face had gone the colour of off milk. "You want us to go into the forest? Forget it. You think you're invincible, you go right ahead. Leave the rest of us mere mortals back here."

"Stop that," I snapped. "I'm not forcing anyone to do anything."

Another howl ripped through the night. Closer. I shuddered violently. It felt like it came from right next to me, not miles away. I put my hands over my ears, and was alarmed when frost cracked on my knuckles. I hadn't even known I was that cold.

"The fortune-teller," I said. "She—dammit, we can't

just let them keep her prisoner while this is going on. Whatever it is."

"She *must* know," said Leo. "Even if she's underground."

"We have to get her out," I said. "Guys, you don't have to come with me, but this is *wrong*. I don't know what's happening but it feels like..."

"Like something's past the defences," Leo finished. "I think so, too. And I'm in."

Claudia nodded. "Me, too."

"Oh, for *heaven's* sake!" said Berenice. "Fine. If we get caught—"

"There might not be anyone left to catch us," Cyrus pointed out. "They've been leaving headquarters in droves. If we get in through the tunnel, then we might be able to get to her."

"Safer down there than in that blasted forest," said Howard. "All right."

Still, we moved as fast as possible, through the hidden entrance and into the tunnels. Down the winding path that seemed ever-longer in the urgency. Nobody was about, but who knew what could be happening on the surface?

"She must be somewhere in the cells," I whispered to the others, as we reached the barred doors. "David said he was guarding her."

"That doesn't give us much of a clue, though," said Claudia. "She could be anywhere in here."

"Well," I said, "we already know she's not near the Angel Box room. Unless they moved her."

"This way, then," said Leo, indicating a path we hadn't taken before. I wished I'd thought to memorise the way. For all we knew, time could be running out. *How* could the Venantium have just left her here, knowing that she could save their lives?

The tunnel ended at a metal door, like the one to the Angel Box room. I hesitated to try the handle, knowing they sometimes put demon-proof protection on their doors, which would also affect me. Leo pushed on the door, and it opened.

A glass case filled most of the room, and inside was the fortune-teller. She sat on the floor, somehow still managing to look graceful and composed, and her eyes met mine.

"Ashlyn," she said.

"Oh my God." I turned to Leo. "Any idea how to get this thing open?"

He shook his head. Of course, if even the fortune-teller couldn't get out, then there was nothing *we* could do.

Unless… the demon stirred at the back of my head. I studied the glass door, found the hinges.

"Can you guys back me up?" I asked. "I don't know if this'll set off an alarm, or…"

"Of course," said Leo. To the fortune-teller, he said, "I don't suppose you know how exactly they sealed you in?"

She shook her head. "It can't be opened from this side, but perhaps… I will try, but they put a partial block on my connection to the Darkworld."

Of course. A wave of anger went through me, and the demon's presence turned sharply cold. I moved to the side of the cage and pushed at the door's hinges, letting icy fire flow from my fingertips. I'd melted the bars off a prison cell this way before. *Burn.*

The glass wall sizzled under my touch. *It's working!* The fortune-teller approached the door and pressed her hands to the other side of the glass, pushing. The door came clean off its hinges, and I quickly moved to stop it shattering on the floor. Leo and Cyrus took hold of one side and the fortune-teller helped them carefully slot it back into place. Then she looked at me, and nodded.

"They're gone," I said quickly. "There are shadow-beasts in Redthorne. But there's something happening up there, too."

"Yeah, we need to get out," said Leo, turning back.

The demon heart burned against my chest, so sharply and suddenly I cried out in pain. The others blurred around me, faces frozen in alarm, or maybe I was the one who was frozen.

Then pain tore through me again and I could feel nothing else. The closest I'd felt to this was when Jude had set my demon heart on fire—purple flashed across my vision and along with my human voice, I felt another scream somewhere deeper. I couldn't even hear Leo calling my name.

WHEN I RETURNED to full awareness, a fresh wave of terror swept over me. Somehow I wasn't in Blackstone any more. I stood on the cliff behind the forest, my feet half-over the edge. The waves writhed beneath me like a nest of serpents waiting to swallow me whole.

How did I get here?

I looked up and saw something that almost startled me into falling into the devouring ocean. Jude grinned up at me from above the raging sea.

"I thought you'd like to see your own demise, Ashlyn," he said.

He stood *on top of the water,* like on a solid surface, several metres from the shore. His violet eyes were alight with malice.

"Like my new skill?" he said. "Your annoying Barrier ends here, so this is as far as I can go. Still, the irony amuses me. They say Jesus walked on water, don't they? It's hardly a singular talent."

"Where are my friends," I said. "How did I get here?"

I backed up from the cliff's edge and the swirling waves, keeping my eyes on him in case he tried anything else.

"You don't remember? What a shame. I might have gone overboard on the pain, but it's been too long since I had a body to play with. This one had some interesting abilities. Together we make a great team—but he's starting to smell a bit, being dead."

He lifted an arm and surveyed it critically. "Not much left under there…"

My stomach turned. The skin was peeling away from his arm, revealing pinkish muscle and purple veins beneath.

Jude smiled, and the skin on his face cracked. "As for your friends, I'm sure they'll be along shortly. I wouldn't want them to miss the fun. The expression on that young man's face when you revealed your demon eyes!"

An icy fist gripped my heart. "No," I whispered. "You bastard."

"You're the one who lied. Better hope they get a move on—you don't want that to be his last memory of you, do you? His girlfriend as a monster?"

God. No. Leo.

"There they are," Jude whispered, veins standing out around his cracked mouth as he stared at a spot somewhere behind me.

I turned in time to see Leo, Claudia, Berenice, Howard and Cyrus emerge from the forest. They stopped short when they saw Jude.

"I knew you were behind this!" Leo shouted. "Bastard. Let her go!"

"She's in her own mind," said Jude. "Ask her yourself."

I backed away towards the others, not taking my eyes off Jude for fear that he'd attack.

"I don't know what happened," I said. "I just blacked out."

"As I said," said Jude. "This young man has some interesting abilities… although this one was my own. Anyone can control a demon if they are in possession of its heart. But it turns out that this body remembers handling a *particular* demon heart very clearly. So I took that magic for myself. It's handy." He laughed.

He'd—Jude had—held my demon heart. That meant he could control me even now?

Anger surged inside me and almost before my thoughts caught up with me, I'd raised my hand and thrown a handful of ice-fire at him. Jude dodged aside, still grinning.

"What the hell's he doing?" said Howard. "How's he on the water?"

"He can't get past the barrier," said Claudia. "Am I right?"

"Perceptive," said Jude. "Now this is an interesting situation, isn't it? I have you all as bait. I'm sure the *venators* will not hesitate to sacrifice your lives to maintain their defences, but I wonder…" His gaze travelled over the others, one at a time. "Interesting choice of friends, Ashlyn," he said, softly. "Very interesting. None of you have any ties to the Venantium, but you are all blind to what's in front of you all the same." He looked directly at Berenice, who'd convulsively grabbed hold of Claudia, gaping at Mephistopheles in sheer horror. "Except one of you, perhaps. One of you knows the darkness that is coming, do you not?" He smiled widely. "I have to admire your resistance, but your time will come shortly. After I deal with Ashlyn, that is."

My demon heart seared again and I winced. This time I felt and saw my own feet move closer to the edge of the cliff.

"Ash!" Leo shouted.

"Let's make this a little more dramatic," said Jude, raising both his arms.

The sea surged upwards, waves rising higher, higher, then crashing back down with an ear-splitting repeat. Then again. Higher they rose every time, and each jarring crash sent a wave of icy water arching over me. I trembled as the water drenched my skin, but I couldn't move. My feet in my sodden shoes had locked in position, curled over the edge of the cliff.

I could hear the others yelling at him to stop, but their voices were muted beneath the roar of the waves.

"Shall I drown everyone in the village?" shouted Jude over the noise. "Shall I bury it beneath the sea?"

"*Stop!*" I screamed—and my vision flashed purple again.

"There she is," said Jude. "There's the little demon. You're strong for a fledgling, but too conflicted with your mortal body. You need time to practice." He held out a hand. "Come with me."

"No!" I shouted, at the same time as another voice inside me, both mine and not mine, cried, *"No!"*

"I'm offering to spare you, human-demon," said Jude. "Your choice."

The waves rose again in a roaring tide. It seemed as though the very sea itself stood upright, a mass that blocked out the darkening sky.

I stared, my mind a blank space of horror. *No…*

Then, everything froze.

Another voice spoke. "This ends here."

Someone took my hand and pulled me away from the cliff. I stumbled backwards, hardly daring to breathe.

"You always have to spoil everything," Jude snarled, and I turned to look at my saviour.

The fortune-teller's eyes raged like the ocean, her slightly ragged black coat billowing around her.

"You do not belong here, demon," she said.

"Rather hypocritical, don't you think?" said Jude.

In answer, the fortune-teller moved closer to the cliff's edge, into the same position I had been in a minute before. Her eyes never left Jude's, and it was clear from her dragging steps that it took all her effort to keep the waves back.

Then she stepped over the edge. My breath caught in my chest. But she didn't fall. She walked towards Jude, as though on an invisible platform only they could touch.

Jude looked disappointed. "Lucifer taught you a few tricks, did he?"

The fortune-teller raised a hand.

Jude sighed, theatrically. "Pity. I'd grown fond of this vessel, but they say parting is such sweet sorrow."

He grinned and the skin fell away from his face, in layers, from tissue to muscle to bone. Bile rose in my throat. "I'll scc you in the Darkworld, Ashlyn."

Fire shot from the fortune-teller's palm, directly at Jude's forehead. The demon screamed, and Jude's body dropped like a stone. The waves shifted and the fortune-teller made a series of complicated motions—I could almost see her physically holding the waves back, calming them. Slowly, the sea returned to its former level, taking Jude with it. His body drifted, briefly, then sank as the waves climbed again.

Silence fell.

"Is he dead?" Berenice sounded faintly nauseated. I

glanced at her; she'd sunk to the ground, heedless of the mud, as though her legs had simply folded beneath her.

The fortune-teller turned to face me, nodding. She looked exhausted, and before the black mass of the ocean, almost insignificant. She stepped back towards the cliff, staggering as her feet touched solid ground.

"He is dead. Blackstone is safe tonight."

The relief was so intense it made me weak-kneed. But other thoughts clamoured for attention, such a conflict of emotions that I couldn't speak. Joy battled terror and dread, reducing me to speechlessness.

"How in hell did you do that?" demanded Howard.

The fortune-teller sighed. "I was driven to play my final hand. As of tonight, I'll be wanted as a dangerous fugitive. But I've always known this is the way things must be."

"They can't arrest you," I said.

"They already did," said the fortune-teller, simply. "I have places to hide. The Venantium's influence does not cover the entire community of magic-users, thankfully. I will continue to help where I am needed."

"So… Mephistopheles is gone? For good?"

"You have nothing to fear from Mephistopheles anymore. But it's only a matter of time before the *venators* come back. I have to leave."

"Wait," I said. "There's something I have to ask you. They wouldn't let any of us come and talk to you."

"I was afraid of that. Come. We should not linger here." She looked at the others. "I must speak to Ashlyn alone."

"Why?" Berenice demanded. "We have as much right to the truth as she does. If it's about how she's not really human, we all know that now. Thanks to Jude."

I flinched, not so much at the venom in her words but

at the fact that no one contradicted her. I sneaked a look at Leo. He was staring at his feet. I felt sick, and a deep pain built in my chest. *Leo…*

But I needed answers from the fortune-teller first. And so I followed her into the forest.

16

THE UNFORGIVEN

I walked beside the fortune-teller, through the woods, weaving around thick oak trees whose arms blotted out the star-flecked sky. I didn't know where we were going, but we followed a noticeable track, trodden into the fallen leaves. Strips of moonlight barred the path. The night was eerily silent now, and when a crow let out a sudden cry, we both jumped.

Soon, we reached a clearing. A lopsided wooden bench sat in the centre, and the fortune-teller motioned for me to take a seat beside her.

She turned to face me, her pale hair gleaming in the moonlight. Everything else around us was smothered in shadows.

"This may be the last night I am safe in Blackstone," she said, as calm as though she merely made an observation on the weather. "If you have any questions, now is the time to ask."

The shock of everything had burned away my hesitancy, and I asked, straight out, "Are you Melivia Blackstone?"

The fortune-teller's face flinched inwards in pain, and she nodded. "Yes. That is my real name. The individual I once was. But I am her no longer."

I didn't doubt that.

"You meant for me to find the diary?"

"I felt you had earned the right to the truth. It's never easy to hear, and yet... having lived a lie for so long, I know the value of honesty more than most."

"I didn't guess until the end," I said. "I thought... I don't know what I thought. I just didn't think there was any way it could be you."

"We change," said the fortune-teller. "You know I am far older than I appear. I was little more than a frightened child when I left this world behind, and over years... I have still been blind to Lucifer's faults, but you cannot glimpse human history through demon eyes and not develop a sense of perspective."

"I guess," I said. "The others didn't believe me. Howard said I thought you were a time-travelling ghost."

"Ghost, perhaps," she said. "I am from a time dead to everyone today. Perhaps I would be a fascination for historians, but I did not want my diary exposed to public view. To an outsider, of course, it sounds like it was written by someone on the brink of insanity." She sighed. "The Venantium have changed less than I hoped in a hundred and fifty years. If they were more open, I might have considered offering to work for them, to teach others what I have learned. I did not truly grasp the nature of demons until I lived amongst them. But they would never allow it. I did not dare reveal the truth of myself to them."

"I still can't believe it," I said. "You've been... there."

"It does seem unlikely," she said. "Yet here I am."

"Why did you do it?" I said. "Why did you come back?"

"Because I was tricked," said the fortune-teller. "You cannot imagine what it is like existing in the Darkworld, having known this world. Lucifer always planned to make his return, and I begged him to bring me with him. I believed in him even after a century in the Darkworld— although of course such terms are meaningless there; time does not exist. It passes, but the Darkworld is an endless present, and a century in our time can pass in the blink of an eye.

"To exist as a spirit is almost to forget how to be human. I was pulled from my body, and yet I remembered what *life* felt like, and desired to come back. But if I had known it would cost another life…" Her face creased into deep sadness. "The woman whose body he stole was in a coma. Perhaps, if I had not usurped her body, she would have woken up. No one will ever know. Her name… was Eve Temple."

"Aunt Eve," I whispered. "So… she *was* a real person? That makes no sense…"

But why didn't it make sense? Something nagged at the corner of my mind.

"She was comatose for years, but I have always wondered about her. When I realised what I had done, the grief consumed me. That was the first time I saw Lucifer for the demon he truly was, and finally took my powers back into my own hands. I began a new life, under a new name, a new face. I wanted to help other magic-users, initially as penance for what I did. It was… hard. The world had changed so much over the century. I barely recognised it, even Blackstone. That was my curse. I lost everything in order to carry on living. Death would be preferable."

"So… what happened to Lucifer?"

"He returned to the Darkworld after William Melmoth

and I defeated him. That was the last time Lucifer was seen inhabiting a human body. That was… a difficult time. William cared for me deeply, but I could not give him what he wanted. The guilt was too strong."

"I still don't understand how that works," I said. "You… possess the body? Can the original person still be alive?"

"Yes, it's perfectly possible, just like when a demon possesses someone. But the demon rarely lets the host live, just in case they break free of its control. In any case, it's incredibly difficult for the host to kill the demon without destroying themselves."

"What happened with you?" I said. "You were going to walk into the fire and kill yourself to kill the demon. I… saw you. In a dream."

"I thought you deserved to witness part of what happened for yourself," she said.

"So *you* made me dream that? How is that even possible? I thought only demons could…"

"My time in the Darkworld taught me some skills, many of which I will never use. Dream manipulation is a branch of subliminal magic, Influence, and few know how to use it, for which we should be thankful. But I knew that the diary only revealed part of what happened. It disappeared for years, and I only found it again when I returned to this world. I had concealed it, near the house after Lucifer took me away."

"But what happened to the demon possessing you?" I asked.

Her eyes darkened. "It escaped. I didn't know. He has influence over demons and persuaded it to let me go… but it stayed in this world, and that's how the Demon Wars started. I claim full responsibility."

"It was Lucifer's fault," I said. "You didn't know what you were doing."

"Naivety is not an excuse. Hundreds were killed. The Venantium have never been the same since. Even now, their numbers are minimal. They're not ready to face Lucifer again."

"But where is he?" I said. "If he could come back whenever he wants, why hasn't he?"

"I do not know for certain, but I believe he is trying to find the perfect human host. It is an obsession of his."

"He's a… spirit? Or soul? Are they the same thing? Does that mean there's some kind of afterlife?"

"No. Only magic-users can separate from their bodies, because it requires a connection to the Darkworld, and the use of spell that draws one's essence and magical energy into an incorporeal form. I have studied it extensively. At death, one's magical energy is left behind, but I retain all the skills I had before I left the world behind."

"There's one thing I don't quite get," I said. "I know you're a powerful magic-user—hell, probably the best I've met—but I didn't see… I mean, when I was reading the diary, I'd never have thought of Melivia as you. Why did Lucifer pick you as a target?"

"I have often wondered that myself," said the fortune-teller. "Perhaps he could see potential that even I myself was unaware of. Most of my skills I have learned since my return; I knew little of the Darkworld before I went there. Either way, he also saw a way to bring low the country's strongest and best-respected magical family from within. I believe it amused him. I was an easy target. You and I are both alike in that we are victims of circumstance."

"That's just…" I shook my head. "Do the Venantium know?"

"No. Just you."

"So why did you let yourself get taken in?" I said.

"I knew they'd come after me eventually. It was the only way I could ensure that I would still be here when Mephistopheles attacked."

"Is he dead?" I said.

"I hope so. His demon heart is lost. I didn't manage to catch it before Jude's body fell into the ocean." She looked at me, and not for the first time, seemed to see right through into my inmost thoughts. "You're worried about what the others will think, knowing the truth."

I knew she didn't mean about herself, but about me. *You don't know the half of it.*

"I know I should have told them," I said, swallowing. "They deserved to know. But… they *hate* demons."

"Have we not already had this discussion? You are no demon, Ashlyn. You are far less guilty than I. Do we not all tell lies to protect the ones we love? If they truly understand, then they will forgive you. It is hindsight which is the most unforgiving of all."

She stood, imposing once more.

"When will I see you again?" I said. "*Will* I?" I felt like we'd barely scratched the surface of all the questions… yet I feared that the longer I waited, the more likely it would be that the others would disappear without giving me a chance to explain.

"You will. I hope I can help when you have need of me. Now go. Return to your friends."

My heart ached as much for her as for myself as I walked the path back through the forest, the path that led to the grave of everyone she'd ever known.

17

HUMAN

The others waited by the cemetery. I wondered if they'd been talking about me. I could almost see Berenice's gloating smile already. But that didn't bother me. If Leo looked at me with disgust, even disappointment... I couldn't face it.

Sure enough, Berenice wore a self-satisfied smile on her face. "Well?"

I tried to speak, but no words came out. My throat felt like sandpaper. I swallowed.

"Look, guys, I... I wouldn't blame you if you hated me right now. I never meant to lie to you."

Cyrus was the first to speak. "How long have you known?"

I swallowed. "Since last December. It was how Terrence got to me. I didn't know it at the time, but he stole my... my demon heart. This."

I held up the amethyst crystal around my neck for all to see. *Leo. Please look at me.*

"I don't know how I'm part-demon," I said. "Some ancestor of mine—I really don't know, there's no way to find out, and obviously, I'm not in the *Sorcerer's Almanac*. There was literally no way I could know. I wasn't lying when we met, when I said I didn't know I could use magic or see demons before it happened. Then Terrence tried to get a demon to possess me, but I can't be possessed."

"I knew it!" said Berenice, whose triumphant expression grew even more pronounced. "You're like a kind of super-human. No wonder the demons all want you on their side. You're like their superior, am I right?"

"I don't *want* to be," I said. I needed them to understand. "I never wanted this. I've been telling them to piss off for the last year and a half."

"You never did tell us everything that happened that night," said Howard suddenly—I backed away in case he swung a fist at me. "When that sorcerer died? Did you kill him?"

I had to think for a moment to figure out who he meant. "Who, Terrence? Of course not. The demon did." I shivered at the memory. "I killed the demon before it could go for anyone else. I wanted to tell people when I got back, but I thought you'd see me as a monster, too. Like the doppelganger, she was part demon as well, and she was killed for it because people thought she was possessed. But she was human. She just had demon magic, like being able to freeze things, same as me. I mean... true demons are human-hating, heartless fiends. I *hate* that I'm connected to them like this. But it's why they keep pestering me. They seem to think they can get me on their side." I looked up, feeling as tired as though I'd just run a mile. "So now you know."

This time, Claudia met my eyes. "Honestly?" she said. "I think... I think I'd kind of guessed."

Leo nodded. My heart contracted. He studied the

ground, making no other acknowledgement that I was there.

"Leo," I whispered. "I'm so sorry."

He didn't say anything.

"We'll leave you two alone," Cyrus said.

I didn't think my heart could sink any lower. I'd lied to him. Lied to everyone, but especially to him. And worse, I was partly the creature he hated, the creature that had killed his mother and driven his father away. I couldn't even begin to imagine what it must feel like.

I opened my mouth to speak, though I wasn't sure if I would apologise, or just promise never to come near him again, never remind him of what I was. But he spoke first.

"Sorry, Ash."

The last words I expected to hear.

"What?" I choked out. "What do you mean, *you're* sorry? I'm the one who—Leo, I understand if you never want to speak to me again. I should have told you from— from when I found out. I should have…"

"Hang on," said Leo. "I can't pretend this isn't—*when* did you find out?"

"Last term." I closed my eyes, tears pricking. "Well, twice, because Terrence messed with my memory the first time. And I couldn't—I already knew you guys by then. If I dropped that on you then, I didn't know if you'd report me, or…" *I was too scared. Too scared of losing you.* My throat closed up again.

"We'd never have done that," Leo said, and I jumped when his hand touched mine. It was warm, so warm compared to my own ice-cold skin. "*I* would never have done that. Ash, I was already falling for you by that point."

Was. My fingers clenched around his hand, almost like I couldn't help it, like if I held on tight enough, he wouldn't pull away from me.

He didn't.

"Ash, I can't pretend it's not a shock, but it's *not* your fault. Like you said, you couldn't have known."

Tears filled my eyes. "Seriously? You don't mind that I'm—"

"Human," he said. "You're not possessed. You're you."

The knot in my chest loosened, and suddenly everything—Jude, the fortune-teller, the demon inside me—seemed like nothing. I genuinely felt lighter, like I could walk on air.

It seemed far too good to be true.

"Look, let's just get back to campus. Everyone's tired, and we've a hell of a lot to talk about, but we'll do it tomorrow."

There was so much I wanted to say, but my mind kept repeating over and over: *They don't hate you. He doesn't hate you. It doesn't matter that you're part demon. It never mattered. Everything's okay.* I wanted to break down and cry with sheer relief and happiness, and hug Leo, but I was conscious that I was in dire need of a shower; my clothes were soaked in seawater and I had mud up to my knees from the flight through the forest.

Shower first. Sleep on it, if I could. And then...

EARLY NEXT MORNING found me dishevelled and tired as hell, waiting on Leo's doorstep. *Really* early, actually. The little sleep I'd had had been interrupted with nightmares of Jude flooding the town, and when the text from Leo had come at 4:00 a.m. I wasn't about to complain. For another thing, there was an ungodly racket coming from down the corridor. Sounded like Pete was throwing a party.

Oddly, another text from Claudia came through a few

minutes later: "Help me. Berenice and Howard are REALLY LOUD next door. I don't want to hear this!"

"I don't want to know, either!" I texted back. But at least it meant she didn't hate me.

"Hey, Ash," said Leo, answering the door. He pulled me into a hug.

"Sorry. Again."

"Ash, you really don't need to apologise."

But the guilt was still there. I'd lied to him and the others. There was no getting around that.

"Claudia's texting me, too," I said. "Guess she has questions." I would, too, if one of the others had revealed something like that.

Would *I* have trusted them? If, say, Cara had suddenly told me that she was part-demon, before I knew I was one?

I didn't have an answer to that. It wasn't like I could read Leo's mind. Maybe there *was* some doubt there. I wouldn't blame him if there was.

We ended up gathering in the Games Room. Most of the others looked like they hadn't slept, either, though Howard made a half-hearted attempt to set up the Xbox. Berenice sat at his side, leaning on his shoulder. Cyrus, who wore the manic expression of someone who was on a last-minute deadline, typed away at his essay, but one eye was on me. And Claudia and Leo watched me openly.

"Okay," I said, as nobody seemed to want to break the silence. "I'm open for questions. Hit me. Uh, not literally."

"Well," said Claudia. "I always thought it was strange how the demons always seemed to go for you in particular. You can't help what you are. So… who was it?"

"Who was what?" I said.

"One of your ancestors must have been a demon, right?"

"I don't know. The fortune-teller thinks it might have been Lucifer."

"As in, the higher demon, not the crazy sorcerer?" said Howard.

"Yeah," I said. "The higher demon. I don't even know how it happened. I'll probably never know."

"Doesn't explain why you in particular inherited the demon powers," said Cyrus.

I shrugged. Something nagged at me, but I pushed it aside.

"Why did the fortune-teller want to speak to you alone?" said Howard. "Is she like you, too? Half-demon?"

"No." I shook my head. "But it turns out I was right. She's Melivia Blackstone."

The others' expressions ranged from incredulity—Howard—to grim acceptance—Leo.

"So she killed her family?" said Berenice. Even she was looking at me now.

"Not deliberately," I said. "Lucifer tricked her. She was ignorant of everything to do with the Darkworld, and he manipulated her into summoning a demon. When it got loose and possessed her family, killing them one at a time, she still didn't know what was going on. She couldn't have known what would happen, no one taught her anything. It's no wonder Lucifer was able to get to her."

"What, she met the higher demon?" said Berenice.

"No… this was a different Lucifer. Human. Well, at least, she's pretty sure he is."

"How many Lucifers *are* there?" Howard demanded of no one in particular.

"Just two. It's the same Lucifer who's supposed to be threatening the Venantium now, and who attacked it twenty years ago. He's like her—he lives in the Darkworld most of the time."

"Wait, *in* the Darkworld?" said Claudia. "How *old* is she?"

"No clue. It isn't her body," I said, and explained what she'd told me about her return to this world after over a century in the Darkworld.

There was a long silence

"It seems really improbable," said Cyrus. "But you're right, it does fit."

Claudia nodded. "It explains her being so maddeningly cryptic, really. I mean, if you were taken out of your own time, of course you'd find it hard to trust people. Who would have believed her?"

"Did the Venantium know?" said Leo.

I shook my head. "No. She wanted to tell them, she wanted to teach people what she knew, but she said they haven't changed in a century and a half."

"Sounds about right," said Howard. "So is she on our side, or Lucifer's?"

"She's against Lucifer," I said. "That much I know. She didn't realise until after she came back that he'd tricked her, and that the Demon Wars started because of the demon possessing her body. That's what turned her against him. She helped Melmoth defeat him."

"Of course," said Leo. "I did have another look in his journals, but he's pretty vague. I don't think he knew who she was."

"He was in love with her," I said. "I think."

"*What?*" said Cyrus.

"Is she the mysterious woman he kept mentioning?" said Leo. "Ah. That'd explain it. Poor guy."

"I kind of feel sorry for her," said Claudia.

"Same," I said. "I think that's why she spends all her time trying to help out young magic-users. She doesn't want anyone else to make the same mistake she did."

"Why'd she tell *you* all this?" said Berenice.

"I don't know," I said. "She didn't say. I guess she thought we had something in common. We're both cursed, in a way."

"Hers was a choice," said Leo. "Yours wasn't."

Leo. I could hardly believe I'd ever doubted him for a second. Of course he was on my side.

"Right," said Claudia. "We've established that none of us hate you. But… the Venantium. They don't know, do they?"

"They don't know," I said. "At least, I don't think so. I reckon they'd lock me up if they did. The reason they thought I was the doppelganger was because my eyes turned… into a demon's."

"Yeah, that was pretty freaky," said Berenice. "So can you switch it on and off? Because if the world's overrun by demons at least you'd be able to blend in."

"Berenice!" said Cyrus.

"She has a point," said Howard.

I'd never thought of it as something that could ever be useful, but come to think of it, in that situation it might actually save my life. Hopefully it'd never come to that…

"What d'you want to do?" said Leo, after we'd said goodbye to the others.

"Anything," I said, and meant it.

"We can watch a film?"

"Sounds perfect," I said.

It *was* perfect. I felt like I'd taken a shot of something that had melted away all my anxieties to nothing and left me buzzing with giddy relief. It didn't even faze me when Rachel answered the door to Leo's flat with her creepy wide-eyed smile and paint-splattered overalls and said, "Congratulations!"

We ended up watching a marathon of comedy films in

Leo's room. Half the time I barely even noticed what film it was. I just shut my eyes and enjoyed being there. All boundaries had completely fallen away. There was nothing to come between us now. Nothing.

The demons can keep their eternal life, I thought. *It's all about the moment.*

"You could have told me any time, you know," Leo said.

I tilted my head up at him. "I thought you'd freak out. Berenice did—I thought she was going to tell you."

"Berenice freaks out if she breaks a fingernail. Seriously, Ash, I thought you knew me better than that."

"I know. I do. I just couldn't find the words to tell you. It seems stupid now."

I'd known all along, really, that Leo wasn't one of those people who put on one face then turned out to be judgemental dicks. Not like David.

"I understand. Believe me. I know some people like to talk crap about you if you're different. My dad ditched Cyrus and me after Mum died, and we were stuck under a spotlight for at least a year. Cy actually changed schools to avoid it."

"That's awful," I said. "Kids could be so mean."

"Eh." Leo shrugged. "Could've been worse. Though Melmoth didn't make it any easier. He was reclusive, and snapped at anyone who came near the house. Of course people talked. Well, they didn't know he was a vampire, but to be honest, that was less ridiculous than some of the rumours. I wasn't sorry to leave that school."

"I felt the same, I hated my school," I said. "They never saw me as anything more than a candidate number, a grade-making machine. The teachers only noticed me after I said I was considering Oxbridge, and everyone else just kind of avoided me. I'm pretty sure they thought I was crazy in the end."

"Because of the demons?"

"Yep. I just thought I was having a mental breakdown. I think the librarian thought the same, that time I threw an OED at a demon in the school library."

"You tried to take out a demon with a dictionary?" Leo laughed. "You're something else, you know that?"

"Is that a good or bad thing?"

"Need you ask?" he said, and leaned in to kiss me, which naturally caused my heart to forget how to beat normally.

"For the record," he said, "I don't think you're crazy."

"Good to know," I said. "Well… that's why I never dated anyone at school."

I'd not told him that before, but now seemed as good a time as any. It wasn't like this was the most shocking thing he'd heard about me tonight.

"Never?" he sounded surprised.

"Yeah. Well, I was at an all-girls' school for most of my life, but I guess I always used that as an excuse. I just wasn't interested."

"I hope you're interested in me." His smile alone was enough to make my heart stutter.

"Of course I am."

And I kissed him again. Softly, he pressed his lips to mine, coaxing my mouth open with his tongue. My entire body tingled in response to his touch.

It got progressively more difficult to concentrate on watching the film.

"You don't have to go back to yours tonight," he whispered. "You could stay."

My heart was practically in my throat. "Really?"

"Of course. But you don't have to do anything you're not ready for."

He was giving me the option. But I wasn't stupid. I knew rational thinking wouldn't help in *this* particular situation. I'd faced my own death yesterday, and that made me see everything a little clearer.

I trusted Leo. Absolutely trusted him. There was only one answer really. I knew what I wanted.

"I'll stay," I whispered, and then his arms were wrapped around me, and mine around him. I could feel myself shaking with nerves and anticipation.

"You sure about this?" he murmured, lips brushing my ear.

"Yeah," I breathed.

18

HINDSIGHT

For the second time in a week, I woke up in Leo's arms. I usually had trouble sleeping if there were other people in the room, let alone in such close proximity—and in the middle of the day. But the first thing I saw when I woke up was his sleeping face on the pillow next to mine, and I felt the overwhelming urge to hold onto him tightly and not let go.

I hadn't the heart to wake him up yet, so I just listened to his steady breathing, and enjoyed the feeling of his arms around me; even asleep, he held me like I was something precious, important, like no one else ever had.

Even before the demons, I'd never considered that I could ever get this close to someone. After the demons, there was always the worry that they'd think I was crazy— and since discovering the truth about myself, the additional worry that they'd find out I wasn't pure human. But Leo didn't care. Besides, only humans could feel love.

"Morning, Ash." Leo smiled at me. Hell, I could fall in love with that smile alone.

"Technically," I said, grinning, "it's afternoon. Or evening."

I wanted to feel him, to run my hands over his skin. Just looking into his eyes made every nerve tingle. His lips pressed to mine, and my heart thrummed in response.

Then things went pretty much the way they had yesterday.

Afterwards we lay side by side, hands locked together, hearts beating fast.

"It's Sunday," said Leo. "We could just lie here for the rest of the day."

"True. Or we could go back to mine. I have a Nintendo Wii. With Lego Star Wars."

"Did I mention you're awesome?"

"Now you have." I grinned.

A whole glorious world of possibilities was open before us. I didn't even care when Alex and Sarah cornered me that evening, after Leo had gone home, and demanded to know where I'd been for the last day.

"At Leo's," I said, to get it over with.

"I knew it!" yelled Alex, and ran up the corridor, whooping.

"Keep it down!" I said. "It's not a big deal."

"Yeah, it is. Unless you're one of those people who says sex is overrated."

"No," I admitted. "I'm not."

Maybe it was different for people who went in for one-night stands than if you were with someone who meant something to you. I didn't know, but I sure as hell wasn't complaining.

"Good. So, what happened? You used protection, right?"

"I'm not an imbecile," I said. "Of course we did. What more do you want to know? I'm not giving a graphic description. I think Pete's account of wanking over a photo of Danielle has downgraded this flat enough."

"Ew. Why'd you even have to bring that up?" said Sarah.

"Did you know he's taking his guitar to the open mic night in the bar tonight? He's going to serenade her in public."

"He does that anyway," I pointed out. "Outside her flat."

"Well, this is a big event. It'll probably be painful to watch, but what the hell. Want to go?"

"Always good to laugh at the expense of others," I said, grinning.

"That's my life motto," said Alex. "Also, Sarah's singing."

"You are?" I said to Sarah.

She flushed. "Yeah. It was that or go on a blind date with someone from LitSoc, because Alex wouldn't leave me be."

"Hey, now," said Alex. "Jake's nice."

"I told you, I'm not ready to start dating again. Ash, you've got to keep her under control. She tried to set me up with Mandeep earlier, too."

"What's wrong with him?"

"We live in the same *flat*," said Sarah. "Where is he now, anyway?"

"Probably hiding from Alex," I said.

"Your conversation is scarring," came a voice from behind his door. "Also, I'm trying to sleep."

"Sleep?" I echoed.

"You were lucky you didn't see the end of Pete's party," said Alex. "Everyone turned up for the free booze, obviously, but they got thrown out by the porters at five in the morning for making a racket. It wasn't even the loud music or anything, it was because some bright spark decided to set up a Ouija board in Terrence's old room."

"Wait—what?"

"Yeah, idiots. They were wasted and managed to convince everyone there were evil spirits everywhere, and someone was moving the furniture. It did kinda sound like someone was throwing things around in there."

I couldn't share her flippancy. Terrence's room had been the place where he'd repeatedly tried to contact demons, using god knew what method. Though he'd long since gone, I wouldn't want to be the next person to move in there. Apparently, I'd been so focused on meeting Leo and the others, I'd missed out on all the action.

"I slept with earplugs in," said Sarah.

"Yeah, me too," said Alex. "Danielle showed up and Pete spent the rest of the night chasing after her. She left him on the lawn with no money and no clothes."

"No clothes?"

"You don't want to know. Last I saw him he was running out of Terrence's old room screaming about ghosts."

"Okay," I said. *It's nothing*, I told myself. *Terrence is gone, and demons can't come onto campus.*

"Yeah, you've missed out on a lot when you've been screwing Leo," said Alex.

"Hey!" I said, flushing. "That's not all I've been doing."

"Yeah, did you go for a swim in the pond? I saw you sneaking around with wet clothes on yesterday. Unless you and Leo decided to take a fully-clothed shower?"

Crap. "No, it was just raining. Were you spying on me through the peep-hole?"

"Maybe."

I laughed. "Okay, I shouldn't have asked. I've got to tidy my room now, anyway. Leo's coming over."

"I'll put my earplugs in again," said Alex, grinning. "You left your door unlocked last night, by the way."

"I didn't, did I?"

I pushed at my door and it swung open. "Oh." I cast my mind back, but unsurprisingly, that wasn't the most vivid memory of last night. Shrugging, I went into my room.

Something nagged at me. Perhaps it was because the last time my room had been unlocked, someone had broken in, but I couldn't help looking around to check nothing was missing.

Of course, nothing was. Paranoia had ruled my life for so long I'd forgotten I lived at the safest university in the country.

I laughed. Everything seemed absurdly funny now. I hadn't realised what a weight it had been, carrying the burden of being a monster, but for the first time in months, I felt free.

Even if Alex *had* signed me up for the open mic night behind my back.

"You what?" I said, as the guy running the open mic read out my name. Stifled giggles answered me, and I turned to face my friends. We sat in the corner of the student union bar—me, Alex, Sarah, Mandeep and some of the English Lit society members who'd joined us.

"You're up, Ash!" said Alex.

"Is this a joke?"

"Ashlyn Temple!" called the guy again.

"Not many people with that name," said Sarah, also giggling. As nice as it was to see her laugh again, I wished it didn't have to be at my expense.

"Blow us away with your amazing verse," said Alex.

"I didn't even bring any of my poetry with me," I said, in a last-ditch attempt to get out of it.

"We did," said Alex, shoving a piece of paper into my hand.

"Where did you get that?" I said, staring at the hand-writing—definitely mine. One of the poems I'd written in the middle of a sleepless night, by the look of it.

"Well. You left your door unlocked..."

"I did not."

"You're up, anyway. Go!"

Sighing, I gave in. I'd already faced more than enough fears that week to make this one seem irrelevant, and it would hardly be as bad as Pete's singing.

"She walks along this dark hallway by night;

Footsteps tracing the path of memory;

Vanishing with the blush of dawn's first light.

The house falls into ruin and decay..."

It wasn't a bad poem, as far as they went. It helped that I'd had a few drinks, but I'd come up with worse in the middle of the night. Plus I'd channelled my inner literary nerd and written it in iambic pentameter, which I thought was cool, even if no one else did. A poem about a ghost under a curse.

"To walk by night and vanish in the sun;

Imprisoned in this world she wanders yet."

It might not have been literary genius, but I still got a round of applause that left me feeling flushed. Plus, Alex had also put Sarah in for singing, and she looked even more nervous than me. But she pulled it off, far better than Pete did. The latest chapter in Pete's failed romance saga ended in Danielle storming from the bar, and the crowd booed him off stage less than five minutes in.

I thought the person who stole his guitar while he sat at the bar in a total stupor might have taken it a step too far, though.

"Better for the guitar's sake," said Alex. "Oh, shit, he's looking this way. Don't come near us."

"Poor guy," Rex commented.

"This has been going on for ages," said Alex. "Six months, at least. Hell, how have we been here that long? It feels like only yesterday when we moved into our flat."

"Time flies," Sarah commented.

"Hope the next two years don't," said Alex. "Crap. It's only two weeks till Easter, then exam season starts. I still gotta tell my parents when to pick me up."

"Me too," said Sarah. "We're going to Paris over the holidays, so I'll be going home a day early."

"Paris? Nice. Yeah, I guess I'll be getting picked up same day as you."

I rubbed my forehead, frowning. That strange headache had sprung up again. I ought to be thinking about going home for the holidays, too, but something felt... off, every time I tried to think about it. I stared into my glass of cider, puzzled.

"Yo, Ash," said a voice. Oh, God. Pete.

"Yeah?" I said.

"You're glowing."

What? "Um, okay? I'm taking that as a compliment."

Sarah and Alex giggled uncontrollably.

"Seriously, man. You should get that checked out. You have two shadows."

"Uh..." I turned to look at him. His eyes were way out of focus, but any mention of *shadows* always made me wary.

"Yeah, man." He stepped forward but misjudged the distance and fell on his face. In the uproar, I twisted, trying to see my shadow, but couldn't see anything out of the ordinary. Strange. Was *Pete* of all people sensitive to the Darkworld? What did it mean?

It doesn't matter, anyway. I turned my thoughts back to the present. And Leo.

~

THE NEXT MORNING, I woke far earlier than I'd have liked to my phone buzzing.

Next to me, Leo groaned. "What's that?"

"The Venantium," I said. "Crap." I should have known. They were aware we'd been about that night, and although I didn't think we'd been seen in the tunnels, I still worried. Surely if they knew we'd set the fortune-teller free, they'd have already contacted us. Unless they'd been busy cleaning up after Jude.

It turned out the Venantium wanted me to come for questioning that evening about the events on Saturday night. I should have known; of course they knew we'd been in Blackstone when the fortune-teller broke out of Head-quarters. Nothing escaped their notice.

"Should we just tell them she just appeared, killed Jude and vanished?" I said to Claudia as we walked down the country road into town. "They'd get suspicious if we mentioned she'd stayed any longer and talked to us."

"Yeah, I'm thinking that's the best way to go," said Leo. "They'll probably suspect we helped her escape anyway, but at least we'll be telling the truth."

The sun had begun to set, and golden light now gilded the rooftops of Blackstone; even the cathedral appeared to wear a bright halo. Blossom littered the path, suggesting that spring was finally on the way. Crocuses peeked through the soil and buds had sprung up along the tree branches. The cemetery, however, looked as gloomy as ever, shadowed by the enormous cathedral.

Even Berenice agreed that we ought to keep the fortune-teller's secret away from the Venantium's ears.

"Duh," she said, as we jumped over the fence to the graveyard. "I'm not getting locked up because of *her* lunatic theories." She gave me a malicious glance. Okay, so maybe I hadn't quite convinced her yet—but who gave a crap what Berenice thought?

Because the tunnels had been blocked off while the venators conducted an extensive search, Dr Philips and another *venator* questioned us in a small room off the hallway. The Venantium seemed to have given up on using trickery and even the Angel Box. Even Dr Philips looked unusually subdued, as though they'd lost more than an escaped prisoner, and had seen defeat rather than Jude's death. Apparently they'd been combing the coastline trying to find his body, but with no luck.

It seemed natural for them to accept that the fortune-teller had just pulled another disappearing act; it was what she did, and no one had seen us in the tunnels. It didn't take too long even though the two questioners insisted on talking to us one at a time. In less than an hour, we sat in the Coach and Horses.

Howard seemed to have latched onto the idea that the Venantium had been trying to get us to contradict each other deliberately.

"It's what investigators do, Howard," said Claudia.

"Yeah, well, I don't work for them, I shouldn't be obliged to keep answering their questions."

"I know, but it's the best way to get them to leave us alone," said Cyrus. "Personally, I can't wait to get away from here. They can't harass me if I'm in the middle of the jungle."

"Aren't there other branches of the Venantium abroad?" I said.

"Course," said Leo, "but they don't exactly keep tabs on travelling sorcerers. Ours are more paranoid than most because the Demon Wars started right on their doorstep."

"When were the Venantium actually formed, anyway?" I said, realising I'd never asked this particular question before.

"Sixteenth century," said Cyrus. "They were in London originally. There was a mass demon outbreak back then that they managed to pass off as part of the plague. A sorcerer tried a major experiment that went wrong, and some others banded together to prevent it from happening again. There have always been barriers ever since the first sorcerers, but the first *venators* collectively created one strong enough to completely block demons from our world indefinitely."

"That's why they don't actually need to be there to maintain the Barrier," said Leo. "It's automatic."

"Which is why it's so obvious that they're only there for the power and making trouble for the people who don't follow their rules," said Howard, to no one's surprise.

"Yeah. And to claim all magical knowledge as their own," said Leo. "Personally I'm in favour of a blatant raid on their library. The way they are now, they probably wouldn't even try to stop us."

"What for?" I said.

"I dunno. Books on magic? They like to make out that it's all evil and demon-related, but I'll bet there are things they just don't want us to find because they're scared we'll use it against them."

"You know what happened to Doctor Faustus when he went after forbidden knowledge," I said, but he had a point. There must be more to magic than using it to fight against demons.

"I looked in a bunch of books last year," said Howard. "Mostly boring theory crap."

"Exactly," said Berenice. She and Howard sat next to each other, as if they'd never argued. Perhaps she had finally talked to him. "It's not worth it. You'd be stupid to break in again."

"The *venators* are lost without Madame Persephone, they aren't exactly at full power," said Leo.

"Is now really the time to be taking unnecessary risks?" said Cyrus.

"They've been more lax recently about people using magic without their permission," said Leo.

"Whatever," said Berenice. "I'm not being a part of this. Just because you want to walk on water like Jude did."

"That wasn't what I had in mind, but good idea," said Leo. "What's wrong with a bit of experimentation with the laws of physics?"

"I think that was the demon, though," said Cyrus. "Any sorcerer could probably figure out how to do it if it was easy, and I don't think the Venantium could cover up every minor use of magic."

"I imagine they probably don't," said Leo. "Not if the user's in Antarctica or something. Hmm."

"Don't get any ideas," said Cyrus.

But underneath the joking, I detected an undercurrent of unease. Like it hadn't quite sunk in for all of us that Jude was really dead, that the demon had gone. That tension still lingered.

Still, tonight belonged to us. We'd fended off the *venators'* questions, and with the demon gone, life had returned to the way it had been before all the trouble—well, before Jude, the doppelganger and the Skele-Ghouls, anyway. Barring the fortune-teller's absence, of course. But I no longer felt the burning need to question her. She'd told me more than I'd ever expected to know, and I still wasn't totally sure what to think. I didn't blame her for her mistakes, but at the same, I was glad not to be in her position—whatever connection she seemed to think we had.

She might never be free of her guilt, but maybe talking to me had helped. I didn't know. It was the one blot on the otherwise perfect days that followed the questioning. Without constant drama and night-time excursions, I managed to get back on track with all my reading, even though Leo reminded me that I didn't need to get so stressed at the prospect of exams coming in a couple of months' time, because we only needed a passing grade to get into our second year.

If I hadn't been a workaholic, I might have given in to the temptation to spend even more time playing on the Wii and watching films than I already did. But there were other things to keep me busy, from working on articles for the student newspaper, going out with my friends, and the weekly meeting in the Games Room. Not that anyone had anything to contribute other than tired arguments about the fortune-teller and whether she was telling the truth or not.

In hindsight I'd look back and berate myself for not seeing what was coming—even though even later on I couldn't deny that this was the happiest I'd been at university, the happiest I'd been in years, even. The phrase "too good to be true" came to mind several times, along with the sense that there was something slightly off, something major I'd overlooked overlooking. It wasn't exactly an unfamiliar feeling with me, but on occasion I'd have the overwhelming feeling that somehow, somewhere, there was something horribly, fundamentally wrong.

Later, I'd reflect that perhaps another person might try to salvage something from the situation and say they were lucky to get those few weeks of relative calmness before it all kicked off and everything fell to pieces. But in the end, I couldn't help but wonder if I'd made a different choice, or been more observant, I could have done something to prevent it. The fortune-teller was dead right when she said that hindsight was a bitch.

19

THE FESTIVAL

A lake spread out before me, a rippling carpet of pure blue. My reflection stared at me, clear as though I looked into a polished mirror. I wore an elegant black dress unlike any I owned in real life. It reminded me of the one Melivia Blackstone wore in the portrait that had hung on her wall. My demon heart amethyst pendant hung around my throat.

I looked across the lake, expecting to see Leo, but no one waited for me on the other side. An ache spread through me. He wasn't coming.

Ice wrapped around my hands, coating my fingers, the cold biting to the bone. I tried to break my connection to the Darkworld, but as I pushed it away, tendrils of darkness only moved closer, like living shadows. They latched onto my feet and climbed upwards, and coldness spread where they moved, ice-fire that writhed and hissed. Like I wore a robe made up of a thousand snakes, pure white and flexible and insubstantial as mist.

When the flames reached the base of my spine, they flared outwards, and the figure in the lake smiled at me. It rose from the water and stood there, smiling, violet eyes gleaming. The doppelganger.

"You're back," I said.

"Yes, Ashlyn," said my double. "But are you?"

"What the hell does that mean?"

"It means you're not entirely here." She reached out and stroked the shadows spiralling from my fingertips, and I shuddered even though she hadn't laid a finger on my bare skin. "You poor thing. What have they done to you?"

"Who's 'they'?" I said, even though I'd long-since learnt that demons didn't manipulate my dreams to give me answers.

"Tell me, Ashlyn, when was the last time you spoke to your parents?"

I looked at her blankly. "Huh?"

"I said, when was the last time you spoke to your parents?"

Again, my mind came out blank. That feeling of wrongness descended on me again, and the shadows seemed to wrap tighter around me like thick ropes.

When *was* the last time I'd spoken to…?

"What have you done?" I whispered.

"I haven't done a thing. It's like you said. I can't hurt you. It wasn't me who lied to you."

The shadows rose again, gripping me, and turned red-hot, searing my skin all over. The shadows became flames and spread outward. The lake sizzled, water evaporating, and in the sinking reflection I saw the university, burning, a torrent of flames consuming everything.

The flames consumed me, too, and I woke up, choking back a scream. It took a minute for me to realise that someone was banging on my door.

"It's today!" screamed Alex from outside.

"What?" I said, jumping out of bed. I opened the door, still breathless.

"It's the Blackstone Spring Festival! I know you've been too busy lost in your lover's eyes to keep track, but Jesus. Get dressed and get ready! We aren't going to miss this."

"'Lover'?" I said, rolling my eyes. I looked at my clock. It was midday, which considering my erratic sleeping pattern, didn't surprise me in the slightest.

"Get your ass out here ASAP!" Alex said, as she closed my door.

I felt totally disorientated. The memory of the dream slipped away even as I tried to grasp it, but the sense of absolute *wrongness* remained.

I took a quick shower to clear my head. It had been a while since I'd had a dream that vivid—I didn't even really dream about Melivia Blackstone any more. But that was understandable given that those dreams had been planted by the fortune-teller...

Again came the crushing sense of wrongness. A headache built behind my temples. *Oh, no you don't.* No migraine would ruin this day.

The sight of the first real sunshine of the year drove the last remnants of the dream from my mind. Alex's excitement was infectious, and she, Sarah and I were in high spirits as we walked down to the fields where the festival was being held, midway between the campus and the town.

Spring had definitely arrived in Blackstone. The trees were dressed in white blossom, and daffodils and daisies had sprung up in the fields, seemingly overnight. Birds sang above, and wagtails flew fearlessly right in front of us in the woods. We even saw a group of baby rabbits in the undergrowth as we emerged from the forest path, which distracted Sarah for a good ten minutes until Alex dragged her away, insisting that we were already missing the festival.

It looked like a toned-down version of the local travelling fair at home. Stalls selling candyfloss and popcorn were scattered amongst locals giving out freebies, and several small—and not particularly safe-looking—rides had been set up, including dodgems. A large crowd surrounded a man juggling fire. I grinned, imagining what Leo would say.

On cue, my phone buzzed. Leo was on his way.

We watched the fire-juggler for a while. Despite his obvious skill, he was definitely not a magic-user. His expression of concentration was too intense for that. Still, the crowd whooped and gasped as he balanced flaming torches on his head, tossed them around in a whirling dance. For a second, an image from last night's dream flashed before my eyes: me wearing a coat of shadowy flames.

"Hey, Ash." My heart fluttered. Leo had sneaked up behind me.

"Hi." I hugged him, breathing in his musky scent.

"It's the mysterious Leo," said Alex.

"Mysterious?" said Leo. "That sounds like my stage name. I could do a better job than that guy."

I knew it. But of course I couldn't say anything with Alex and Sarah there. I settled for exchanging a wink with him behind their backs.

"Cy's walking up from town, too," said Leo. "He said he'll be here in a bit. My brother," he added, for Alex and Sarah's benefit.

"Cool," I said.

"What about a go on the dodgems?" he said.

"No thanks," I said. "Last time I went on dodgems I managed to lose control of the damn thing and cause a pile-up; it was the most humiliating thing ever. Plus it looks like it could collapse at any moment."

"Fair point," said Leo, nodding.

"Yo," said a voice. Howard appeared, with Berenice at his side, actually holding hands. "Anything interesting happening?"

"Aside from the guy juggling fire?" said Alex. She eyed Howard with dislike, even though I knew they'd never met before. I hadn't been in a hurry to introduce my friends to the people they thought were in the Gaming Society.

"Nothing special," Howard said, shrugging.

"Your creepy flatmate's about, Leo," Berenice remarked.

On cue, Rachel wandered past, wearing a long daisy chain in addition to her usual paint-splattered overalls. She looked totally out of it.

"She's baked," said Leo, as she waved at us. My heart sank as she started weaving her way towards us. *Come and join the party!* I thought.

"Hi, Ash!" she said. "I'm so sorry!"

"For what?" I said, blankly, but a chill went through me. I detected a cold undercurrent to her voice, and remembered how accurately she'd impersonated a demon.

"Bye, Leo," she said.

It's nothing, I told myself, as she wandered off without another word, leaving us staring after her.

"Oh… kay," said Alex. "Thought I'd seen it all, but I guess this place really does have more than its fair share of characters. Was she an art student?"

"Given the paint, I hope so," said Sarah.

"Yeah, she is," said Leo, frowning. "I'll have to tell her to stop creeping people out, it's not the first time she's done it."

"Could be worse," I said, attempting to keep my voice light. "She could have impersonated Jigsaw."

"Yeah, that was memorable," said Leo. "Want to go get a drink, Ash?"

"Sure," I said. Alex and Sarah were still gawping at me, and Howard and Berenice had disappeared whilst we'd been looking at Rachel. That figured.

We walked over to the drinks stand, stopping short as someone ran in front of us. David. Not bothering to apologise to people he bumped into, he pelted across the grass to where he'd parked his bike.

"What's he up to?" said Leo.

Howard stepped right in front of David, nearly sending him flying. Even from here I heard him ask loudly, "Where the hell d'you think *you're* going?"

I didn't catch David's reply, but I hoped Howard didn't start a public fight. Leo and I made our way over through the staring crowd.

"Look," David was saying in a low voice. "It's urgent. I have to go."

"We have the right to know if there's any danger, too!" said Howard.

"People are staring," I said.

"Yeah, let it go," said Leo, glancing about.

"Look," said David. "It doesn't affect you anyway. We've just received word that someone's possessed by a demon in Manchester. They're in the town centre—a lot of people saw them. I'm warning the other *venator* students, okay?"

"Right," said Howard, but he didn't try to stop David as he ran off again. "Alright, at least that's not here."

"A real demon?" I said, taking care to keep my voice down. People were still looking curiously in our direction. "Someone's actually possessed?"

"Like he said," said Berenice, tossing her hair. "None of our business. We're ages away from Manchester. I have nothing to do with it." But her tapping foot betrayed her anxiety.

"Cara lives there," I said. "She'll be there now…"

And there was something else. The feeling from last night's dream came back. The sense that I'd overlooked something important.

"And *you* live there," said Leo.

Pain shot through my head. "Something's wrong." A throbbing built up behind my temples, like a headache, but something more—like I struggled to remember something long-forgotten.

"Ash, don't worry," said Leo. "It's a big city. You don't live in the town centre, right?"

I shook my head. "In the suburbs." But the words felt forced, rehearsed, like I only repeated something someone else had told me to say.

"Well, you have nothing to worry about." And despite the others' eyes still being on us, he kissed me. Slightly surprised, I stumbled backwards.

"Ew. Get a room," said Berenice.

"You're one to talk," I said, indicating her and Howard.

"Whatever." And the two of them walked away, abruptly drawing the conversation to a halt.

I went with Leo back to find Alex and Sarah, even though my head still throbbed and a sense of urgency prickled at me. I wondered if I should text Cara and ask if everything was okay. Was she even at home yet, anyway? I couldn't remember if term ended earlier or later for her than it did for us.

The end of term. Why did that feel like an omen to me?

And speaking of omens…

A flock of harpies soared overhead, unnoticed by the chattering crowd, although a couple of people did look up in surprise. Most people had their attention on the fire-dancer, who now had three companions and tossed flaming torches to each of them in turn. The flock of birds disappeared in seconds, but I knew Leo had seen it too.

There must be something serious going on for that many harpies to be on the move.

It's none of our business, I reminded myself again.

The fire-dancers had reached the final act of their performance now. Flames leapt in the air, and they weaved amongst them in an elegant dance which dazzled the eyes to watch. Even Leo looked impressed.

It took several minutes before I realised my phone buzzed in my pocket. Cara. Despite the heat from the flames, a quiver of foreboding went through me. I flicked the touch screen to unlock my phone.

"Hey, Cara," I said, trying to sound calm. Normal.

"Ash! Have you heard?"

"Heard what?"

The image of a demon flashed in front of me. *No way. She'd be freaking out more.*

"Someone set your house on fire! Your parents were out, thank God, but it's totally burned down."

"What—someone set my house on fire?"

"I'm sorry, Ash, I thought you'd know! I thought your parents would call you…"

A throbbing built up behind my temples again, this time almost unbearable. My vision flickered, and I clutched Leo's arm.

"Ash! What's wrong?"

"Someone burned down my house," I said.

"They what? Why?"

Very good questions. But I couldn't think past my blinding headache.

"I don't know. My head hurts… I think I need to go home. To Cara."

"You sure? I'll come with you. We can get the train from Redthorne, right? Or Preston?"

"Whichever." My voice sounded oddly distant.

"Ash?" said Cara. "You don't need to come! Just give your parents a ring."

"Something's wrong," I said. "I've got to come. Now."

"Okay. Well, I guess you're coming home soon for Easter, anyway, right? I thought you were coming home today, actually."

Come to think of it, Alex and Sarah had been talking about going home tomorrow earlier. Why hadn't I thought of that?

Why did my head hurt so much?

"If you're sure, I'll meet you in town, okay?"

"No! Not town! Wait—"

My connection cut. I looked at my phone in disbelief. "Shit."

"You sure about this?" said Leo.

"Positive." But I had no clue. I just felt—knew—that I had to go home as soon as possible. "Let's go."

20

INTO HELL

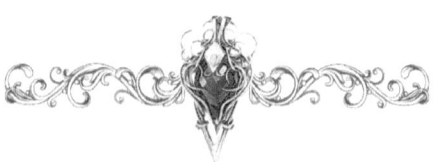

W e jumped on the first bus to Redthorne. I frantically redialled Cara's number, but my phone still refused to acknowledge a signal. The bus flew downhill, lurching over speed bumps and I held onto Leo for support; he was the only solid thing left in the world.

We got off the bus and ran through the town centre. The security guards at the train station eyed us suspiciously as we sprinted into the station, down the corridor and onto the platform. Leo bought all our tickets whilst I checked for the next train. Ten minutes to go.

Those ten minutes stretched out agonisingly. I kept checking my phone, but Cara hadn't tried ringing me back, and I still couldn't get through to her. If something had happened to her, I didn't know what I'd do. I'd sworn never to get her involved in this…

"Ash, relax," said Leo, who seemed as usual to know exactly what was on my mind. "Odds are the demon will have been caught by the Venantium before we even get there. They have a head-start on us, and from what David said, it doesn't look like the demon's taking any great pains to stay hidden. If you ask me, it's just an arrogant sorcerer who's bitten off more than he can chew. He'll get caught soon if he hasn't been already."

"I know," I said. "But still. Cara doesn't deserve to be dragged into this. I'm such an idiot."

"You'll meet her in town, right? Just get the train home together. She'll understand, you need to find your parents."

I didn't say anything. I'd gone ice-cold all over, as though someone had turned down the temperature to freezing. Dark shapes clustered on the outskirts of my vision. With every heartbeat I felt like I walked towards the cliff's edge again. I wrapped my arms around myself in a futile attempt to keep the Darkworld at bay.

Leo put his arm around me, which worked a thousand times better.

"It's okay, Ash."

I shook my head. "Can't you feel that?"

"The Darkworld? You're shivering. That means the connection's getting stronger, right?"

I nodded. "Yeah, it's like it's *inside* me. It's been getting worse. I can see shadows everywhere."

"I'll bet it's Mephistopheles's doing," said Leo. "It's the demons manipulating you."

I tried to cling to this idea. It wouldn't do any good to get all panicky.

But even as we boarded the train, fear gripped me as I saw dark spaces open up everywhere, holes forming in the universe.

"Shit," said Leo, looking into a carriage. The other passengers carried on with their business, utterly oblivious to the gaping darkness around them. "Okay. This looks... a little more serious than I thought. Let's sit out here."

We sat precariously on a pipe that ran along the corridor, opposite the door—a prime position to make a run for it. Not that it made much difference, we couldn't jump off a moving train.

I jumped to my feet at every stop, but started to feel like an idiot. The dark spaces weren't doing anyone harm. I hadn't even seen any demons. I made myself relax, leaning against Leo. He made an effort to talk of other things on the journey, like the first time we'd spoken, when he'd made fun of me for admitting to accidentally stopping a clock's hands during an exam using magic.

"I kind of wanted to punch you then," I admitted. "You were being really annoying."

"It is a specialty of mine. But you were interesting, Ash. I'd never met anyone quite like you before."

"Guess I'm probably one of a kind now," I said. "Not that I really want to meet another human-demon like him."

"That's how I know you're more human than demon," said Leo. "That guy was on the demons' team from the start, but it's a choice."

"I know," I said. "I just wish other choices were easier. Should I really be going home right now?"

"I think you need to figure stuff out," said Leo. "Do you think someone's messing with your mind?"

"It wouldn't surprise me. I feel really weird when I think about home at all. Like something's missing. It's been happening a lot lately. Like I've been missing small details. The same thing happened when Terrence messed with my head." I sighed. "I'm an idiot—I should have realised sooner."

"Don't blame yourself. The whole reason people use mind-magic is because it's hard to see through, especially for the person it's being used on. An expert can fix it so you pass things off as coincidences, or gloss over things you'd normally think were strange. Melmoth had to deal with that kind of shit all the time. It's what the Venantium do to people who witness demon attacks."

"It can't be someone from the Venantium," I said. "They don't know what I am. But how can I take it off? It's driving me mental."

Now I knew it was there, the truth lurking at the edge of my mind kept bothering me like an itch. Every time I tried to get close, I got the mental equivalent of a Taser.

"It depends who put it on you," said Leo.

I sighed, again, then jumped about a foot in the air when the robotic overhead voice announced that we'd soon be pulling into Manchester Piccadilly Station.

"Want to get off here? Or Oxford Road. That's closer, right? It's been a while since I've been here."

"Either. Cara's more likely to be at Oxford Road, her train will have got in ages ago though."

It was only five more minutes, but watching the city centre flicker past stirred new depths of fear within me. The corridor filled with people waiting to get off, commuters; people coming into town for a shopping trip; businessmen; families with small children. I wished I could do something to warn them.

I hoped to God the Venantium were there—and I never thought I'd ever hope that.

We legged it through the station and out into the open. I'd thought it was unusually sunny in Blackstone; here, it felt like an early heat wave had struck. The sun blazed above the high-rise buildings, dazzling light reflecting in the rows of windows. I'd forgotten how *big* everything was—even the smallest shops were two stories high. I saw the giant Starbucks where Cara and I had spent many a weekend, and the walkway to the shopping centre where I'd been so many times over the years…

I looked around, trying to spot Cara—or any signs of a disturbance. The town centre was heaving; we couldn't stand still without colliding with people. Of course, Saturdays in the school holidays were the worst time to come to town. Every child's scream of delight set my teeth on edge. I couldn't see any *venators*, but there were so many people in suits about that I might have overlooked them.

"Shit," said Leo. "Ash—look!"

A large number of people stood clustered near the shopping centre, looking up at something. A figure stood on the roof.

"God, no," I whispered, starting to push my way towards them. A roaring rose in my ears. *Where the hell are the Venantium?*

Unless we'd wandered into some ordinary person's suicide attempt?

No. Not an ordinary person. Normal people didn't float.

The woman stood on the air, on a level with the shopping centre roof. A familiar coldness gripped me, and the pendant burned against my chest.

"It's her," said Leo. "She's possessed."

"What's she doing?"

"God knows. There are so many people…"

The crowd had become too dense to see any more than the backs of people's heads. No *venators* appeared to be nearby.

My phone buzzed, startling me. I fumbled over the keypad.

"Ash!" Cara screamed down the phone. "Finally, dammit. Where are you?"

"I'm in town!" I turned my back on the floating figure. We had to get out of there, before Cara saw something I couldn't lie my way out of. And I needed to find out what had happened at home.

"Me too, but I can't find you!"

My heart plummeted. "Whereabouts are you? I've… I've just come out the station."

And I started running in that very direction.

"Not so fast, Ashlyn."

The connection cut out, and coldness shot through me. The floating woman appeared in front of me, eyes aglow with violet light. How had she moved so fast?

"You thought I wouldn't notice you?"

She looked to be in her mid-twenties, and wore a pencil skirt and a long black coat. Maybe she worked in the town centre. Maybe she was on her way to an interview. I couldn't infer that much from her appearance. She could be anyone. She had family, maybe even children. And she was dead. Worse than dead—possessed. The third eye in the centre of her forehead was proof enough of that.

Anger surged inside me. She was an innocent victim. She didn't deserve this.

"What's your game here?" I said, my voice shaking with rage. "Why do you want to draw attention to yourself? Why kill that woman?"

"It is no business of yours, human-demon."

Mephistopheles used his own voice rather than the woman's, which sounded chilling coming from her mouth. She stood like an automaton, simultaneously lifeless and animated, limbs hanging like dead weights.

"I want you, Ashlyn. Join me and you won't have to die when Lucifer brings in the new order."

"You can't have her," said Leo, stepping forward. The woman turned her demon eyes on him, and renewed fear shot through me. He wasn't immune to possession. Only I could face the demon.

The Darkworld closed in around me, shadows clinging to me like a living cloak. Coldness pierced my skin, and the demon smiled at me.

"This vessel is weak, but I can still break you. Your choice, Ashlyn. However invulnerable you might think yourself, breaking humans is what I do best."

She lifted off the ground, head bobbing like a puppet, hands outstretched. In one whip-like movement, she'd seized me and we were flying through the air, high above the town centre. I screamed as the ground dropped away. My head span with vertigo.

"I can use subliminal magic, too. No one sees us. It's just you and me."

"Ash!" Leo shouted from the ground, a tiny figure amongst thousands. But he couldn't do anything; if he hit the demon, I'd fall, too.

"Let go of me!" I shouted, but her hands gripped me with strength only a demon could give.

"Agree to join me, Ashlyn. Agree and I might spare your friends."

"No! Never!"

"Then you leave me no choice."

The woman's grip loosened and I slipped, seconds from falling to the ground. I shifted, tried to connect to the Darkworld.

"Come out and play, little demon!"

And she let go.

I should have fallen. A scream jammed in my throat as I dropped a foot, then rose, supported by a cloud of darkness.

The Darkworld held me up. Through the shadows, the world below looked unreal, like a dream landscape. My vision flickered to purple.

"ASH!"

I tried to call Leo's name, but my voice choked in my

throat, and instead, another, alien voice spoke through me. *You won't defeat me, demon. I'll never join you.*

"*You want to play, Ashlyn? It's been a while since I had a human body to break. Jude's was too important to damage, but this one…*"

Blood leaked from the corners of the woman's eyes, beneath the violet. Streaks of red appeared in her skin, like something had dug sharp nails into her face.

"Stop," I whispered.

There was a jarring *snap*, and a shudder of revulsion went through me. The woman's arm had broken, seemingly by itself. It hung at a right angle, a dead weight. The hand spun on itself with another horrible *crack*.

"*I could do worse to you, demon. Your human vessel is vulnerable. I told you I could break her.*"

And she grabbed my left arm, squeezed hard. I screamed, a wrenching scream that tore at my lungs. The demon pulled my hand upwards and placed it on the demon heart on the woman's forehead.

"*You can feel it, can you not?*"

I felt it. The power pulsing in the crystal was fathomless, far beyond my own. It was almost a living essence itself, and it seemed to laugh at me, with Mephistopheles's voice.

The strength of a true demon resided in the crystal. I'd become attuned to the feel of my own amethyst; when I touched it, I felt protection and security emanating from the core. This felt like a store of pure fear. Faces flashed before my eyes, people Mephistopheles had tortured and killed. Thousands of lives ruined over centuries. The sheer weight of it threatened to knock me out.

"*You feel it, Ashlyn. I am the oldest of demons. I am Mephistopheles. And this world is ours for the taking.*"

"Never!" The shock turned my vision back to normal,

but it brought a new vulnerability. I felt horribly, nakedly human, like a fly next to a god.

A sudden burst of fire ignited the air around is. The woman turned her head with a surprised sound. Her feet had caught fire.

"How—"

Leo. He'd somehow managed to reach us with magic, and the demon cried out as the flames crept up the woman's body. I pulled my hand out of the weakening grasp, wincing at the pain. I could still move my arm; even though it hurt like a bitch, it wasn't broken.

"Ash!" Leo's voice rose through the darkness. "Can you get down? I'll catch you!"

Shit. I had about half a second before I fell, so I did the only thing I could, I contacted the Darkworld and cried out for help.

The shadows around my legs held me as I dropped through the air, slowly. My mind spun, my throat burned from trying not to scream, my heart was about to burst out of my chest—

And then Leo held me in his arms and I could breathe again. I clung to him, and he held onto me tightly.

"Thank god," he whispered. "Thank god, Ash."

I tilted my head and saw the woman fall, just behind us. She hit the pavement with a horrible *crack* and a spray of red. I looked away, bile rising in my throat, even though I knew she'd been dead long before.

Leo looked sickened. "I had to burn her…"

"Not your fault," I coughed. "Put me—put me down, I can walk."

He nodded, walking over to the woman's body. I staggered after him, clutching my bruised arm.

Blood seeped out from under the woman's head. Her limbs were twisted at odd angles, and the bones of one arm poked through the skin like a snapped candy stick. Gore was spattered around her in a halo-like pattern. I gagged, shutting my eyes.

"Shit," said Leo. "What do we do with the demon heart? It can't be the same one as before, right?"

"Just take it." I swallowed, hard. "Give it to the Venantium."

Leo bent down and pulled at the now lifeless crystal. It came away easily, like peeling off a plaster.

Someone screamed.

People ran towards her. We backed away from the corpse and tried to look as stunned as everyone else did. I felt like I barely had control of my own body, like I experienced this through someone else's eyes. That feeling when I'd touched the crystal had thrown everything else out of whack. Now Leo held it, but he was already walking away.

"Did anyone see?"

"Where did she come from?"

"Did she jump?"

"Who saw?"

We needed to get out of there.

"Train station," I said to Leo, who nodded.

We pushed our way through the crowd. No one gave us a second glance, to my relief. As we entered the station, someone grabbed my arm——thankfully, not the injured one.

"Ash." Cara stared at me, wide-eyed, like she'd seen a ghost.

Oh, crap.

21

STOLEN LIFE

"**T**here you are!" I said. "Did you see——"

"Ash, seriously. We need to talk."

"About what?" I struggled to bring my mind back to normality after what had just happened.

"I just spoke to your parents. They didn't know who you were."

My heart dropped. "They what?" I turned to face Leo, who looked as aghast as I felt.

"I'm not stupid. I know something's going on. I saw you *flying* just then. Are you going to tell me what that was about?"

My voice seemed to have deserted me. *Crap.*

"Look, I'm sorry," was all I could manage. It sounded like a stranger spoke. My head throbbed. Maybe I was going into some kind of shock. I had just nearly died, after all.

"I'm your best friend, Ash. I'm not an idiot. I know there's been something going on. But you can tell me. I can take it."

"I need to see my parents," I whispered, and I felt tears pricking at my eyes. "I don't understand."

"You're not the only one." Cara's face said it all, she'd persist with questioning until she had answers.

"I'll explain," I said. "Honestly. I just… I really don't know what's going on."

"You said you thought someone had messed with your memory," said Leo, who didn't seem to care that Cara was listening. She'd seen enough, and we had bigger problems to worry about.

"Yeah——it must be that, but… my parents…"

"They said they didn't have kids," said Cara. "Gave me a hell of a weird look. You know what that's about?"

I shook my head. "No. I need to go to the house."

"They've cordoned it off," said Cara. "But yeah. Let's get on a train."

Leo bought the tickets; my arm hurt too much to operate the ticket machine. It was beginning to swell; I wondered if it was broken after all. I still felt detached, in a dream, despite the pain. We just made the train, jumping on seconds before the doors closed.

"Right," said Cara, as we found a mercifully almost-empty carriage. "Spill it."

I drew in a deep, calming breath, and unconsciously stroked the crystal around my neck with my hand. Surprisingly, it helped, like it anchored me back in reality.

Leo gave me a look as if to ask if I felt okay to talk, and I nodded.

I gave Cara a basic rundown of the insanity——from the start. Firstly, I told her about seeing the demons in the assembly hall at school, and how they'd dogged me ever since.

"I knew there was something bothering you besides the exams," she said, to that. "I hoped you'd talk to me about it, but when you went to uni, I thought you might be okay."

"I was," I said. "Because I met the others. But…"

"You remember when I came to visit?" Cara interrupted me, and I could tell this was something she'd wanted to say for a while. "I heard you yelling in your sleep, begging demons not to kill someone."

"Seriously?" I never knew I talked in my sleep. But that night, I'd dreamed of Melivia Blackstone for the first time.

"Hell yeah. Also, I saw your book."

"What book?"

"I can't remember the title—seven demons of something. It was shoved down the side of the bed."

"What—the *Seven Princes of the Darkworld?*"

"Yeah. I thought it was a story at first. I couldn't sleep, so I just had a look inside. But there was something a little too *real* about it. It creeped me out. I couldn't figure why the hell you had something like that in your room. So I did a little research. It's amazing what you can find on the dark corners of the Internet."

"So you knew about the demons?" I said, disbelief colouring my voice. Cara had once accidentally gone onto a poltergeist-spotting website and when her computer had subsequently crashed, she'd refused to go near it for weeks, fearing it was possessed by an angry spirit. But she'd willingly researched demons?

"Not exactly… the site I went on sure as hell didn't mention *flying.* But I found this forum. Mephistopheles's lair, or something."

"Mephistopheles has his own website?" said Leo. "Man, no one better tell him that. He's egotistical enough, thinking he's king of all demons."

"I want to hear your version, anyway," said Cara. "Knock me out."

So I launched into a repeat of the events since I'd come to Blackstone, from the first week. I told her about my first encounter with a shadow-beast at Satan's Pit; about meeting the fortune-teller; finding out about the Darkworld; Claudia teaching me magic. I told her about the group meetings, about the Venantium, about Terrence and how he'd almost killed me. Cara didn't flinch once, not even when I revealed that I was half-demon. Of course, to an outsider, it would be seen as irrelevant, not that I was a monster.

Then I told her about Mr Melmoth's murder, about the Ghouls, the doppelganger, Jude and the night I'd almost died. Finally I mentioned Lucifer, and told her that we'd just defeated Mephistopheles, Lucifer's second-in-command.

This took most of the journey. I had to keep backtracking to explain things like demon hearts, and higher demons, and even the fortune-teller's past—I didn't want there to be any more secrets. It was selfish, but I wanted her to understand. And amazingly, she did. Cara, who feared things that went bump in the night more than the average ten-year-old, sat calmly as I told her about the horrors that lurked beneath our world.

"You're taking this way better than I pictured," I said.

"Yeah, well, I have a lot of experience dealing with the unseen." It amazed me at how flippant she sounded.

"You're not going to perform an exorcism on me?" I said.

"From what you tell me, exorcisms aren't much use. You're not evil. I might not totally understand what it's like, but I get that much."

"You're the best friend ever, you know that?"

"Glad to be. You weren't ever going to tell me, were you?"

"I just didn't want you to worry about me. Most people can't even see harpies, let alone the Darkworld. There's like a one in a million chance."

"And it's hereditary?"

"Huh? I think so. It's the only way it makes any sense. Most magic-users are from the Blackstone area."

"I mean, you're part demon. Your parents are totally normal, aren't they?"

It hurt my head to think, but I knew she was right. Which meant…

"So they're not your parents," said Cara. "Jeez, what's wrong with you? You're not freaking out."

"I am freaking out," I said quietly. "Someone's screwed with my memory. Every time I try to think about anything related to my parents—"

I winced as a jolt of pain lanced through my head.

Cara stared at me. "What, they made you forget about your parents? And *they* forgot about you?"

"Or it could be the other way around," said Leo, in a low voice. "They made your parents forget about you, which made you forget… unless there was *already* a spell there, and it got removed."

Ice curled around my heart at what Leo implied.

"Everything… everything was a lie? My entire life? It was just a spell?"

Leo squeezed my hand. "To be honest, I've never heard of anything like it. I'm sorry. We'll figure it out."

He hugged me, but for the first time, it didn't make me feel all right. I didn't see how things could possibly be okay ever, now.

After a short walk from the station, I saw two fire engines parked at the end of the road where I used to live. I quickened my pace, Cara and Leo behind me.

Several people gathered around the house at the end of

the street. The smell of burning hovered around the road, and smoke lingered in the air like mist. The fire had been put out, although as we drew closer I saw the living room windows thrown wide open, and the room inside reduced to charred ashes. A rush of deja-vu reminded me of the Blackstones' house.

The area had been cordoned off, so we couldn't get any closer. My heart jumped into my throat as I saw two familiar figures.

My parents stood talking to one of the fire fighters. I both recognised and didn't recognise the two people in front of me, like they were strangers I'd passed once on the street. And it felt wrong, like the world had shifted on its axis and left me behind, spinning in a black void.

"Ash," said Cara, "are you sure you want to…?"

I stumbled towards the house. The woman—Mum—was shaking her head. She looked like she'd been crying. Dad said something to the fireman.

"Mum," I said, choking out the word before it slipped back down my throat.

She didn't look up.

The fireman did. "Excuse me, can I help you with something?"

I looked at my parents. They regarded me blankly, with no recognition in their expressions.

"No," I said. "Sorry. I was just looking."

And I walked away, my heart breaking because I couldn't feel a thing, like I'd just had a passing conversation on the street. Tears overflowed and streaked down my face. But I felt frozen inside.

Cara and Leo exchanged glances and hurried after me towards the train station again. I kept my head down, tears flowing freely, mind in free-fall. Rushing onto the platform,

I collided with someone, and looked up to find myself face to face with the fortune-teller.

"You," said Leo, from behind me. "This is your doing, isn't it?"

The fortune-teller looked at me with the same deep sadness on her face as she'd had when she'd been telling me about her past.

"Ashlyn. I am truly sorry."

"Tell me what's going on." Anger made my voice raw. "Tell me."

She gave a deep sigh, and gestured. The Darkworld moved, closed in around us, cutting us off from the outside world.

"No one will hear us now."

She sat on one of the platform benches and gestured for me to sit beside her. Leo and Cara did, too, the former eyeing her with anger, the latter with suspicion.

"You messed with my memories," I said, hollowly. "Why?"

"It was—"

"Let me guess. It was a 'necessary deception', am I right? Has anything you said not been a lie? Is my entire life a lie? Who the hell are you? *Who the hell am I?*"

And to my horror, I felt another voice ask the second question, an echo of my own. The demon inside me.

"Ashlyn. Believe me when I say that it was for your own safety that I deceived you. None have come to any harm from this, but your very life would have been in danger if I had taken care of you myself."

Once again, I felt myself spinning in a black void. I shut my eyes.

"You're my *mother*."

She nodded. "I had to keep you from Lucifer. I did the

only thing I could: I found a young couple whose child had been stillborn. The man was the brother of the woman whose body I had inadvertently taken on. They had no plans to have any other children. It was easy to get close to them, to use Influence to persuade them to take you, and they raised you thinking their child had survived. Meanwhile, I posed as your Aunt Eve. The spell was simple to maintain, and I never thought it would break. But when I was imprisoned, the majority of my powers were cut off. I didn't realise what had happened until now, when the anti-demon defences around your house activated. I knew Mephistopheles was here."

"Who was I in danger from? Lucifer? *Which* Lucifer? Who's my father?" Horror gripped my heart. It couldn't be…

"The true demon Lucifer is your father. It's why you were in danger from the human sorcerer who also calls himself by that name. He would do anything to possess you. You're half-demon—half-*higher* demon. He would have used you as a weapon, or killed you, taking your magic to fuel his own. When he learned that I had betrayed him to the higher demons, I was lucky to escape with my own life."

I shook my head. "Were you ever planning to tell me? What if Lucifer had come back?"

"He *is* coming back. I will do everything in my power to keep you safe."

"Bullshit. You've been doing everything in your power to ruin my life. I have *nothing* now." I laughed humourlessly. "I have no family. I have no home. I *certainly don't have a mother*."

She flinched, and I felt a bizarre surge of gratification. She deserved as much pain as I could give her.

"You were too much of an unfeeling bitch to raise me. Did you ever wonder what I would grow up to be?"

"All the time, Ashlyn. I sent you the pendant. I talked to you as your aunt, and when forced to drop that disguise, I obtained your new phone number. I tried to warn you when you were in danger, but…"

"You sent me those cryptic messages?" I stood, shaking all over with rage. "What *are* you? I was totally alone. I thought I was mad, when I found out I could see demons. You might have had a fucked-up life, but at least your memories are right. How the hell am I supposed to know if *anything* is true now?"

She didn't have an answer. I knew I shouted at her like a child in a tantrum, but I didn't care. This woman had destroyed me, broken me apart from the inside, and I'd never—*never*—look at anything the same way again.

Even Cara and Leo, who watched, lost for words.

"He's looking for me," the fortune-teller said. "Lucifer, the human. He wants me back."

"He can have you," I said coldly, and the demon's presence bolstered my anger. "I hope he feeds *your* life force to the demons, *demon lover*."

She winced.

I stood up. "I'm going home. Not that you'd know what that is."

"I know I can't force you to trust me, Ashlyn."

"Screw you," I said. I walked out of the circle of darkness. She didn't try to stop me.

The journey back was a blur. I said goodbye to Cara beforehand, and she hugged me. She was crying, too. "I'll call you later, Ash. It'll be okay. It's fucked-up now, but it'll be okay."

It wasn't, but it'd be easier to let her believe it.

Leo held my hand all the way back, but it still felt ice-cold.

22

FIRE AND ICE

I jerked back to reality when the train stopped in Redthorne. The sun had set whilst we were on the train, giving way to a clear night. The stars shone, bright pinpricks in the inky sky. I stared up as we walked to the bus stop to catch a bus back to campus, as if hoping for some answers in the depths of space.

Leo had texted Claudia, and she met us at the station.

"Did something happen?" she said, eyes widening as she took in my appearance. Like I needed reminding of what a mess I looked. Like someone whose world had fallen apart.

I tuned out as Leo started to explain. I didn't want to hear about it. I didn't want to think about it.

My phone buzzed in my pocket. An anonymous number, but I knew who it was.

Ashlyn. You may never forgive me, but I'll always be here if you need my help. I set up a bank account in your name, in which I deposited a substantial amount of money for any future expenditures—you know that my family is rich.

If there is anything else you need, I can be reached at this number.

Like money could solve anything.

I barely paid attention to where we were walking. It didn't even register that barely anyone stood on the street, that eerie silence followed us, and I didn't notice the gaps in the universe until something gripped my ankle.

A long, scaled hand reached out of the darkness, its fingernails digging into my leg. I jumped back with a cry, pulling my foot out of its grip.

There were *things* in the darkness, clawed things, scaled things, everywhere under my feet. I couldn't see anything; the Darkworld had crept up like miasma, shadowing the buildings around me.

I heard Claudia shout, "Shit!"

"Ghouls!" Leo's voice said. "Ash—get out of there!"

Where was I? I couldn't see the real world beneath the darkness. I stumbled forwards, kicking clawed hands away as I did so. More ghouls, moaning, hunched creatures breathing darkness, clawed at me.

"Get out of it!" I yelled, kicking at them again. I tried to draw the Darkworld around myself like a cloak, but the creatures came with it; a thrill of horror went through me as I realised that the ghouls held onto the Darkworld itself, like they'd melded to it.

I ran, and that seemed to work; the Darkworld remained static, and although I couldn't see where I was going, the ghouls were forced to let go. I jogged at random, feeling cobblestones strike my feet and hoping that I wouldn't run into anything. I heard the ghouls behind me, their piteous moans echoing in my ears. I moved further into the fog. Deeper.

My phone buzzed again. *For God's sake.*

I hoped irrationally that the message would be some

kind of explanation—but it was just from Cara, asking how I was. Not the fortune-teller.

Wait a minute.

I'd never replied to any of the anonymous messages… but now it was the only thing I could think of to do. I typed one-handedly, **We're being attacked in Redthorne, help!**

I pushed my phone back into my pocket. Then I summoned light.

My hands blazed and illuminated the area around me. Ghouls were sensitive to light, and this hit them directly in their weak half-demon eyes. Screeching, they retreated into the withdrawing shadows.

A voice cried out ahead.

"*Leo!*" I shouted, and ran.

I saw glittering demon eyes wherever I looked, unconcerned by the light blazing from my hands. I followed the sound of Leo's voice down unfamiliar streets, panic rising.

A line of ghouls waited in front of me, hideous bodies woven into the darkness. Flickers of the real world appeared through the Darkworld. I'd thought I ran toward something familiar but I'd headed in the opposite direction from the shopping district, near the canal. I saw a bridge up ahead, and my feet alternately hit stone and scabbed hands as I flew over it, and right over the ghouls clinging to the shadows. I wouldn't let them stop me getting to Leo.

Below, the water surged, and the image of hanging over the edge of that cliff flashed through my mind. I ran faster, kicked another ghoul out of the way—

And nearly ran headlong into Leo. He stood at the end of the bridge, his back to me.

"Leo!" I all but threw myself at him. "Thank God you're—"

The words stopped. Everything stopped. Leo had

turned his head, and looked into mine with violet demon eyes.

I couldn't breathe. My lungs felt frozen, and my head swam, my vision flickering like I looked through a distorted window.

Leo. *Leo.*

"Looks like you were too late, Ashlyn."

Even though he spoke with Leo's voice, I had no doubt it was Mephistopheles. Leo's forehead now bore the demon heart he'd been carrying, winking like a third eye.

I couldn't take it in.

"Leo," I whispered.

"I'm afraid not," said the demon. "You thought you had me this time, didn't you? It was all a trick, Ashlyn. A set-up. I knew you'd come to your family's aid—admittedly, I thought you'd be there earlier, but I enjoyed toying with the humans for a while. But it was staged to bring you to the demon heart. You and the one person you'd do anything to save."

And for a minute, the violet eyes disappeared, and Leo's grey-blue, human eyes looked into mine.

He was *alive.*

"It didn't take me long to persuade him, but the Blake family have quite a history with us. I knew it wouldn't take much. Who in their right mind would turn down an offer of immortality? Of limitless power?"

"You're lying," I said. "Leo would *never*—"

"Would he? Do you humans ever truly know each other's hearts?" He tilted his head.

It wasn't possible. I'd imagined a contract with a demon as like a kind of Faustian pact, something formed over time, like with Terrence. *This isn't real*, a desperate voice told me, but the evidence before me screamed otherwise.

Leo smiled, and my heart simultaneously flipped and twisted inside me.

"Is it possible to trust someone absolutely, without access to their every thought, every emotion, every dark secret? I know this boy better than you ever could, Ashlyn. I've read his mind."

Icy hatred surged through me. "Like hell you do," I said.

He smiled, and my insides twisted at the sight of Leo's face distorted like that.

"Leave him alone," I said. "If you want me so badly, why didn't you try to possess me?"

I was aware that I played for time, but I'd never felt so helpless as I did right then, knowing that the slightest whim on the part of the demon would mean Leo's instant death. I remembered Terrence, dying without as much as a whisper, his life snatched away by the creature that possessed him. I remembered Jude, sinking into the ocean. I remembered the anonymous woman, falling from the sky.

I couldn't let that happen to Leo.

I wouldn't let it happen.

"Pathetic, human-demon," said Mephistopheles. "You assume I would fall for such a feeble deception? Immune to possession you may be, but your human ties are your weakness. Let them go."

I shook my head. "No…"

"Lucifer is impatient. So am I, come to that. Your stubbornness does you no credit, and certainly will not help you when he returns. Give me your heart, demon, or he dies."

Slowly, watching Mephistopheles's flickering eyes, I reached to the pendant around my neck. It seared my skin, as if guessing what I planned to do.

I didn't care what happened to me. Leo was the one person I couldn't afford to lose. The fortune-teller might have broken my life from the inside out, but the truth was, she hadn't taken everything from me. My friends were still there. And so was Leo. If I lost him…

"Predictable," Mephistopheles crooned, and I hated him for using Leo's mouth to speak. I hated him for invading my boyfriend's mind. The hatred felt like something living inside me, a beast lurking under the surface.

When my hand moved to lift the pendant over my head, the anger froze my arm.

You'll never take me, said a voice. My voice, but not mine. *Not again.*

I tried to move my arm, but it was locked in place.

"Feeling a little conflicted?" said Mephistopheles. "I meant what I said. Demons don't lie."

Move! I told my arm, like I battled sleep paralysis again.

Don't be an idiot, Ashlyn. I'm trying to save your life.

And my body moved by itself, ice fire spinning into life in my palm.

NO!

Leo moved out the way of the fire just in time—like Mephistopheles wanted to see how far he could push me. I stared, horrified, at my own hand. The demon inside me wanted to kill Mephistopheles—even at the cost of Leo's life.

Stop that!

You don't know anything Ashlyn. This demon must die.

I know that! But Leo has nothing to do with it.

He's as good as dead.

I shook my head fiercely. *Shut up.*

"I'm getting bored, Ashlyn," said Mephistopheles. "How about I give you an incentive?"

Fire flared from his hands.

"Interesting. This one has particular skills with pyromancy. Even I don't burn! Imagine, a demon impervious to fire. This has to be a first. Perhaps I won't let him go so easily, after all."

He took a step closer to me. "Hmm."

The Darkworld moved around me, tendrils locking around my body from behind like a straitjacket. I couldn't move—could only look into Leo's empty eyes as he summoned fire, and touched my forehead.

I screamed. The pain tore me in two; I was simultaneously there, writhing in the grip of the Darkworld, and above, floating in a haze of pain. My vision flashed purple, then black. I flickered in and out of consciousness as the pain branded me like a searing-hot iron.

Then it stopped. The Darkworld let me go, and I fell to the ground, limp and shaking.

"Wasn't that fun, Ashlyn? Do you want to go through that again?"

"Never." Something moved my legs to stand up. *"You won't kill me, demon."*

Coldness seeped through me and I felt ice form on my hands, by itself. It became liquid, still clinging to my palms, and coalesced into the form of two daggers.

"I'll kill you, *Ashlyn, you and your demon both."*

No! I shouted at the voice, but my body was moving by itself, raising the twin daggers.

"Rather showy," Mephistopheles remarked, and summoned fire again. This time it danced around him, forming a sword of flickering flame. He smiled, and fear gripped my heart to see Leo's face distorted with malice. "You want to do battle, human-demon?"

"Stop!" I shouted, as my hands moved and ice met fire in a clash that jarred the Darkworld itself.

23

WALKING ON ICE

M y hands burned. I screamed at the demon inside me to stop, not to attack—I couldn't risk hurting Leo. But the rational side of me told me I had to kill Mephistopheles, and this was the only way.

The voices warred within my head, but as the flaming sword forced me to step back, again and again, I realised that I'd be lucky to escape with my own life.

My feet hit something solid and I stumbled back. I'd almost forgotten that we stood on the bridge over the canal, and I'd narrowly avoided stepping into empty air. The demon seemed to realise the same thing.

"Reached your limit, Ashlyn?" said Mephistopheles.

The demon took control again and the Darkworld responded. The two daggers melded, forming a long sword equal to the one Leo held. Icy flames danced along it.

It was all I could do to keep out of reach of the other flames. I felt them burning my hands, and if it hadn't been for the magic of the Darkworld binding my palms to the sword, I'd probably have dropped it.

This has to end.

I couldn't even tell whose thought I heard, mine or the demon's. But I felt my connection to the Darkworld surge upright like a torrent of pure coldness, engulfing me inside and out. I could no longer feel the pain in my arm, the exhaustion, even the heat from the fire. Desperation pushed me forwards.

Leo moved without warning, and the ice-sword flew out of my hand. I jumped back as the fire grazed my skin—and suddenly there was no ground beneath my feet, and I was falling.

Too stunned even to scream, I fell toward the abyss. I felt everything move in slow motion and reached out to the Darkworld just in time to re-connect with the ice-sword. Coldness pierced me and I felt ice solidify on my skin, cocooning me, as the water rushed at me like a black tunnel.

But I never slammed into the water. My outstretched hands brushed the surface and it froze at my touch; I barely had the chance to feel a modicum of surprise before I was skidding across the canal, which had turned into a sheet of ice, smooth as polished glass.

Holy shit.

Even as I watched, the ice continued to spread across the surface.

"Wow, Ashlyn." Mephistopheles called from the bridge. "I'd never have expected the human part of you to show such resourcefulness."

He moved in a blur, and then Leo stood on the ice, a couple of metres away. His violet eyes shone against the dark backdrop of the city.

"A very nice idea, Ashlyn. It's too bad that I'm the man on fire."

My heart twisted at Leo's own words spoken in the monotone of a demon.

And a spark shot down his outstretched hand, curled into a flame. The canal beneath his feet hissed as the ice melted, leaving two foot-shaped holes.

"Isn't this fun?"

Leo ran at me, outlined in flame. I snapped back to my senses and backed away, feet skidding on the ice, but I couldn't out-run a demon, let alone on a frozen canal. He tackled me and threw me to the ground, and I screamed as I landed on my injured arm.

"Does it hurt, Ashlyn?"

He pulled my head forward then slammed it into the ice. Stars winked before my eyes.

"Leo," I choked, desperate. "Fight him… please…"

"No human can fight a demon, little fledgling. You should know that."

He slammed my head again and this time, my vision flashed to violet.

"There you are."

Through the haze I saw his hands blazing. His face was twisted in an expression of cruelty.

He really does mean to kill me.

"Only one way out, demon," he whispered. "Will you give up?"

My demon side already had its answer, and this time, I wasn't sure I'd be able to stop it. I squeezed my eyes shut, as if to deny there was something else controlling me.

"Ash!" yelled a voice.

I turned my head, still fighting for control over my own body.

Claudia stood on the bridge, looking down at us. "Leo! What're you doing!"

Leo turned to face her, and she gasped.

"No!"

While he had his face turned away, I scrambled to my feet. The back of my head throbbed and my ears rang, but I slid away across the ice. I half-skidded, half-fell onto the bank, and, pushing the pain to a dark corner of my mind, struck out for the bridge where Claudia stood.

Of course, I should have known I wouldn't get away that easily. Leo appeared in front of me before I could take a step onto the bridge.

"Going to run like a coward? How about I stop your boyfriend's heart?"

"Get away from him, you bastard," I said.

"I'm having rather too much fun to leave now," said Mephistopheles. "Your human entanglements amuse me. I wonder…"

He paused. I tensed as he reached out a hand and gently stroked my face. I cringed, expecting pain——but it didn't come.

"How did that feel?"

"What?"

"You get the same physical response as you would if he were himself, do you not? He's still *here*. Even if he were dead, your emotions would still be there. You'd still feel… attraction, wouldn't you?"

I realised what he meant, and the implication sank into me like a stone. "I'd never be attracted to you," I said. "Never."

"Does your heartbeat speed up when I do this?"

He reached out to stroke my face again, and I punched him on the jaw.

It *hurt*. I'd never hit anyone before, and the *snap* as my fist connected with his face jolted through my entire body. Even though I'd used my uninjured hand, it throbbed at the impact, and even the demon looked momentarily startled.

Mephistopheles laughed. "Well, now, I didn't expect that."

"Get away from him, demon!" Claudia had crossed the bridge to stand beside me. She regarded him with a mixture of pity and revulsion.

"I have no interest in you," said Mephistopheles. "I want the human-demon."

"You can't have me."

"You're willing to risk his life?"

No. I wasn't, and I knew he could read it on my face. There wasn't any way I could win this.

The Darkworld shifted around us, and a strong breeze swept past me. Leo's expression turned to one of surprise.

"You again?" he said.

The fortune-teller stood behind him as if she'd dropped down from the sky, and she held two threads of darkness in each hand.

"What—?" Claudia gaped at her.

The fortune-teller moved so fast she appeared blurred—one second Mephistopheles stared at her, horror etched on Leo's face—

And the next, she'd seized his demon heart.

The demon screamed, a horrible, piercing cry that turned my blood to water. I swayed on the spot, my eyes fixed on Leo's face, which was distorted in pain—then went blank. The violet lights winked out, and he fell backwards.

I dropped to my knees.

He was dead.

I clutched the ground, as if compelled to grab onto something solid. *No...*

The fortune-teller was at my side. "Ashlyn. He's alive."

I raised my tear-streaked face and met Leo's ordinary, grey-blue eyes. A sob choked me. I couldn't speak, but flung myself at him.

He held me by instinct, staring as though seeing the world for the first time.

"I'll take the demon heart," said the fortune-teller. "He won't dare try to possess *me*… I should have foreseen this. He must have manipulated someone into retrieving the heart from the ocean—that, or he had another helper. It doesn't bode well." She sighed. "The Venantium will doubtless be here shortly, but the ghouls will bother you no more. You should go."

I heard her speak, but cared for nothing other than the certainty that Leo was really here, that he was alive, that he'd survived possession.

I saw her nod at Claudia, then disappear into the night.

"Ash, your arm's really swollen," said Claudia. "I think you need to get it looked at."

All the injuries of the past few hours seemed to crash down on me then. My head throbbed from where it had struck the ice, and my wrist looked twice its normal size.

"Good idea," I said vaguely, and more or less passed out there and then. Good job Leo was there to catch me.

I came to a moment later. He held me, but his face was still blank. Maybe he was in shock.

"Leo?" I said, tilting my head to look at him.

"Ash," he said. "Sorry. I'm so sorry."

"It wasn't you, Leo," I said. "It was the demon."

"I saw myself hurt you." He swallowed. "I couldn't control my own body—it was like being trapped behind a wall."

"I hurt you, too," I said, and then I was crying again. "The demon inside me wanted to kill you. It didn't care if you got hurt, it just wanted to kill Mephistopheles. I could hardly fight it—if the fortune-teller hadn't come—"

Why had she saved us again? It was always her. I couldn't hate her, not now that she'd saved one of the few good things left in my life.

"Can you walk?" said Leo, in that same flat tone.

"Huh? Sure."

"We should get you to a hospital."

"Okay. Right."

He wouldn't meet my eyes, and barely spoke as we walked towards Redthorne town centre. If I hadn't felt on the verge of passing out again, I'd have attempted to reassure him that it *wasn't* his fault. But it was all I could do to keep my feet moving, and when we finally reached the hospital, my legs gave way altogether. Leo carried me, and his face was the last thing I saw before I blacked out again.

24

HOMELESS

They made me stay overnight, to my annoyance. I just wanted to fall asleep in Leo's arms, but I had to be checked over to make sure I didn't have a concussion. My arm wasn't actually broken, just badly bruised, but I still had to have a cast fitted.

I didn't expect to sleep very well on the uncomfortable hospital bed, but in the end exhaustion won out. There was no one there when I woke up. Claudia had gone back to campus; I vaguely remembered that from the night before; and I guessed Leo had left whilst I was asleep. For some reason, this made me uneasy, but I tried to quell the feeling as I was discharged and left the hospital to catch the first bus back to campus.

I went back to my flat first, to shower and change. The hospital had leant me pyjamas for the night but my own clothes were soaked and filthy. I changed into a clean outfit, but my skin still felt ice-cold.

My room felt a cage now. Things I didn't want to think about kept coming back to me. This was my only home now. I no longer had anywhere else to go. Everything I owned was here.

And I had no family.

That was the hardest part. I assumed the fortune-teller had erased every trace of evidence for my existence from my parents' lives, but she'd forgotten that I had all my photo albums, all my old diaries with me. I felt tainted, like I was holding pieces of someone else's life. But I couldn't bring myself to throw them out.

In the end, I decided to check on Leo. Luckily, I didn't run into my flatmates on the way out; I hadn't yet thought of a cover story for my injuries.

Rachel answered the door again.

"Hi, Ash. Congratulations!" She gave me one of her creepy knowing looks, and I shuddered. Whatever Leo said, she plainly knew *something* about what had happened.

Leo's door was open, and a number of bags leaned against it. I saw a half-open suitcase inside, and Leo threw objects into it haphazardly.

"Leo? What're you doing?"

"Leaving," he said brusquely.

I'd forgotten it was the end of term. Without a home to go to, it had completely slipped my mind that most people would be leaving campus behind for four weeks. I hadn't even thought about my own plans. I wanted to see Cara again, but could I face going back to familiar places knowing I had no real ties to them anymore?

"Now?"

"Yeah. I mean, I'm not just going home. I'm going out of the country." He didn't meet my eyes.

"You what?"

He still didn't look at me as I skirted the pile of bags and stepped into his room, closing the door behind me.

"I can't—I can't stay here. I'm going travelling with Cy."

"For Easter break?" My own voice sounded dull, now, as dread curled around my heart.

"For longer. I'm leaving uni."

"What?"

"I can't stay," he said simply.

"I don't understand. Is it about…" I swallowed. "No one blames you for what the demon made you do."

I stepped forward and wrapped my arms around him, but he didn't respond. It was like hugging a statue.

"I mean it!" The hurt choked me; after everything, I needed him to understand. I had no blame left. Mephistopheles had manipulated both of us.

"You should blame me. I let the demon in."

"You…" I didn't know what to say. Deep down I'd known this conversation was coming, but I'd thought we'd at least be able to forget about it for a while. "It wasn't your fault," I settled for saying.

"I made a pact with a demon. It wasn't anyone else's fault, that's for damn sure."

"How? What did Mephistopheles tell you?"

"The demon told me that it was the only way to save you from them. That… the half-demon part of you was going to join them no matter what."

"What? You believed that?"

"It's not whether I believed it or not. The demon was *in my head*. You don't know what that's like—you only get a split second, and you'd say anything, do anything to spare your own life. That's all I was thinking about."

Leo. Shivers raced up my arms, like the Darkworld crept up on me, even though bright sunshine shone through a gap in the curtains.

"I don't know what it's like?" I repeated. "I'm half

demon. There's a demon in my head *all the time*. Did you forget?"

"That's different." He looked past me, as though I wasn't even there, and half-heartedly picked up a book and threw it into his suitcase.

"Maybe, but it wanted to attack you. It didn't care if you died as long as it killed Mephistopheles. That wasn't me."

"I remember seeing your eyes," said Leo. "I thought… I thought you were trying to kill me. And I thought… well, I'm just glad the fortune-teller stepped in when she did."

"Me too," I said. "I wanted to hate her after she ruined my life, but now…"

"So how does it feel for you, having the demon inside you?"

"Terrifying," I said honestly. I didn't want to talk about it right now. "I couldn't fight it—I was helpless."

"Me too," he said. "I never really understood what you meant until now. There was no way you could fight it?"

I shook my head, wondering what he was getting at.

"Then I guess it's a good thing I'm going away."

I looked at him blankly. "What d'you mean?"

"We nearly killed each other, Ash."

"So? We're both still alive. The demon's gone."

"Your demon isn't."

"It's not *my* demon. It's… like a part of my personality, I think." *Except it can control me.* I'd never trust her again. Never.

"That's kind of the problem. If I got possessed again, it'd attack me, wouldn't it?"

"I…" This wasn't what I'd expected at all. "I don't have any control over the demon. I don't know what would happen."

"Yeah…I don't know about you, but I don't want to die." He threw a video game box into his suitcase.

I gaped at him. "What the hell kind of logic is that? You're not… seriously dropping out of uni, are you?"

"I don't belong here. Hell, I only came here because Cy did and I didn't want to spend forever stuck with Melmoth. But he's dead now. I haven't got anywhere else to go."

"That makes two of us. I don't have a home either, remember? Well, except here. Don't you consider this your home?"

For the first time I really understood what it meant to be rootless. Tears pricked at my eyes as the dam threatened to burst.

"No. Not really. I don't think I've ever had a home since Mum died. And there's no way I want to be anywhere near the Venantium ever again."

"Look," I said. "At least think about this first. It's Easter break. You have four whole weeks to consider. Next term, they'll have forgotten about it."

"They don't forget," he said.

"You'd leave me to face them alone?"

"You're strong. You can face anything." But he still spoke in that awful monotone, so it didn't sound convincing.

"Bullshit. I nearly lost you. I couldn't face that again, not for the world." I was properly crying now, tears running down my face. "So you're just going to run away?"

"I'll see you again. Just not for a while. I need to get over this."

"Over what?" I choked. "I thought you were dead! I nearly lost you already—more than once. Talk to *me* about it. Don't just…"

"Sorry, Ash."

I felt like I couldn't get enough air into my lungs. "Leo," I croaked. "Don't do this."

"Goodbye, Ash." He still refused to look at me.

"You're messed up in the head!" I sobbed. "You aren't yourself. Please just think about——"

"What if another demon came along? Face it, you're more equipped to deal with that kind of shit than I am. If we're both here, it has leverage over both of us. It's pretty damned obvious the Darkworld itself is working against us, and if we carry on like this, we'll have all the demons on our tail. They watch you, Ash. They'll be watching us now."

A sour taste filled my mouth. "So freaking what?" I said. "It's a necessary risk of being connected to the Darkworld. It hasn't stopped Berenice and Howard——"

Bad example.

Leo winced. "Um, Ash, I don't know what happened to Berenice any more than you do, but I'm willing to hazard a guess that the Darkworld had something to do with it. Those two are both messed-up."

"What's wrong with messed-up? This whole situation's ridiculous," I said. "So the demon tried to kill you... I won't let it. Never again."

"Jude——Mephistopheles——controlled you, Ash. How do you explain that?"

I stared. "That was... that was because Jude had touched my demon heart... don't ask me how demons work."

"You have one living in your head," he pointed out. "Look, I know you're, well, human, but the part of you that isn't is unpredictable. I'm not saying you'd do anything on purpose..."

"Don't you even think of finishing that sentence," I said, sharply. "Don't you dare."

Leo shrugged. "I've always wanted to go travelling. I have no patience for university. I never should have come here in the first place."

"Aren't——" I choked on the words. "Aren't you glad you did?"

"No." He shook his head. "I'm not."

I couldn't see through a haze of tears. Whether he was in his right mind or not, his words struck like a knife in my chest.

"Then I guess there's no point in me staying." I stumbled towards the door. My chest ached horribly as though my heart was literally breaking, and numbness made my limbs clumsy.

I reached for the door. He still wasn't looking at me. I felt a surge of rage.

"Look at me!" I shouted. "At least have the courtesy to look me in the eyes when you break up with me!"

"I don't want to look into your eyes."

And I'd thought it wasn't possible to feel worse than I did. My heart splintered.

"You didn't just say that," I whispered, stupidly. "You'll regret it." I wanted to hurt him as badly as he'd hurt me, but suddenly words were meaningless. I felt like I yelled at the walls of the Angel Box. I wanted—needed—to get away, before I lost it completely. I fell into the endless void again, and this time there was no one to catch me.

So I ran. I ran right out of the flat—nearly colliding with Rachel—and out of the student village. I kept running, through the woods towards town, and didn't stop until I reached the Blackstone House.

It stood, lonely and sad, and watched me cry.

I crouched on the grass, not caring what I might look like to passers-by. I thought the tears would never stop. It was like a dam had been wrenched open inside me, and I cried until I could barely breathe. They were selfish tears, true. I cried for Leo and myself, and for everything I'd lost. I'd given him everything, and yet that wasn't the worst of it. The last few weeks had been like a crazy, wonderful dream, but in the end, my entire life had been a fabrication. I didn't deserve happiness.

Eventually I got bored of being self-pitying, and trudged back uphill to campus. I ran into Sarah just as she was leaving the flat.

"Ash! I wondered where you were. I'm going home now—"

Her eyes widened. I wondered how bad I looked.

"I broke up with Leo," I said, by way of an explanation. The rest of it wasn't something I could tell anyone.

"No way!" said Alex, coming out the door—she was clearly in the process of moving her stuff to her parents' car, too.

"Ash, I'm so sorry," said Sarah.

"So am I." *God, not again.* I'd thought I had no tears left in me.

"What happened?"

I shook my head. "It's complicated. I'll explain later."

"I'll be online tonight. Tell me then?"

I nodded, though I didn't intend to go on Facebook or any social media site at any point in the future. Not when Leo had doubtlessly changed our relationship status.

Fresh tears gathered in my eyes.

Get a grip.

I said goodbye to Alex and Sarah and went back to my room. Almost immediately I wanted to leave again. Possibly I was going crazy, but it smelt like him. He hadn't been here for at least a week, and yet…

Definitely crazy.

My phone buzzed. I groaned.

Cara demanded to know why I hadn't answered her message the day before, and if I was alright. I loaded up Skype and texted her asking for a chat. At least I could tell her everything—even if she didn't truly understand it all.

To her credit, she barely interrupted as I told her the whole story. I was crying so hard I could barely get the words out by the end, and she looked like she wanted to come out of the screen and give me a hug.

"Okay," she said. "I think you need to get away."

"I know," I sniffed. "But I can't—I can't come back home."

"You can stay at mine. Seriously, stay as long as you like."

"The—the fortune-teller left me money. I could rent my own place."

"She left you money? How much?"

"I don't know. A lot. Her family were loaded, and she got it all."

"She did? Hmm…" Cara's voice had the tone that meant she'd thought of some kind of plan. "Did I mention I got an extra grant from the university for my grades? You did, too, right? If your uni does that kind of thing."

"Yeah," I said, hesitantly. "I don't know if I'll get any student funding any more though—now that I'm not technically connected to my parents. God, it's a mess."

"Let the fortune-teller worry about that," said Cara. "She deserves to have to deal with those finance idiots, right?"

"Right." Ordinarily I might have smiled. As it was, I was kind of half-laughing, half-crying at the ridiculousness of the whole thing. Worrying about student finance when my parents didn't know I existed anymore, for crying out loud.

"Anyway, I'm thinking you and I should go on holiday. A long one."

"What, right now?"

"Maybe. Nah, I have essays to write over Easter. But summer, definitely. We have three months off, might as well go wild. How about we go to Australia? I've always wanted to go back. A week there wasn't enough."

"Australia?" I repeated. "Are you crazy?"

"Are *you* crazy? Who'd turn down a trip to Australia? It's an amazing country."

"I need to think about this."

"Sure. But the answer's obvious, isn't it? You don't have anything holding you back. You have a shit-ton of money. Loads of people would love to be in your position. I mean, money-wise."

I hadn't thought of that. I didn't relish the idea of owing anything more to the fortune-teller... but she'd never dictated that I couldn't spend the money on whatever I wanted.

It wasn't like she owned me, anyway.

"Cara, you're amazing. Seriously, you're the best person ever." This time, I managed a smile.

"Proud to be of service. So, you're in?"

"Hell, yeah," I said.

ABOUT THE AUTHOR

Emma is the New York Times and USA Today Bestselling author of the Changeling Chronicles urban fantasy series.

Emma spent her childhood creating imaginary worlds to compensate for a disappointingly average reality, so it was probably inevitable that she ended up writing fantasy novels. When she's not immersed in her own fictional universes, Emma can be found with her head in a book or wandering around the world in search of adventure.

Find out more about Emma's books at
www.emmaladams.com.